Jessica Huntley

My True Self

Book 2 of The My ... Self Series

First published in 2021

ISBN: 978-1-7397697-8-9

Third edition
Website: www.jessicahuntleyauthor.com

Cover Design: GetCovers
Edited and proofread by: Jennifer Kay Davies

About Jessica Huntley

Jessica is, and always has been, a huge fan of psychological and suspense thrillers. Her favourite authors are Chris Carter and John Marrs. She loves the twists and turns and shocking reveals and uses the books she reads as inspiration to write her own.

Jessica wrote her first book at age six. Between the ages of ten and eighteen, she had written ten full-length fiction novels as a hobby in her spare time between school and work.

At age eighteen, she left her hobby behind and joined the British Army as an Intelligence Analyst where she spent the next four and a half years as a soldier. She attempted to write more novels but was never able to finish them.

Jessica later left the Army and became a mature student at Southampton Solent University and studied Fitness and Personal Training, which later became her career. She still enjoys keeping fit and exercising daily.

She is now a wife and a stay-at-home mum to a crazy toddler and lives in Newbury. During the first national lockdown of 2020, she signed up on a whim for a novel writing course, and the rest is history. Her love of writing came flooding back, and she managed to write and finish her debut novel, The Darkness Within Ourselves, inspired by her love of horror and thriller novels. She has also finished writing the My … Self trilogy, completed a Level 3 Diploma in Editing and Proofreading and has worked with four other authors on a collaborative horror novel entitled The Summoning.

She is now working on a new novel in her spare time, reads every day (thrillers...obviously) and is also a Thriller Ambassador for Tandem Collective.

Other Books by Jessica

The Darkness Series

The Darkness Within Ourselves
The Darkness That Binds Us
Book 3: TBC

My ... Self Series

My Bad Self: A Prequel Novella
My Dark Self
My True Self
My Real Self

Standalone Thrillers

Jinx

Writing in collaboration with other authors

The Summoning

HorrorScope: A Zodiac Anthology

Acknowledgements

To all those who have helped make this book happen.

My twin sister Alice, my best friend Katie (who convinced me to turn this into a series), my dad for always supporting me and my husband Scott who allows me the time to write.

Thank you to my lovely editor Jennifer Kay Davies who has taught me so much.

To all the lovely fellow self-published authors I've met who help and support me the whole way.

Special thanks go to Stuart Knott and Harriet Everend.

To all my new fans who I've met through writing my books. Without you these books would not be what they are today, so thank you all!

Connect with Jessica

Find and connect with Jessica online via the following platforms.

Sign up to her email list via her website to be notified of future books and her monthly author newsletter:

www.jessicahuntleyauthor.com

Follow her page on Facebook: Jessica Huntley - Author - @jessica.reading.writing

Follow her on Instagram: @jessica_reading_writing

Follow her on Twitter: @jess_read_write

Follow her on TikTok: @jessica_reading_writing

Follow her on Goodreads: jessica_reading_writing

Follow her on her Amazon Author Page - Jessica Huntley

Chapter One
Alicia

I am Alexis Grey.

You may know me better by my original name – Alicia. Yes, I am still a psychopath – that has not changed, nor will it ever change. I, however, am not the same person I once was. Everything and everyone must evolve in order to survive. It is human nature and so I have adapted in order to blend into society and its social norms. There is still a darkness within me, but I have become very adept at hiding it, a skill I know I must continue to develop. This body used to be inhabited by my identical twin sister Josslyn, as you may remember, but since I regained my rightful presence within it I have become a more rounded and stronger individual. I believe I am a better version of who I was before. I am not just a killer and a psychopath. I am so much more than that now. You should be proud of me.

Josslyn was removed from this body as a tumour (a foetus in fetu – a rare condition where one twin is absorbed by the other in utero, but not completely, leaving a small group of abnormal cells), but a small piece of her remained due to being located too close to a collection of nerves and vital organs. I was told that the tumour would eventually be absorbed by my body, or it would remain there but cause me no serious harm, however, this scenario was less likely to happen. I did not expect any part of her to have survived. It was not in my original plan for her to return, but return she did. A year and a half after she was removed she somehow clawed and fought her way back to the surface, back to life, as it were. I will not lie – her determination and perseverance have both surprised and impressed me. I always pegged Josslyn as the weak one, the pushover, but she has evolved too.

Josslyn returned, but she is not the Josslyn I remember. Yes, there are parts of her that I recognise (she still annoys the hell out of me), but I have come to understand that sisters are generally annoying, especially twin sisters, because while they may have different personalities their similarities are what make them stronger and we are more similar than I originally thought. Therefore, when we argue we are both stubborn, strong-willed and not afraid to speak our minds. This is the main change that I have noticed in Josslyn. She is not exactly the same as she used to be and that is something you must understand before we go any further. The Josslyn you once knew is gone. This may be hard for you to accept at first, as it was for her. The past month has been challenging for both of us. I cannot stress that enough.

Josslyn had been blissfully unaware of the events of the past year and a half: her removal at the hospital, my moving to Tuscany, the virus sweeping across the planet, the death of her parents, my renovating and starting up of the wine bar business – all of this was thrust upon her in a split second. She came back to me, we spoke for a few minutes and then her *mind* appeared to catch up and all of my memories started flooding her consciousness and she was inundated with vision after vision, memory after memory of what my journey up until that point had entailed. It had been too much for her to handle all at once and she had quickly retreated into the depths of her despair, unwilling to talk to me for days. I allowed her the space she needed. I felt I owed her that much.

Eventually she began to surface and asked me questions and I revealed the truth – that I had tricked her into removing herself from this body; my body. She had never been the true host and this was difficult for her to accept. Josslyn blamed me, hated me, shouted at me. She told me to go and throw myself off a cliff. Her emotions overwhelmed her. She still blames me now. I know she does. She blames me for everything ... especially for her parents dying, but, as I told her, that was not my fault. I had no control over what happened. She hates me—

I don't hate you ... I just ... it's hard to explain. You ruined my life, you stole my body, you moved to another country, you abandoned my parents, you quit drinking and you sold my vet practice ... how do you expect me to feel? You threw my whole life away like it meant nothing.

This was always *my* body, not yours. You were merely renting it.

So what! I think I deserved ... you know what, I'm not going to start all this up again. The fact is that you could've told me the truth right from the start. I would've understood—

I disagree.

Okay, so maybe not at first, but you should've trusted me. We're twins who share a body. I think I should have some say over what we do with it.

I disagree.

There's a shock.

As you can clearly see our relationship is somewhat strained.

That's the understatement of the fucking century.

However, I believe we have eventually arrived at a mutual understanding.

Not like I have much of a fucking choice anyway.

As I mentioned earlier, a month has now passed since Josslyn came back and we have been attempting to adjust to this severe change. It has not been easy. I had grown accustomed to the silence in my head, but now I have a constant reminder that I am not alone ... and it is slightly disconcerting. There is, however, one individual who is ecstatic about Josslyn returning – Oscar.

The joy on his face when he realised his true owner had returned was ... I am unable to explain exactly what emotion I felt, but there was a part of me, deep down inside, that felt *happy*. The animal could not stop licking my face and yapping. However, Josslyn has been unable to stroke him herself, as it appears that she cannot take me over—

Yet.

There is no way you will ever be able to take over, Josslyn, because you are not strong enough. It is not possible. I do not even know *how* you have survived—

Maybe I'm stronger than you think.

I decline from answering.

I have established many theories as to how she may have survived, but none of them have been proven, nor can they be proven. There is no way I can clearly explain any of them. The only one that makes any logical sense is that the tiny piece of *tumour* that was left behind was enough to enable her to stay, but because the bulk of the *tumour*—

Will you stop calling me a fucking tumour? I'm a human being!

What do you want me to call you?

Anything! Just not a tumour.

Fine ... but because the bulk of the ... foetus—

No!

... Life-form—

No!

... Individual—

I guess that's about as good a name as any ...

... Because the bulk of the *individual* was removed it loosened her grip on the control of the body, allowing me to gain complete control. I still have no idea how she came to have the majority of the control in the first place. It is a mystery, but one which, thankfully, I have rectified. Now everything is as it should be.

Except for the fact I'm still stuck in your body and there's no way I'll ever be able to get out.

Are you not happy to be back? You could have stayed away forever.

I don't know how I'm supposed to feel. I'm still trying to wrap my head around the fact that I'm now blonde and have a banging body, I live in Tuscany and my parents are dead.

I told you if you put the work in and stopped eating takeaways and drinking alcohol every night you could look and feel so much better.

Silence.

Josslyn still has a difficult time admitting when I am right.

It is late at night and I am carrying out the close-down procedures for my wine bar, *A Slice of Paradise.* All the customers have left, thoroughly intoxicated and, I assume, satisfied, and I am alone with my thoughts. Josslyn does approve of my new lifestyle and occupation, which is not surprising considering her enjoyment and love of wine. I often feel myself dreaming of travelling the world again, now the virus is easing and tourism is beginning to revive itself. I was never supposed to remain in one place, settle down and start a business, but that is how my life has developed, and as I mentioned earlier, in order to survive one must adapt and evolve. One day I shall continue my quest for adventure and leave all of this behind when the time is right.

At first, when I informed Josslyn about the virus that had brought the entire world to its knees, she did not believe me. She said it was like something out of a horror movie and had asked if anyone had turned into a zombie yet – I assured her that they had not. She did not believe me and was convinced for nearly two days that the apocalypse had come and that we were all doomed. Of course, she was in a complete state of shock and eventually accepted that the virus was not turning the world into flesh-eating zombies.

It could still happen.

The idea of staying in Tuscany forever is not appealing to me. It was only due to the virus that I have been forced to live in one place and, to be perfectly honest, I have also wanted to get as much distance between myself and Peter as possible. I do not often think or talk about that man. He is not worthy of my time and effort. Josslyn says she feels nauseous every time she thinks about him, especially because I believe him to be the cause of Ronald's death. I have no proof, but there is a part of me that believes he wants to get my attention and lure me out of hiding somehow. I assume he does not know where I am, but, again, I cannot be certain. I have received no creepy phone calls, neither have I felt like I am being watched or followed ... yet. I would like to think that I have developed a sixth sense and would be able to tell if someone was watching me.

That doesn't mean he isn't here. He spent over five years watching me without me knowing about it. What makes you think he couldn't do it to you?

I am more intelligent and more aware of my surroundings than you are.

Still as tactful as ever.

I am still a psychopath Josslyn. I do not care what you think nor do I care about hurting your feelings.

Are you sure about that? I mean, I think you've changed quite drastically over the past year and a half, Alicia. You've kept Oscar for a start. You interact with your customers and what's even more amazing is that they actually seem to like you.

My name is Alexis, not Alicia. I have told you enough times.

Well you'll always be Alicia to me. I'm never going to stop calling you that. It's your real name. Why did you change it anyway?

I told you. I changed my name because this body belonged to you and I required you to disappear. I am now Alexis and, hopefully, it will be enough to cover my tracks so that if anyone is searching for you, or me, they will not find us.

Of course, I did not officially have my name changed via deed poll because otherwise the authorities would be able to work out that Josslyn Reynolds is now called Alexis Grey, so I had to be careful. Technically, Josslyn Reynolds still does exist, but she has disappeared. I used her passport to fly to Tuscany, then I destroyed it and everything with her name on. I closed down her bank account (after transferring all her money to my new one). I cancelled and deleted every online account she had, including her social media pages. Then I managed to get myself a new passport and ID (if I told you how I would have to kill you). I keep my online presence as small as possible. It is not the perfect cover up and I am sure that if someone were to look into her disappearance more closely they would eventually find out the truth, but for now, as long as I lay low, I should be safe.

So basically you used a brand new name so you could hide from Peter.

I did not say that.

Then who are you hiding from? Why would you go through that much effort in order to erase me? Are you scared of him?

Do not be ridiculous. I am not afraid of anything or anyone.

Then why are you still hiding and not going back and kicking his ass like you should have done before you left?

I told him to stay away from me and that is what he is doing. I have no reason to go back and see him as long as he keeps to his end of the deal.

Even though you think he killed my dad to try and get your attention ... if he did that then he deserves to die.

Despite what you may think I do not go around killing people randomly for sport. I only kill a person if they are a threat to me or my livelihood.

And you don't think that killing my dad warrants enough of a threat to you?

He was not my father.

Fuck you, Alicia.

I do not respond to Josslyn's temper tantrum. We still have a few issues to iron out, but generally we get along. Some days are tougher than others.

I ignore her and get back to work wiping down the tables. It is the height of summer, the middle of July and so it is only beginning to get dark now at eleven o'clock at night. A warm breeze gently tickles my skin. I have left the sundeck doors open while I tidy. The view from the sundeck is extraordinary during the day – vineyards, mountains and valleys stretch out far into the distance. At night, tiny specks of light illuminate certain areas of the valleys, highlighting where other members of the population live. I do not have any close neighbours – the exact reason why I chose to buy this property. At the time of purchase the whole world appeared to be keeping its distance from one another, which suited me perfectly and still does to this day. However, the world is healing and coming closer together again and I feel trapped here, like I do not belong.

The villa I live in is a sand-coloured, two-storey building with two bedrooms, a spacious open-living lounge/kitchen/diner and a small swimming pool situated in the back garden area, and when I say it is small that is exactly what I mean. It is barely big enough to do four adequate swimming strokes before reaching the end, but it is satisfactory for cooling off after a long, hot day. The gardens are modest with a few orange and lemon trees and very little grass, which makes it easy for me to maintain.

The wine bar itself is a stand-alone building, separate from the villa, located at the end of the courtyard. The bar is tastefully decorated. I was able to complete almost all of the work myself, having had

Josslyn's skill and knowledge from when she and her father renovated her vet practice. I chose classic wood panelling teamed with modern appliances and decorations. Simple, yet effective and elegant. There is a large chandelier hanging above my head made solely out of empty wine bottles all of varying shapes and sizes, which glitter and catch the light perfectly. It is a common talking point among the regular customers who appear shocked that I was able to hoist it up there by myself with only a rope and a pulley (and a few choice swear words). The bar itself is stocked with various wine bottles, red, white and rosé, all lined up neatly on the shelves in alphabetical order. I do not serve any other type of alcohol. I like to consider myself as a budding wine connoisseur. I am not an expert, but I have learnt a few things about wine while I have lived here.

I finally finish wiping down the tables, so I move on to washing the used wine glasses. I do not have the luxury of a dishwasher so I am forced to wash them by hand every night. It is a laborious chore, one I utterly despise. I turn on the hot water tap and wait for the grey metal sink to fill with soapy water.

Oscar is in his bed underneath the bar to my right. He is somewhat of a celebrity to the customers, who always say hello to him before they interact with myself. Oscar thrives on the attention and has happily made himself at home here. Early every morning after breakfast we take a stroll through the vineyard to the end and then join a well-worn walking trail, which circles around the local area, branching off every so often in different directions. We walk in silence for an hour or so and then head back to the villa to begin the daily routine. After Oscar has been walked I begin my daily exercise. Walking is suitable exercise of course, but it is merely a warm-up for me. I have built my own small gym located in the spare room of my villa, complete with dumbbells and a punch bag. I usually do whatever exercise I feel like doing depending on my mood. After an hour I take a shower and then tend to any jobs that need my attention, whether it be invoicing, fixing something that has broken or ordering more stock for the bar. I keep busy, but this life, as you know, is starting to lose its allure and I am becoming more and more agitated about staying in one place.

I am casually washing the wine glasses, not looking down at what I am doing, instead staring ahead into the growing darkness outside. That is when I feel it: a cold shiver running down my spine. It alarms me, as it is not a pleasant feeling, but it is one that Josslyn used to feel often when she was in this body. I stop washing and remain still, listening as intently as I can ... there is a scuffling sound coming from outside the double doors leading to the sundeck. It may be an animal searching for food, but if it were then Oscar would have sensed its presence by now and chased it away. As it happens he is still snoring peacefully.

What is it Alicia?

Josslyn has sensed my uneasiness, being completely aware of the feeling herself.

I do not know. I feel like ... someone is out there. The customers left half an hour ago, so it cannot be any of them.

I brush off the cold shiver running down my spine, the hairs on the back of my neck standing to attention, dry off my hands on a tea towel and begin to take tentative steps towards the open doors.

'Who is there?' I call out. 'Show yourself.'

I reach the doors and step out onto the sundeck. The darkness has crept in quickly. The light from the inside of the bar is casting strange shadows on the deck and up the sides of the building. I stop and listen.

Silence.

Okay, I don't know about you, but I'm slightly creeped out right now.

I do not respond directly to Josslyn. I am not afraid, but I do not like the feeling of the unknown. If someone is out here watching me, then I want to know who it is and why they are here.

'Show yourself!' I order.

There is a sudden movement and sound behind me, like claws tapping on wood. I spin round on the spot, my fists clenched, my body rigid, ready for a fight.

Oscar is standing in the middle of the bar looking at me and wagging his tail. I unclench my fists and relax my shoulders, breathing a sigh of relief. I walk up to him, bend down and give him a stroke. He licks my hands and face.

Don't do that to us Oscar! You scared the life out of me.

There was definitely something or someone outside just now. That was not Oscar.

Yeah, you're right. So much for saying that you haven't felt like you're being watched lately. Do you have CCTV set up on this place?

No, but maybe it is time I installed some.

Chapter Two

Alicia

Half an hour later I lock up the wine bar and walk across the small courtyard to my villa. I can see the pool lights flickering nearby, casting spectacular shadows across the surface of the water. Oscar cocks his leg on the plant pot beside my front door and then takes himself upstairs to my bedroom and promptly curls up into a ball and goes to sleep. I, however, am too wired to go to sleep yet, so I dress into my cotton pyjamas and head back downstairs. I pull out my yoga mat from under the sofa, lay it out and adopt the cross-legged position on the floor.

And breathe.

I miss the days where we'd crack open a bottle of wine and watch serial killer documentaries and then fall asleep.

I ignore the voice in my head and take another deep breath, feeling my body relax and unwind. I usually do yoga before bed, especially if I have had an exceptionally long day. It is nearly midnight; I would say that classifies as a long day.

And breathe.

A glass of wine is good for relaxing and unwinding too, you know.

I sigh in frustration.

What? Yoga has never been our thing. Remember that time I went to that yoga class and I ended up shouting at you and we were asked to leave? You wouldn't stop talking then either. It's stupid.

I have changed. I enjoy yoga now.

Why?

It helps me suppress my anger and stops me from killing people in a fit of rage.

Really?

Yes. Now shut up.

You seem stressed.

That is because my twin sister will not stop talking to me while I am trying to focus my good energy and repel the bad. I am attempting to become a better person, is that so hard to believe?

Um ... yeah kinda. Wait, you have good energy? Wow, you really have changed.

I am trying.

Fine, I'll be quiet. Goodnight, Alicia.

Goodnight, Josslyn.

Ten minutes later I finish my short yoga routine and crawl into bed, feeling the warmth of Oscar's tiny body next to me, whilst attempting to ignore the feeling of dread growing from within. That night I am plagued by disturbing dreams and images—

I am laying on a table, cut open, my flesh torn apart and a large tumour is removed from my abdomen. I am conscious as a hooded figure holds up the tumour and shows it to me. It has my face on it – Josslyn's face, but she is ugly, deformed and in pain. The face screams at me. I look down and my body has miraculously healed itself, but there is a scar across my stomach. It is dark and purple and the skin has puckered into the shape of the letter "A". The tumour engraved with her face is behind me, still crying in agony. I get off the table, leaving her behind to suffer and die. I follow the hooded figure out of the room, unaware of where I am going, but knowing that I want to get as far away from the tumour as possible. I can still hear it wailing behind me. The sound never leaves me; it haunts me for eternity.

The hooded figure is ahead of me and it finally stops. I cease walking and reach out my hand towards the entity, determined to reveal who is under the black hood. The figure is large, much larger than an average person. I am forced to balance on tiptoes to reach the hood covering its face. I pull off the hood. There is nothing there. The figure is just a floating black cloak, now with no hood, but its form is human-like.

'Who are you?' I ask.

The floating black cloak does not answer. Instead, it turns and begins to drift away again without a sound, but this time I do not follow. I allow it to leave me—

I wake up with a start and sit up, my heart racing, my skin damp with sweat, my pyjamas clinging to my body. It is the height of summer, so the room is warm and the moonlight is gently illuminating the area around my bed. The hooded figure is standing at the bottom of my bed, towering over it like a humongous shadow. I lay back against my pillow, convinced that I am still dreaming. It is not real. I know that I am merely in that strange place between being asleep and awake. I close my eyes to block out the terrifying image and dream again—

This time I am playing with Josslyn, both of us only children. We are at My Place, the tree in the woods; our favourite place to play and also the final resting place of our sister, Alicia Phillips. Josslyn and I are laughing and having fun. We are identical in every way, from the slightly crooked teeth to the freckles scattered across our noses. The scene before me plays in slow motion. Then, the ground beneath us begins to tremble and the dead corpse of our sister emerges from her grave, covered in soil, her jaw broken, hanging limp, her blonde hair saturated in blood. She is also only a child and wants to play with us, but she cannot speak. Josslyn and I do not care that she is dead and looks like a rotting zombie. She is our sister – so we play together, just the three of us – the normal one, the dead one and the psychopath. We are happy.

I dream again. I am running, but I remain stationary. I can hear footsteps behind me. I am surrounded by darkness and there is an invisible barrier stopping me from moving forwards. I keep trying to run with all my strength, with all my will, but it is no use. The footsteps get louder and louder until they are directly behind me and then suddenly they stop. I halt my attempt at fleeing and slowly turn around. The owner of the footsteps is standing directly in front of me, an evil and menacing grin across his face. His strong, muscular arms lurch towards me and his massive hands grab me around the throat effortlessly. I cannot breathe. He lifts my whole body off the floor while squeezing my neck tighter and tighter.

'You are mine,' he says. 'I have found you and you are now mine.'

Then nothing—

I wake up coughing, unable to catch my breath until I am able to take a few sips of cool water, which I always have beside my bed. The liquid soothes my sore throat. The hooded figure is no longer standing at the bottom of my bed, but this does not remove the fear that is growing substantially fast from within. I am alone ... yet I feel as if I am not.

The next morning I eat breakfast and take Oscar out for our routine walk. I did not sleep after I woke up the second time. Josslyn has not surfaced yet, so I assume that she is unaware of my dreams. It is possible she has her own dreams. I do not know, but she is dormant for the time being so I enjoy the peace and quiet. Josslyn appears to be able to come and go as she pleases. It is a phenomenon that I cannot explain, but one I do not question.

I will not lie, I am rattled by the events of last night. It is not often I will admit that I am afraid; in fact, I have never been afraid before. The morning light has eased my worry slightly. Things always appear worse in the dark. Something is happening to me. Maybe Josslyn's fear is rubbing off on me. I am becoming weak because of her and I do not like it. True psychopaths do not experience fear, so what am I? I cannot be a true psychopath after all ...

I shake the thought from my mind almost as quickly as it appears. I cannot think that way. Being a psychopath is all I have to explain why I am the way that I am. Without that I am ... nothing. I am a psychopath. I am not afraid.

Upon my return to the villa I notice a car parked next to my own, which is a new black BMW. I decided to splash out on a fancier car with some of the money from Ronald and Amanda's will, among other things. The car on the left of mine is a blue Mini, an old version, back when they were small cars and not the size of an average vehicle. It looks familiar. I know who this car belongs to – Benjamin Willis.

Uh, excuse me ... but who's Benjamin Willis?

I see you are awake now.

Yeah. I slept like shit. I had some really weird dreams about you, me, Alicia and Peter.

So did I.

Weird.

Did you see the hooded figure at the bottom of our bed?

Ummmm ... no! What the fuck? There was someone in our room?

No, I do not believe so. I believe it was a figment of my imagination caused by my nightmares.

Are you sure?

Yes.

You're sure you're sure?

My silence is enough of an answer.

Fine ... so who's Benjamin?

I ignore the question and go in search of the man himself. There are certain things that Josslyn does not remember about the past year and a half. Some things (and people) are not important to me and therefore do not form long-term memories in my brain. I know who Benjamin is, of course, but I do not give him a second thought on most occasions – he is the man who delivers my sausages.

Your what?

Sausages, Josslyn.

You're going to have to explain a bit more.

I do not have time to answer before I spy Benjamin standing by my back door. He has a bag of sausages in one hand and a bottle of red wine in the other. Oscar runs to greet him, excitedly sniffing the bag.

'Sorry boy, these aren't for you,' says Benjamin with a laugh, holding the bag up higher out of Oscar's reach. He notices me walking towards him and smiles.

Woah! He's fit. You didn't tell me he was fit.

Benjamin is indeed an attractive man, I will not deny that, however he does have slightly long, curly dark hair, which makes him look approximately twenty years old, even though he is actually closer to thirty. His skin is tanned and his body is strong, yet he always smells of raw meat with a hint of fragranced herbs. He is a butcher and works in the local town at a family-run delicatessen/butcher shop. We met when he came to my bar one night for a drink with a few of his friends. A friend of his attempted to chat me up whilst completely inebriated. Benjamin kindly apologised to me and directed his friend back to their table before I could punch him in the face or throw him out of my window. Benjamin stayed until closing time that night trying to initiate a conversation with me, but I politely told him (even though I wanted to be rude – he was a paying customer, after all) that it was time he left. He asked for my number, but I did not give it. I saw him again when I walked into the delicatessen and since then I have always bought my sausages and various other cured meats from him.

That sounds so dirty.

Everything sounds dirty to you.

No, it doesn't.

Remember what happened to the last guy you fancied?

Right, yeah. He turned out to be my secret stalker.

Exactly. We do not trust men anymore.

Let me guess, you haven't been laid since you've lived here ...

I do not dignify that with a response.

That's a yes then.

'Hey Alexis, sorry, I know I don't usually deliver your sausages on a Tuesday, but I'm totally swamped right now. Business is doing well.' He hands me the bag of sausages – apple and sage flavour, my favourite.

'Glad to hear it,' I say.

'I hope you don't mind your meat a day early.'

'I do not mind.'

Seriously ... am I supposed to ignore that blatant innuendo?

'I also brought you this.' He hands me the bottle of red.

I take it and frown. 'What is this for?'

Benjamin shrugs. 'Just thought you might like it.'

'I do not like red wine.'

'Oh.'

Alicia! Be nice.

'I mean ... thank you Benjamin.'

'You can call me Ben you know.'

'I know.'

There is a silence while Benjamin shifts his weight from one leg to the other and back again. It appears I have made him uncomfortable, something I am exceptionally proficient at.

I thought you said you were getting better at the whole small talk thing?

Neither of us have ever been good at small talk.

True.

'So ... um ... do you have any space for tonight, in the bar, I mean? I was thinking of stopping by for a drink.' His attempt to change the subject is abundantly clear.

'By yourself?' I ask.

'Yeah, well, unless you want to join me ...'

'I am fully booked.'

'Okay, that's cool. It was a bit short notice anyway. How about tomorrow night?'

Is he trying to ask us out on a date?

That is unclear at this precise moment.

'I have a space available tomorrow night at nine.'

'Great, I'll take it ... as long as you can join me for a drink.'

I narrow my eyes at him. 'I will not be able to join you for a drink until near closing time at eleven once the majority of the customers have left.'

'That's okay, I'll wait.'

Is he seriously going to sit at a table by himself for two hours and wait for you?

As long as he pays his tab I do not care what he does.

'See you at nine tomorrow,' I say, hoping that is enough to make him leave.

'Cool, see you then. Bye, Alexis. Bye, Oscar!' He bends down and gives the dog a final tickle before walking to his car. He glances over his shoulder at me and then gets into his vehicle. I watch him intently, my eyes never wandering until he has driven out of sight.

That was weird.

Indeed.

He likes you.

I do not believe that is the case, although he does appear to perspire a lot and his pupils dilate when he talks to me.

Maybe he just wants to fuck you then.

I have no interest in fucking anyone.

Urrgg, you're so boring! What's wrong with a little fun once in a while? Didn't you tell me that once?

I did ... and I was wrong. Sex leads to complications and all I want is an uncomplicated life. If that means I must be celibate then so be it.

Pffft ... we'll see how long that lasts. Well, celibate or not it looks like you have a date tomorrow night.

It is not a date.

I think it is. He's cute. You could do a lot worse.

I sigh in frustration. I can already tell that today is going to be another long day.

Once my jobs are complete and I have done my exercise (I chose boxing today because I am holding onto a lot of pent-up anger and frustration and it needs to be released) I change into my bikini and head to the pool. It is nearing the middle of the day so the heat is rising exponentially, which is why a quick dip in the cool water is exactly what I need. My bikini is black, with a high-waist thong and a triangular-cut top, showing off my toned body exceptionally well. I lower myself off the side and sink into the water, feeling my body relax almost immediately. I swim a few lengths (and since the pool is so small this does not take long) and then float on my back, staring up into the cloudless, blue Tuscan sky.

Is this what it's like to be dead?

Must you constantly interrupt my quiet moments?

Who else am I supposed to talk to?

I sigh and continue to float while we converse.

I believe we have spoken about this before, back when we were children.

Yeah, but that was when you were in my position and I was in yours. I miss my body. I'd do anything to be able to feel the cool water and the heat of the sun on my face.

There is nothing I can do to help you.

I know ... but maybe one day ...

I suddenly stand up in the pool, having just heard a crunching noise which sounded a lot like someone walking over gravel. My courtyard at the front of the villa is gravelled, but from my position in the back garden I cannot see it. I listen and wait, but the sound does not appear again. Oscar is nearby in the shade of a tree, snoozing peacefully.

I think you're a bit on edge. Maybe you need to get laid.

I very much doubt that will help.

Worth a shot though, right?

I spend a few more minutes in the pool. I even sink down and practise sitting on the bottom, something I have almost managed to perfect. My record for holding my breath is one minute and thirty-two seconds.

After I have dried off and showered I make myself a strawberry and banana smoothie and take a seat at my office desk. I enjoy sitting here. I chose to set up my office space in the main open plan living area, overlooking the vineyard, which is slightly off to the left and also the courtyard, so I can see if anyone is coming. I do not expect people to visit me, for I have no one relevant in my life, but I prefer to be on my guard. Just in case.

I wish you'd admit it.

Admit what?

You're afraid that Peter is going to come after you.

Do not be ridiculous.

Then why do you Google him every day?

I purposefully ignore her question and begin my search.

Yes, I use the internet to search for information relating to Peter every single day without fail. I am not an idiot. Without me (his previous obsession) around he has more than likely set his sights on his next victim and I want to ensure he is not hurting anyone else. I need to know where he is and what he is doing at all times.

Now who's the stalker ... It sounds like he's become your obsession now.

Blanking out her voice, I continue.

Peter is still not on any social media sites – not using his real name anyway. I assume he has set up fake accounts in order to stalk his prey, but with my limited knowledge of the internet and hacking techniques I have been unable to trace him. He is, however, on Lampton Boarding School for Boys' website – the school where he works as a teacher. He has his own page on the website along with a picture showing him with a happy smile, combed hair, trimmed beard and wearing a smart suit and tie. There is a short biography about him, which I read for the hundredth time.

Peter Phillips studied History at University College London and joined our school in 2010 as the history teacher. He quickly became known as the History Buff (for his outstanding knowledge of history as well as his exceptionally good looks). Peter enjoys playing golf and in his spare time he likes to bird watch in the local parks, sometimes spending hours watching them in their natural habitat and making notes. He has won the title of Teacher of the Year five times since joining the school. Peter is a well-loved and special member of the teaching team, a favourite with the students as well as the female members of staff.

I lean back in my desk chair and narrow my line of vision at the paragraph. Anger seethes inside of me, as it does every time I read it. The thought of that man being free to do as he pleases and carry on with his pathetic life infuriates me. I also find it rather amusing how he has managed to incorporate his hobby of *bird watching* into his biography – a clear and clever cover-up for his real passion ... stalking and watching women. This paragraph, however, requires updating because a few days ago I came across a newspaper article about Peter and how he had recently won his sixth Teacher of the Year award. I have it saved in my *Peter* folder on the desktop, so I click it open and read it again.

A local history teacher has made headlines today after winning the prestigious title of Teacher of the Year for the sixth time, a record at Lampton Boarding School for Boys. Peter Phillips has not only been awarded this title, but also the Favourite Teacher award by his pupils. These awards have won him a hefty bonus, as well as an all-expenses paid trip to a destination of his choice.

Tragically, Peter has been in the headlines before when his beloved sister, Alicia Phillips, disappeared seven years ago. Her case was ruled as a suicide, but he has never given up the hope of finding her and has been searching for the truth ever since. We wish him the very best and pray that his sister is found alive one day soon and that he receives the answers he is looking for.

I stare at the picture of Peter in the Cambridge newspaper article. He is dressed in a black tuxedo and holding two gold statues – his awards – in his left hand and has a glass of champagne in his right. There is also a smaller photograph of Peter shaking hands with the Head Master of the school – Henry Smith. According to the article the awards ceremony took place over a week ago and there is also a small mention of a black-tie function happening soon which he will also attend. His smile offends me. I grit my teeth.

You really hate him, don't you?

Yes. Sometimes I do I wish I had killed him when I had the chance.

Let's be honest Alicia, you wouldn't have stood a chance against him. He would have killed us. I know I've said you should have killed him back then, but he would've overpowered you.

Maybe.

Why do you keep searching online for him every day? What do you expect to find?

I do not reply straight away. The truth is that I am not afraid for myself. I am afraid of what he might do to someone else and I feel ... what is the word for it—

Guilty. You feel guilty that he might stalk someone else and hurt them. Alicia ... guilt is an emotion ... since when do you feel emotions?

Josslyn, I do not feel emotion like you feel emotion. I am different. You know this. I do not feel guilty, but I do feel responsible for whatever happens to his next victim. I cannot allow him to scare or hurt another woman.

To be fair Alicia, he never actually hurt me or his sister. He just ... okay, yeah, it's creepy. He watched us for years and made us fear for our lives. He may not have hurt us physically, but who knows what he would have done eventually. He could have killed his sister ... but you got there first.

I let out a long sigh.

I killed our sister. At the time it was the right thing to do and I stand by my decision, even now. However, these dreams that I have been having recently are telling me that my subconscious is no longer happy about what I did.

I did what I had to do.

It was the wrong thing to do.

I do not wish to talk about Alicia anymore. Now please can you—

I stop mid-sentence.

I am scrolling through some online searches while conversing with Josslyn and suddenly spot a headline which holds my attention. As well as searching for any news relating directly to Peter I also search for any local news articles about women going missing or being stalked or followed. I do not only stick to the area of Cambridge because Peter stalked Josslyn and myself and we lived three hours away from him. He is capable of anything. Unfortunately, there are dozens of new articles every day about women being attacked or killed or followed. I methodically read and check every single one. It has become a fascination of mine, but I am looking for something in particular that jumps out at me and that is exactly what I have just found—

The Hooded Man – a notorious serial rapist has struck again. Another young woman has come forward with a report that she has been raped by a man wearing a black hood. Rachel Williams was walking home from her job as a waitress at a local bar and was attacked, dragged into an alley and raped. This is now the sixteenth rape of a similar nature that has been reported over a period of approximately twelve years. In each report the women have described the attacker as a man wearing a black hood. He never says a word. The police have given him the name – The Hooded Man. If anyone has any further reports of being attacked, please call this number ...

I stop reading ...

The Hooded Man.

The name sears its way into my brain and will not leave. I cannot stop staring at the headline. There is no photograph of the man, but there is one of Rachel Williams. She is young, merely out of her teenage years, and is smiling and happy – no doubt taken before she was assaulted and her life destroyed, quite possibly forever.

My mind shifts to the events of last night and the hooded figure at the bottom of my bed. It cannot be just a mere coincidence. Before I jump to the conclusion that the hooded man is Peter I think seriously about it and list the facts in my head.

Peter does not rape his victims – he stalks them, makes them feel afraid, calls them on the telephone ...

The attacks have been reported as far back as twelve years ago, which would make Peter approximately nineteen when the first one occurred (if that was indeed the first attack – there could of course be older cases which have not been reported yet).

As much as I want to accuse Peter of these awful crimes I cannot deny that the facts just do not add up for him to be the person responsible.

You don't think that's Peter?

No. It is not him.

Then why'd you stop and read it?

Do you remember that dream I told you about this morning? I said I saw a hooded figure at the bottom of the bed—

Are you fucking serious! You think The Hooded Man is here?

Do not overreact Josslyn. It was a figment of my imagination. I am merely stating that I saw and dreamt of a hooded figure and now I am reading about a serial rapist called The Hooded Man ... it caught my attention, that is all. I do not believe in coincidences.

But it's creepy, right?

Yes, I agree it is ... creepy.

Can you please install a security camera now?

Yes. I shall get one today.

After I am happy that there is no new information regarding Peter online today I close down my computer, put on my trainers, grab my car keys, whistle for Oscar to follow and get into my car. I drive the ten miles to the local town and park outside an electrical store, which just so happens to be opposite the delicatessen/butcher shop. I automatically glance over—

Are you hoping to see Ben?

No ... and his name is Benjamin.

I prefer Ben.

I enter the electrical shop. I avoid all unnecessary conversation and focus on purchasing the best security camera they sell. It comes with five cameras, which I plan to install at the front door, the back door, the courtyard, the bar area and my bedroom. The shop assistant asks if I require help setting it up – I do not. It appears simple enough to install.

A woman, who I recognise as a customer who frequently visits my wine bar, waves at me from across the road as I place the camera equipment in the boot of my car. My usual automatic reaction is to look down and avoid her friendly gesture, but I know I must keep up appearances for the local community. I do not wish to be known as the unfriendly bartender as it will draw unnecessary attention. I smile and wave back … and now she is walking over to me.

Fuck.

Urrgg! This is why we don't talk to people. Why are you so friendly to everyone all of a sudden? You always told me to avoid people like the plague.

I had not realised how much attention being rude to people brings upon oneself … I want to avoid being noticed and that often involves being pleasant to people.

Well congratulations, you're now no longer invisible. I'll leave you to your friend.

Fuck you.

There is certainly now a downside to occupying a living body and not just being a voice in someone's head. I must often endure tedious conversations with annoyingly perky women who seem to want to be friends with me. If only they knew what a bad idea that was … No one should want to be friends with me and I do not wish to be friends with anyone.

'Ciao Alexis!'

She is Italian, but speaks English fluently, however she does like to throw in the occasional Italian word, which throws me off at times. I do not know how she has come to speak English so well because I have never asked her. I do not care. All I care about is that she pays her bar tab at the end of the evening. She usually comes in to my bar with a different man every time, despite wearing a wedding ring. Again, I do not question her about it for it is not my business to know. Her name is Francesca and her male friends are always called *plus one* or *husband*.

'Hello,' I reply with a forced smile.

Francesca is wearing copious amounts of bracelets and necklaces, all of varying colours and designs. They jangle and clatter together as she jogs up to me. It is difficult to define her age due to the ridiculous layers of makeup she constantly wears. Her hair is dyed jet black and her facial skin is tight – too tight for a natural look. She must have Botox injections as often as she switches her male partners, but again ... I do not judge and I do not care. It is merely an observation.

'I'm so happy I caught you Alexis. I've been meaning to call and book a table for tomorrow night, but you know how it is ... you can lose track of time so quickly. Do you have any space *tesoro*?' (I have come to learn that *tesoro* means darling).

'Yes, I do. What time would you like?'

I am aware that I gave the last space to Benjamin earlier, but I usually have an extra table hidden away in the back for overflow. I do not always use it because it means the tables are slightly too close together and I do not like my bar to be overcrowded, but Francesca is a good and loyal customer and more often than not spends a fortune on the most expensive wine, so for her I almost always make an exception.

'Oooh, eight would be perfect. *Grazie tesoro*.'

'Shall I set the table for two?'

'Yes please, I'll be bringing my *husband*,' she replies casually. She glances at me and winks. I do not know if she will actually be bringing her real husband or if *husband* is her codeword for lover, but again ... I do not care, although if he is her real husband I may feel the urge to warn him about his whore of a wife.

'Perfect,' I say with a smile. 'See you then.'

'*Ciao*! *Grazie,* Alexis!'

Francesca flounces off towards the hairdressers. I roll my eyes, mutter a few obscene words, put my head down and drive back home.

I manage to install the security cameras within an hour and have just enough time to take Oscar for another quick stroll before I need to start opening the bar for tonight's customers. The security system is linked to an app on my phone. I can disable the alarm throughout the day, but still have the cameras running to capture any movement, and I can set the alarm function overnight to alert me of any intruders. If only I could set up a similar system to turn off these haunting dreams.

I am about to open my bar when my phone rings. It is not often I receive calls, so I am slightly startled by the noise. I glance at the screen for a clue, but the number has been withheld. I am in the middle of setting the tables, so I put the call on loudspeaker and set it on the table in front of me.

'Hello?'

Silence.

'Hello. Alexis speaking.'

Silence.

Oh my God it's him! It's happening again.

I stop setting the table with the wine glasses and gingerly lift the phone to my mouth and speak very slowly into it.

'Peter, is that you?'

Silence and then ... breathing.

I am so stunned that I cannot speak even though I have been rehearsing what I would say if this ever happened again over and over in my head every day for the past year and a half. The words refuse to form in my mouth, like they have been stolen from me. I hate that he can do this to me without barely doing a thing. Despite my insistence that I am not afraid, I am ... and that is what terrifies me most of all.

The line goes dead and I am left shaking with fear.

Chapter Three

Alicia

I am angry at myself for reacting in such a weak and pathetic way. The phone call last night has shaken me, more than I care to admit. It has upset Josslyn too. She is now jumping at every noise and second-guessing everything I do. It is not her fault so I do not blame her reaction. She has lived through this once before and the idea of being stalked again is clearly having a negative impact. I have decided that, until I know otherwise, everyone is a suspect. I cannot automatically assume that the phone call was from Peter. The logical part of my brain keeps telling me that he has not found us and that Josslyn and I are perfectly safe and the call was only a wrong number. However, the suspicious part of my brain has the majority of the control and is constantly on the lookout for him, or someone else that may be watching us.

I have a dark and sinister feeling inside of me that is growing by the second. I fear that the killer part of me is returning, ready to defend myself and Josslyn no matter what it takes. I have killed people to keep us safe and I will continue to do so if necessary. I am trying to become a better person, but how can I when I feel constantly threatened? Josslyn convinced me to sleep with a knife under my pillow last night, like she used to do on occasion.

She is paranoid, which in turn, is causing me to become paranoid.

I searched online for Peter again this morning; maybe Josslyn is right – Peter is now *my* obsession and I am now stalking him. We even discussed flying back to England and facing him, but that plan was quickly disregarded when I pointed out that it was too risky to show our face. Josslyn finally agreed to remain hidden.

The Wednesday evening events unfold as normal. Customers arrive, sit at their tables, enjoy their wine, comment on the beautiful scenery, make a fuss of Oscar and chat amongst themselves. The evening would be exactly like every other evening if it were not for the fact that I feel as if I have a vice-like grip around my chest, squeezing the life out of me.

Francesca and her *husband* arrive at eight sharp. She is dressed in a tight, sparkly red dress, showing off her no-doubt fake breasts and he is wearing a sharp suit and tie. Some would say they are slightly overdressed for my wine bar, sticking out compared to the otherwise smart/casual style of the other customers, but they certainly do turn heads. I cannot help but notice that her *husband* is not wearing a wedding ring and that he is at least ten years her junior ... none of my business, of course. Francesca orders the most expensive bottle of red wine and tells me to 'keep it coming' so I make a mental note to ensure her wine glass is never empty for the remainder of the evening.

At nine o'clock precisely, Benjamin arrives. I cannot fault his punctuality. I have the bottle of red wine he gave me yesterday stashed behind the bar. He looks like he has made a conscious effort to dress up. He is wearing dark jeans and a crisp blue shirt that has been expertly ironed, the collar open, the sleeves professionally rolled up to show off his tanned forearms. He catches my eye, smiles and waves. I nod curtly to show that I have spotted him as I pour some wine for a table full of businessmen, who have progressively grown louder throughout the evening. Benjamin waits patiently by the bar while I finish, but I notice that he keeps looking over at me and then quickly turning his head away. It looks suspicious ... but maybe that is just my own imagination.

I finish serving the table and walk behind the bar, ready to attend to Benjamin.

'Hi,' he says as he leans against the bar, flashing me his perfect smile.

I purposefully have not added stools for people to sit on so that they are less inclined to stay at the bar and talk to me. It does not work with everyone; some people insist on talking to me anyway. I read in an online article about bartending that the perfect bartender is like a therapist; there to listen. I am clearly not a perfect bartender because listening to people's problems in their own pathetic lives is literally the worst way in which I could possibly spend an evening.

'Hello Benjamin. What would you like to drink?'

'How about that bottle of red? You still free to join me for a glass? I promise you'll like it.'

'How can you possibly promise me that?'

'I can't, but I can promise that after a couple of glasses I'll be much more interesting to talk to.' He grins at me and I mentally roll my eyes. I have never been comfortable with men flirting with me. I find it tedious and unnecessary. If I wished to have sex with a man then they would be aware of that fact straight away. I do not waste my time with flirting, but it appears to be one of those socially acceptable and normal past-times, so I do my best and play along.

'I am afraid I am busy for the next hour, as I said before, but it will begin to get quieter after ten.'

'Then I'll see you around ten. Save the red for later. I'll have a large Cabernet Sauvignon now, if I may, to tide me over until then.'

I nod, impressed at his perfect pronunciation. He watches me intently as I uncork the bottle and begin to pour.

'Where's Oscar?'

'Asleep under the bar. It is past his bedtime.'

Benjamin smiles as he takes the glass from me. Our fingers lightly touch and he lingers for a few seconds before taking a sip.

'Perfection.'

'Your table is over in the corner.'

'I'll see you soon. Bring the bottle.'

I let out an exasperated sigh as he walks away.

This is definitely a date.

I do not wish to date Benjamin.

Can I date him then?

Excuse me?

I've been thinking ... just hear me out ... maybe I can try and take you over. I'm not saying that I'll be any better at talking to him than you will, but I won't lie ... I'm bored of being stuck in your head. I miss my body, you know I do. I miss the feel of the sun on my skin, the smell of fresh air, the softness of Oscar's fur ... the touch of another human being. Please can we try?

Absolutely not.

Oh, come on Alicia! Give me a break. You'd take me over whenever you damn well wanted to. I never had a chance to say no sometimes. Well, now it's my turn.

You are not strong enough.

But if you allow me and let me take control maybe it'll work ... like the first time we tried as kids, remember?

It will not work.

You won't even try, will you?

No.

Fine. Fuck you. Enjoy your fucking date. I hope you have a horrible time.

For the next five minutes all I hear is Josslyn muttering abuse at me.

At ten fifteen the table of businessmen have left (after spending over five-hundred Euros on wine) and there is a lot less noise and customers in the room. Francesca and her *husband* are on their third bottle of wine between them (it will not be long before I cut them off because I do not want customers passing out in my bar despite what I said before about agreeing to keep her glass full) and Benjamin has been nursing his first glass of wine for the past hour and fifteen minutes. I am unable to avoid the inevitable any longer, so I reluctantly retrieve the bottle of red from behind the bar, uncork it, pour out two glasses and head over to the corner table with both glasses and the bottle.

Benjamin sees me approaching and immediately straightens up and smiles. I take a seat and hand him one of the glasses.

'I am still working,' I say. 'I can only have one.'

'I'll agree to that ... Cheers.'

'Cheers.'

We perform the usual ritual of clinking glasses and take a sip simultaneously. He does not take his eyes off me the entire time. He is clearly waiting for me to mention the wine. It is a Cannonau di Sardegna from the island of Sardinia. It is a strange choice for his favourite wine as it is not known for its great flavour profile, however I do taste ripe berries, plums and cranberries with a hint of white spice.

'It is ... nice,' I say, licking my lips.

His eyes darken as he watches me. 'Oh come on, you run a wine bar ... you can do better than that.'

I inwardly sigh in frustration, annoyed that he is pushing me into making small talk. I have no intention of discussing wine, however since he is insisting I decide to be brutally honest with him.

'I think it is rather bland. The flavour is not that strong, but I can see why you like it. It is rich in antioxidant compounds which promote heart health.'

Jesus Christ, Alicia. You're really bad at flirting. Is that the best you can do?

I thought you were angry with me.

So sue me ... I'm intrigued.

I ignore Josslyn's remark as I watch a smile spread across Benjamin's face.

'You know your wine after all.'

'Why is this particular wine your favourite?'

'I don't know. Maybe it's because it was the first proper wine I ever tasted. Back at university my best friend and I went on a wine tasting tour. It was where we forged our friendship I guess. This wine is important to me because of that.'

A completely ridiculous reason for liking a particular wine, but I do not mention this fact. I take another sip and then lean back in the chair.

'What's your favourite wine?' he asks me.

'Guess.'

'Pinot grigio?' He did not even pause to think about it.

I narrow my eyes at him. 'Have you been spying on me Benjamin?'

Benjamin laughs awkwardly and shifts in his chair. 'No, you just look like a pinot kind of girl ... and please, call me Ben.'

Alicia, please stop making this date so uncomfortable.

I do not trust him. How can he know what my favourite wine is?

Maybe it was a lucky guess.

Doubtful.

Okay, fine, you don't trust him. Can you just talk to the man without mentally accusing him of stalking you? Not every man is like Peter.

I disagree. All men are untrustworthy. This is exhaustingly hard work. He is all yours ... you have five minutes and then I need to get back to work.

Then I make a decision that I know I will later come to regret. I close my eyes and relinquish control of my body. I do not know how it happens, but it does.

I am gone and Josslyn is back.

Chapter Four
Josslyn

Oh my fucking God ... I'm back! Holy shit ... uh, what do I do? How do I speak? What's my name again? Where am I?

This feels so weird and surreal. I feel different. I am different. This body has changed so much and I feel so fucking good! This body is awesome and strong and ... tight. I automatically feel my stomach – no fat rolls (not that I had them before, but I definitely had a bit more excess fat than I do now). My hair is shorter, my butt is firmer and ... are my boobs bigger?

I suddenly realise that I haven't said a word yet and Ben is staring at me, as I attempt to not panic at the fact that I'm back in my body for the first time in nearly two years. I can feel myself getting anxious and my face turning red, so I reach forward, grab the glass of wine and down it in one go without pausing for a breath.

Oh my God – I've missed you wine! I don't know what Alicia's talking about. This wine is awesome ... and I never really liked red wine before.

I wipe my mouth after I've swallowed the last gulp and realise my mistake. Shit. I'm supposed to be Alicia ... I mean Alexis ... I mean ... shit! He's staring at me ...

'S-sorry,' I say. 'I was suddenly really thirsty.'

I can see Ben's mouth twitching, as if he's trying his hardest not to burst out laughing.

'Top up?' He picks up the bottle.

'Uh ... I shouldn't. I'm working.'

'You sure?'

'Oh, why the hell not. Fill me up ... I mean, top me up ... I—' It seems I'm still not great at having a normal conversation either.

Ben continues to hide his laughter as he fills my glass. I greedily take another sip, but then try and control my urges. Okay, let's do this. I only have five minutes. I'm on a date with a very attractive man who is happily talking to me and I have a glass of wine in my hand. I've been in worse positions before. Let's see ... what do people talk about on dates?

'So Ben,' I say casually, crossing my legs and leaning towards him slightly, 'how long have you lived in Tuscany?'

'You called me Ben.'

Fuck. Alicia ... I mean Alexis ... never calls him Ben.

'Er ... yeah, you asked me to call you Ben.'

'Right, yeah, I did.' He frowns at me slightly, but then noticeably relaxes. 'I moved here just over a year ago before the pandemic hit to have a bit of time to myself. I've always loved the area. Then I guess I got stuck here for a while. I'm really only here just to say I've lived in Tuscany to try and sound interesting to women. I started working in the delicatessen just to make some cash, but then the pandemic started and I was off work for a while, but I've fallen in love with the country ... and the people.' He sips his wine and smiles. 'What made you move out here and start a wine bar?'

Where do I even start?

'Err ... same as you. I like the area. I like wine.' I feel so fucking stupid right now.

'Good call. Where's home for you? Where did you grow up?'

Okay, this is getting a bit too personal. I'm supposed to be Alexis and she is not supposed to have anything to do with Josslyn who grew up in the New Forest. Josslyn doesn't exist anymore. I must be careful not to reveal too much information. Alicia is right ... I shouldn't trust him, so I decide to be someone else and totally make shit up on the spot.

'I grew up in Cambridge.' I use that city because to be perfectly honest it's the only city I can remember apart from London, and London's boring. Everyone's from London.

'You're kidding!'

I look confused. 'No, why?'

'So did I. I grew up in Cambridge too.'

I laugh out loud because it's just so ridiculous. I'm pretty sure he's just trying to find similarities between us to make me like him. It's an age-old trick that men do to get women interested in them. I'm not stupid.

'Whereabouts did you live in Cambridge?' he asks.

Shit. This was a mistake. I have no idea about the different areas of Cambridge.

Alicia, come back. I need help!

'Err ... the west ... side,' I slur.

I take two big gulps of wine, finishing the second glass and that's when I start feeling a bit woozy. Ah, the blissful fog of alcohol. I blink several times to try and regain some control over my vision, but it's going blurry. I can feel myself slipping away. Ben is moving further and further out of sight ... and then I'm gone.

Chapter Five
Alicia

I knew I would regret giving Josslyn control. She has had five minutes in this body and already she has consumed two full glasses of wine. My head is foggy and Benjamin is staring at me. I need him to leave. I struggle to my feet, clutching the back of the chair for support as the room spins around me.

'I-I need to get back to work.' I can barely speak.

Fuck you, Josslyn!

'Here, let me help you.' Benjamin goes to stand, but I put my hand up to stop him.

'No, thank you, but I do not require your help Benjamin.'

'What happened to Ben?'

'It was a momentary lapse of judgement.'

'Are you sure you don't need any help? You downed that wine pretty quick. I'm not sure whether to be impressed or concerned.'

I straighten myself up and attempt to stand, but my body fails me and I stumble sideways into the chair. Benjamin lunges forwards and steadies me.

'Why don't you let me serve some customers for a few minutes. I used to bartend at university. Why don't you take a seat behind the bar and I'll get you a glass of water?'

I want to decline his offer, but there is no way I will be able to professionally serve my customers while I am seeing double. I nod slowly and he helps me to the stool behind the bar. I perch on it while I watch him fill up a glass with water from the tap. I take it from him and start drinking. He expertly and quickly attends to all the tables, asking them if they require a refill, fulfils a few drink orders and then proceeds to clear up a spilt drink.

I watch him intently, silently amazed as his aptitude.

I'm so sorry, Alicia. I got carried away.

That is the last time I allow you to take over with alcohol around. You seriously have a drinking problem Josslyn.

I know, but it felt so good to feel something again. Thank you. I really appreciate it. I'm just sorry I fucked it up.

I am silent for a moment. I want to be angry with her, but I do know how she feels. I spent twenty-eight years trapped inside this body, only able to feel and do things for myself when the moment arose, and when it did, I always took full advantage of it. I cannot blame her for wanting to do the same.

You are welcome.

Can I take over again another time?

I will think about it, but now Benjamin is on to us. He could tell something was different. We need to be careful around him. Did he really say he grew up in Cambridge?

Yeah, but I don't think it's true. I think he only said it to try and bond with me ... us.

Maybe.

Despite what Josslyn says I am still slightly suspicious.

Five minutes later Benjamin returns with a smile on his face.

'All happy customers. Don't worry, I don't think any of them have noticed that you're drunk. Most of them are wasted themselves.'

'I apologise for my behaviour Benjamin. I do not usually drink to that excess.'

'I guess you do like the wine after all.'

I give him a small smile. 'I guess so. I believe I am feeling better now. Thank you for your help. You may now leave.'

Benjamin ignores my last statement. 'You know ... you're actually pretty funny and a lot more relaxed when you're drunk. It's like you're a different person.'

'I have heard that once or twice before. That is why I do not drink very often.'

'Maybe we can do it again some time. I really enjoyed those five minutes with you.'

I lick my lips and take a sip of water. It is time to break his heart.

'I am sorry Benjamin, but I am not looking for any sort of relationship with you. I cannot give you want you want.'

'And what is it you think I want?' His eyes have darkened and he is staring deep into my soul. I feel vulnerable and I do not like it.

'I assume you wish to have a sexual relationship with me.'

Benjamin raises his eyebrows and a slight red tinge appears on his cheeks. 'I won't deny that I haven't thought about it, but that's not exactly what I want.'

'Okay, then I can only assume that you wish to get to know me, to get me to open up and confide in you, but I can promise you that you will not like what you find.'

'I disagree. I like what I've found so far. Look, I'm not asking you to sleep with me or marry me ... just ... give me a chance. You don't have a lot of friends here Alexis. I can tell that you're lonely. Let me be a friend ... or just have really rough, hot sex with me and toss me to the curb, you know, whatever you want.' He winks at me, clearly hoping that I find his attempt at humour cute and appealing. Annoyingly, I do.

I sigh. Maybe it is the buzz due to the wine, but I feel myself relaxing a little in his presence. I hold out my hand for him to shake it.

'Just friends,' I say.

Benjamin nods and we shake hands. 'Friends,' he repeats. 'With benefits?'

'Do not push it.'

Benjamin laughs. 'Maybe one day soon you'll let me talk to that other girl inside you again.'

My heart skips a beat, but then I realise what he means – he means the stupid, fun, drunk side of me. He means Josslyn.

'Maybe,' I reply quietly.

Oh my God, do you think he likes me?

Josslyn, control yourself. Remember what happened the last time we had a threesome with a man?

Yeah, you took over and scratched his back. Can't we just have a bit of fun?

No. It is too risky. I am trying to keep us safe.

You need to loosen up and get laid. He's harmless.

We shall see.

Benjamin stays with me until the last customer leaves. Francesca and her *husband* call it a night after three bottles of wine. I order them a taxi and help her into it. She calls me a darling again in Italian and winks at me, telling me that the man I am with is 'one hot piece of meat' and that I should 'taste his sausage'. Honestly, drunk people are ridiculous.

Luckily, my wine buzz fades and I am able to get back to work. I begin to wipe the tables while Benjamin washes the empty glasses. As much as I hate to admit it, it feels nice to have him around helping me. We engage in general conversation until the bar area is clean and tidy and I am ready to switch off the lights.

'So,' he says. 'I see you've installed some security cameras.'

I look above my head at the new camera. 'Yes, you can never be too careful.'

'True ... listen, thanks for tonight. I know you've a hard time with people, but ... I like you. I'm happy to be friends for now. I can give you as much time as you need, but if you're not interested in me at all then tell me now so I can begin to pick up the broken pieces of my heart.'

I smile at his further attempt at humour. 'Benjamin ... I am not—'

I am unable to finish my sentence because he leans into me and kisses me, lightly at first, but then he takes both his hands, cups the back of my head and neck and draws me closer. My body automatically responds and I kiss him back, hot and heavy. My breath escapes my body and I feel a tingling sensation all over, the hairs on the back of my neck springing to attention.

Then just as quickly as he kisses me he pulls away, but I am left wanting more. My body physically aches to be touched. I fight the urge to grab him, wrap my legs around his waist and fuck him right there in the open.

'Think about it,' he says.

And then he turns and leaves.

Holy mother of fucking God.

Chapter Six

Alicia

I do think about it. I think about it all fucking night and it infuriates me. I cannot turn my brain off from that kiss and Josslyn keeps repeating *holy mother of fucking God* over and over. I am extremely conflicted, constantly battling my inner and most darkest thoughts, but by the time all the morning jobs have been completed I have made up my mind – Benjamin has to go. I cannot have him around me, muddying my mind. He is clearly a distraction and one which I cannot afford to have.

Please don't kill him Alicia.

I did not say I was going to kill him. He just has to be told to keep his distance. I should have punched him in the face when he kissed me.

But that wouldn't have been nearly as much fun.

I disagree.

You enjoyed the kiss.

I sigh in annoyance. Sometimes I wish Josslyn did not know me so well.

He must go. Besides ... it is clearly you he has feelings for, not me.

He only met me for like five minutes.

Yet he wanted to see you again.

But he thinks we're the same person.

We are.

Oh shit ... you're right.

Of course I am right.

He has to go. It's too fucked up and complicated. I can't deal with another weird love triangle again. Not after the whole Peter thing.

Then finally we agree ... Benjamin has to go.

Yeah ... I guess ... but oh my fucking God ...

It was not that good of a kiss.

Yeah, okay ... you just keeping telling yourself that.

I switch on the computer and watch the screen come to life. It is time for the daily Peter search. Oscar is on my lap. He seems extra affectionate towards me today, possibly due to the fact he can smell or sense that Josslyn is close by. I stroke his soft fur while he snoozes, letting out little happy whimpers as he does so.

I begin my routine search, flicking through the daily headlines on the BBC News website.

You know, maybe you should let Peter go too. You're basically stalking him the way he stalked us. It's been over a year and a half. I doubt he's still looking for us or cares about us anymore.

You clearly do not know a lot about psychopaths.

Are you sure he's a psychopath ... and not just a ... sick, twisted freak?

He and I are very similar in many ways. Once a psychopath forms an idea or a plan in their head then they never deviate from that plan. I planned to take full control of this body, no matter what the cost and I did exactly that.

Yeah, cheers for that. You had me cut myself out.

A necessary cost.

Tell me the truth ... you never expected or wanted me to come back, did you?

No, but then I did not expect the doctor to leave a part of the ... individual—

You were going to say tumour then, weren't you?

Yes. I did not expect them to leave a part of you inside me, but as it happens they did and you came back and now we must live with it.

Are you glad I came back?

I do not answer, not because I refuse to tell her the truth, which is that I am glad she came back, but because I have spotted a new online video article on the BBC News website relating to a very familiar name, but it is not the name of the person I have been searching for. It is a name from the past, one which I had hoped would never surface again.

The young cameraman speaks directly to the camera whilst holding a microphone.

'A body of a man in his early thirties has been found at a landfill site just outside of Cambridge. The body is badly decomposed and experts say he has been dead for well over a year having been stabbed approximately twenty-six times in the chest, neck and face. The man's identity has been revealed as Daniel Russell, who disappeared on the 9th of November 2019. He was last seen at a club in Bournemouth. His family have been informed. A local Cambridge man called Peter Phillips discovered the body while visiting the landfill. He is somewhat of a local hero having recently won the Teacher of the Year award at Lampton Boarding School for Boys. He, unfortunately, knows how it feels to lose a family member. His sister, Alicia Phillips, disappeared seven years ago. Peter is here with me now and would like to speak to the person responsible for Daniel's death ... and is hoping that they see this broadcast and turn themselves in ... Peter, what would you like to say?'

'Thank you Keith. Yes, my sister disappeared seven years ago. I don't know what happened to her. The police say that she killed herself, but I know that's not true. I'll never stop looking for her. I'm just glad I found Daniel Russell's body so that it may give his family the closure they deserve. No one should have to go through the torture of not knowing what happened to someone they love. I want to talk directly to the person who killed this man ... and I'll say this ... come forward and confess. It's the only way that you will find peace and closure yourself. Come forward ... or I promise you ... you'll regret it for the rest of your life.'

'Thank you Peter. And now, back to you in the studio ...'

The video cuts out and everything goes silent.

Oh God, I think I'm going to be sick—

I immediately shove Oscar off my lap and grab the nearest object I can find (the wastepaper bin next to the desk) and vomit up my breakfast. Oscar barks at me in annoyance, but then gently licks my hand while I recover. I hover over the bin for a few seconds in case any more food decides to reappear. It does not. I take the bin and clean it out, then head into the kitchen for a glass of water. I lean against the counter for support as I take small sips, trying to catch my breath. My heart is hammering inside my chest and all I see are black spots dancing in front of me.

I close my eyes and recall the memory of repeatedly plunging my knife into Daniel's body over and over ... and over. Blood had spurted everywhere. I remember the pure elation I had felt at that moment. I had never wanted to stop. He was a bad man and he had deserved to die. I do not regret killing him. My only regret is that I allowed Josslyn to tell Peter about him and I let Peter dispose of the body. It had been a stupid and costly mistake. I had never known where the body had ended up ... until now. Peter has now used his knowledge against me and has gone back, dug him up and alerted the media. Now he has made a public declaration to me to come forward and confess, while at the same time looking like a fucking hero to everyone else.

I am angry – I am more than angry. I am furious and I need a release. I immediately throw the half empty glass of water against the nearest wall. Oscar runs for cover under the desk while I kick my foot through a cupboard door, then punch my fist through the glass cabinet holding a set of expensive wine glasses. Pain radiates through my hand as shards of glass slice their way through my skin, drawing blood. Lastly, I grab my favourite cup (a large one with the words Fuck Off on it) which is drying on the draining board and hurl it against the fridge door. It smashes apart and clatters to the floor. I immediately regret my decision – that was my favourite cup.

I notice that Josslyn has not attempted to calm me down or stop me from destroying the house. She is as angry as I am, but I can sense fear in her too. She is afraid that Peter has found us, that he will tell the media who killed Daniel, that we will be arrested for murder and locked up for the rest of our lives, but I know that this is not true.

How do you know that? You heard him ... he's threatening us.

Exactly. He is merely threatening us. I do not believe he will reveal the truth to the media for it will tarnish his reputation. How can he possibly tell the truth and accuse us of murdering Daniel without making himself look guilty of a crime at the same time? No, he will not tell a soul. Also, he does not know where we are, but he is getting desperate. He knows I am keeping tabs on him. He knew I would watch that broadcast. He is trying to draw us out, to get us to make a mistake. He is not giving up on finding us. We must stay hidden.

You heard him ... he said we'll regret it if we don't come forward.

It is merely a weak attempt at threatening us. It will not work. I will not let him control me.

But—

We do nothing.

But—

We ... do ... nothing.

My right hand is stinging and bleeding so I go to the bathroom and fetch the first aid kit. There are small slithers of glass embedded in my knuckles. I pick up the tweezers and gently begin to pull them out, but I do not flinch. Pain makes me feel alive. I watch as blood trickles down my hand and into the white basin. It creates mesmerising patterns with the water as it swirls down the plughole in beautiful waves. Blood has always fascinated me. It is our life force. We are unable to survive without it, yet it can escape from our body so easily through merely a small slice of our skin. Human beings are weak when you really think about it.

I look up and stare at my reflection in the mirror above the sink. I reach out my bloody hand and stroke my reflection, tracing the outline of my face. I am not the person I once was. I may be stronger physically, but since gaining full control of this body I have weakened mentally. I used to be Alicia – a strong woman who would stop at nothing to ensure she got what she wanted, cold-blooded and vicious. Now look at me. I am weak and I am afraid – a man has rendered me useless. I am consumed by him. He haunts me and he is now hunting me again. I cannot allow him to control me. I must stop searching for him online and get on with my life. Peter is in my past. It is finally time to move on with my future. I will not be threatened by him any longer.

I wrap up my hand in a bandage once I have removed the last piece of glass and head back down to the kitchen to clean up the mess I have created. Oscar appears from under the desk, desperate to see me, but I tell him to stay back to protect his delicate paws from the glass spread out across the floor. He sits and watches me as I sweep and collect the debris and throw it into the bin.

Once the area is clear I sit on the sundeck and look out across the vineyard, taking in the scenery and the smell of the grapes growing. I have been foolish to think that I belong here, trying my best to fit in with the community and live a normal life. Yes, lockdown forced me to stay in one place for a while, but that is over now. The world is opening back up to me again and I am free to do whatever I want.

What are you saying Alicia?

I am saying it is time to leave.

Are you running away?

No. I am doing what I set out to do from the start. I will travel the world. I am not meant to stay in one place, not like you, always tied down to something or someone.

But you've built such a wonderful life here. What about Oscar? He likes it here.

I will give him to someone who will look after him.

No! You can't do that. I won't let you. He's my dog. You can't just give him away.

He cannot come with me. I am leaving, Josslyn. My mind is made up. Peter has made me realise who I truly am ... I am a psychopath and we are not designed to fit in and live normal lives. I was wrong to think that I could.

But maybe you are. Please ... don't do this. We need to stay and deal with our problems and Peter is a big problem. He needs to be dealt with once and for all before someone gets hurt. I don't want anyone else to get hurt.

Peter is not my problem anymore. I do not care about him.

What about the women he may stalk or hurt in the future? He'll never stop. What about them?

Fuck them.

You're a selfish bitch, Alicia. You always have been. I don't know why I ever thought you could change. I thought maybe being a part of me for nearly thirty years would make you more human, more inclined to feel ... something, anything ... but I was wrong. You're heartless and cruel and I hate you.

Say what you will about me, Josslyn. You will not have to worry about it for too much longer.

What the fuck does that mean?

It means that sooner or later you will fade away and I will finally be left alone to live my life the way I want to.

Excuse me? What do you mean by fade away?

Did I forget to mention that fact? The tiny piece of you they left inside of me will eventually become absorbed completely and you will cease to exist, something that should have happened in utero in the first place.

I-I ... you're lying.

No, Josslyn, I am not.

I'm really going to fade away?

Yes.

When?

I do not know the time frame exactly, but I imagine it will not be long.

Josslyn does not respond so I take her silence to mean that the conversation is over. I will allow her to silently hate me. She will eventually adapt, like she did when she learnt the news of her parents' passing. Josslyn is fairly resilient I have come to realise and at times she is more like me than she cares to admit. She may hate me, but I am doing this for her own good ... our own good.

That evening I open the bar as normal, however I have already started making plans to sell the property by contacting the local real estate agent. As you know, once I set my mind on something, I always achieve it, no matter how long it takes. I even had time earlier to browse destinations for where I might travel to first – Thailand, China, America. The world is now at my fingertips and for the first time in a long time I am awakened with the sense of adventure and freedom. I am angry with myself for not doing this sooner.

I glance around my bar at the happy customers as they drink their wine and laugh with each other, some even smile at me. These people mean nothing to me. I do not belong here. I have been wasting my time attempting to live a normal life, but here is a certain fact – I am not normal. How can I possibly attempt to continue this charade any longer? I have been lying to myself, attempting to cover up who I really am.

No more.

The appearance of Benjamin walking through the door causes me to awaken from my dark thoughts. This asshole needs to disappear. I am tired of men trying to control me.

'Hey,' he says as he stops at the bar in front of me.

'Benjamin,' I reply with a sharp nod.

'Listen, I'm just dropping in to apologise about last night. I shouldn't have kissed you like that. I know I don't know you that well, but I kind of get the feeling that you like your own space. I shouldn't have just assumed that you wanted me to kiss you. I apologise.'

I lift my chin ever so slightly, wanting to get angry with him, to start spitting insults, but I refrain from showing him my true feelings. After all, he is also a part of my plan, so I am required to be polite to him for the foreseeable future.

'You are forgiven Benjamin.'

'Thank you and listen, whenever you're ready to—'

'I am leaving.' I cut him short of finishing his sentence and watch as a confused expression takes over his face. He blinks several times.

'You're ... what? You're leaving?'

'Yes.'

'Why? Is it because of me?'

I sigh in annoyance – typical man assuming that everything is about him. 'No, it has nothing to do with you. I have just decided to leave.'

Benjamin does not respond. He merely looks like a pathetic puppy who has just been left by the side of the road. Speaking of which ...

'In fact, I have a favour to ask of you,' I continue.

'Um ... okay.'

'I am unable to take Oscar with me where I am going and was wondering if you would take him and look after him for me.'

'I ... really? Well, sure I can, but ... are you coming back for him?'

'No.'

'So you want me to look after him ... forever,' he states rather than asks.

'Yes.'

Benjamin scratches his head and sighs. 'Alexis ... I don't know what's happened in the past day that would cause you to suddenly up and leave, but you love Oscar. You can't just leave him. Of course I'll look after him, but ... he'll miss you.'

'He is a dog. He will adjust.'

Benjamin stares open-mouthed at me for a few seconds, clearly battling some inner dialogue that he wishes to say, but then he finally closes his mouth and nods slowly.

'Whatever you want, Alexis. I'll look after him for you. When do you leave?'

'As long as I can get all my affairs in order then I am hoping to be gone by the end of the month.'

'Where are you going?'

I do not reply.

Instead, I begin to fill up some glasses with a fresh bottle of white wine. There is an odd silence between us, one which I wish would be over as soon as possible, but I refuse to answer him. It is none of his business where I am going. I would rather no one know of my destination. I am just going to disappear.

'Okay, clearly you don't want to talk about it, but can you at least tell me why you're leaving so suddenly? You said it has nothing to do with me ... then who or what does it have to do with?'

I pick up the two full glasses of wine and walk over to the table in the corner where a man and a woman are waiting. We exchange smiles (theirs are real, mine is fake) as I hand them their beverages and then I walk back to the bar. Benjamin has not taken his eyes off me. I get the sense that he is slightly upset about the news of my leaving. That is not my fault.

'Alexis ... will you talk to me please?'

I stare at him and he takes a small step backwards. 'Benjamin, I do not know you. We have barely spoken before now. We are not friends, so—'

'That's funny because didn't we agree that we were friends only last night?'

'Things change.'

'In one day?'

'Look, I am sorry you feel angry about me leaving, but I do not owe you an explanation. All I need is for you to look after my dog. I wish him to live out the remainder of his days happy and with someone he likes and trusts. Can you do that for me?'

Benjamin bites his lip and frowns. 'Yes,' he replies slowly.

'Thank you.'

I turn and get back to pouring some more wine for my next set of customers. Benjamin is still refusing to leave, so I ignore him and continue with my work.

When I return a few minutes later he is gone.

Alicia, you've gone too far this time. You've really hurt his feelings and mine. Why has that video made you react this way? Admit it ... you're scared.

I am not afraid.

Then don't run, don't leave. Let's go and visit Peter and have it out with him.

There is no need.

Josslyn screams in frustration inside my head.

Chapter Seven
Alicia

Over the course of the following week I spend my time booking flights, selling unnecessary items (my car for one) and talking with the estate agent who comes to do a viewing. We agree on an adequate selling price for the villa and it is put up for sale. I arrange with him to take care of the sale via email and phone, so that I can leave the country as soon as possible. I inform my customers that I am selling my bar and am surprised by their disappointment. They say they will miss me, but to have a wonderful time wherever I am going. Luckily, they do not ask too many questions.

Josslyn is very quiet and barely says two words to me throughout the week. I refuse to let her take over again, as I do not desire a repeat of last time. I arrange with Benjamin to come and collect Oscar on Saturday, the day after tomorrow. I have booked a flight to Croatia for Sunday the 25th of July and plan to travel from there to Hungary, then to Poland and finally up to Norway and Sweden. I have money in my account and will acquire more once the villa has been sold. I have packed only the essentials – a week's worth of clothes, necessary toiletries and my sturdy walking boots. I plan on doing a lot of walking and living and staying in hostels. It will not be glamorous, but it will enable me to live under the radar and be free from conformity and rules. I will make my own rules. I will live my own life, the way I should have always lived it, not tied down to one place and obsessing over pathetic men. I am extremely enthusiastic and find myself excited by the prospect of travelling, something that has been a dream of mine ever since I was a child.

Today is Thursday and it is my last night officially running the wine bar. It will be closed from tomorrow until a new owner can acquire it. It may never open again. The new occupants may wish to transform the building into something else entirely. I do not care for it is only a building. I have no emotional connection to it, nor anything here anymore. Josslyn thinks I am avoiding my true emotions, but she is wrong. I have no emotions. She and I were wrong to think that I have changed. I will never change – true psychopaths do not change.

The night begins like any other – my customers arrive, some with farewell cards and gifts for me (mostly wine) and some even wish to give me a hug to say goodbye. I reluctantly accept, but only in order to keep up appearances. I despise contact with fellow human beings.

Benjamin shows up with a bouquet of flowers and hands them to me with a solemn look on his face. I take them and stand there awkwardly, not really knowing how I should be reacting. It is the first time I have ever been given a bouquet of flowers.

'I'm sorry,' he says. 'I'm sorry for snapping at you. I overreacted. It's just ... I'm going to miss you. I wish you were staying. It was all just so sudden.'

'Thank you,' I say. I place the flowers down on the bar. 'I shall miss you too.'

'Really?'

'No.'

'Oh.'

'I just said that as I assume it was what you wanted me to say.'

Benjamin sighs. 'You're a difficult woman to talk to at times, you know.'

'I am aware.'

I glimpse a flicker of a smile. 'Anyway, I just brought the flowers as a good luck and goodbye sort of thing. I'll be back on Saturday to pick up Oscar.'

'See you then.'

'Where is the little guy anyway?'

'He is in his bed under the bar—' I glance briefly at the dog bed in the corner, but it appears that I am mistaken. Oscar is not there. 'Actually, I do not know where he is.' I look around the bar area in case he is begging for treats and attention from the customers. He is not. Benjamin helps me search for the dog, but he is nowhere to be found in the general area.

'He's probably outside having a pee,' says Benjamin. 'I'll go and check.'

I watch him leave through the double doors out onto the sundeck. The sun is beginning to set, creating glorious colours across the horizon. I walk up to the nearest table of customers.

'Have you seen Oscar?' I ask.

The old couple shake their heads. 'Not since we came in earlier about an hour ago,' says the old man.

'Okay, thank you.'

I back away and walk out onto the sundeck. I can see Benjamin walking around at the bottom of the courtyard. He is calling Oscar's name. That is the moment when I get a tight sensation across my chest and it continues to get tighter as I watch Benjamin walk towards me, shaking his head.

'I don't think he's out here. Maybe he's back at the villa? Do you want me to check?'

'No, I will do it. Can you stay here with the customers? Francesca and her ... husband ... should be arriving soon. They are to be seated at the back left corner table.'

'Of course.'

The vice around my chest continues to tighten as I walk towards the villa. It is very unusual for Oscar to go missing. The one time he did I found him at the bottom of the vineyard digging a hole, but that was during the day and this is the evening. Oscar likes to sleep during the evening under the bar. He hardly ever leaves the warm comfort of his bed except to go outside to relieve himself or to greet a friendly customer. He has his routine and he very rarely deviates from it, which is why I find myself confused as to his whereabouts.

What's going on?

I am unable to find Oscar.

What? He never goes missing.

I am aware.

Maybe he knows you're going to abandon him.

I push open the front door, glancing above at the security camera as I do so. A part of me thinks I should check the security app on my phone for any movement, but I resist for the time being. The villa is lit dimly by the setting of the sun, casting shadows all around. I do not turn on any lights as I make my way through the rooms and upstairs into my bedroom. I had expected to possibly find him asleep on my bed, but the room is empty, the bed undisturbed since I made it neatly this morning. Again, I glance briefly at the camera in the top right corner of the room, which is pointing in the direction of my bed. I can see the tiny green light blinking, a sign that it is working as it should.

I turn to leave and that is when I feel a cold breeze skim past my right shoulder. I turn my head quickly, but there is nothing there. I do not know where the breeze came from as the windows are not open in my room.

I have a strange feeling.

As do I.

Please hurry up and find Oscar.

I hastily walk out of the villa and make my way across the courtyard and towards the vineyard. Oscar has a favourite spot at the bottom of the rows of vines. I assume an animal lives around the area as the ground is usually disturbed in some way. That is where I am headed now. I involuntarily start to speed up, not because I want to find Oscar quickly, but because I feel as if I am being followed and it is unnerving me slightly. Josslyn is correct – it is a strange feeling.

I arrive at the beginning of the vineyard and slow to a casual walk. I call his name a few times, but there is no happy bark in response, nor the jingle of his collar as the tags clash together. I glance behind me at the bar area where I can hear a faint hum of happy conversation and wine glasses clinking and then keep pressing on. The vines are growing big and tall and are blocking the natural path so I gently push them aside. I call his name once more, as I know I am near his favourite spot and that is when I hear a quiet and gentle whimper. I tilt my head in the direction of the sound and wait for another. It comes and this time it is slightly louder.

'Oscar,' I whisper. 'What are you doing all the way out here?'

I reach the end of the vineyard and stop. The sound has now ceased, but I believe it originally came from the long grass ahead. I take a few steps forward ... and that is when I see the spots of blood on the ground. At this point I feel Josslyn's panic and fear rise up from within and without her ordering me to do so I start to run and follow the trail of blood spatters across the grass. My heartbeat is deafening in my ears, my heart thumping so hard it could easily push through my chest. The blood stops and starts several times, causing me to lose track on one occasion, but I quickly find my way again.

I can see a clearing up ahead, which is lightly illuminated by the final light of the day. I do not need to see the scene up ahead to know what has happened. The vice-like grip on my chest squeezes so tight that I stop breathing for several seconds as I lay my eyes on the poor, helpless creature on the ground in front of me.

Oscar's fur is matted and covered with fresh, sticky blood, which is pooling around his trembling body. His breaths are short and sharp and he is letting out low whimpers that are barely audible. I hear Josslyn scream his name as I fall to my knees beside him. I do not know what to do. I am completely helpless. Josslyn is screaming and crying, and I try to remain calm in my movements, but inside there is a white-hot burning rage growing, one that will not stay buried for long. Oscar does not have a lot of time left.

Alicia, please! Let me take over. Let me say goodbye. I need to say goodbye to him.

I close my eyes without a second thought.

Chapter Eight
Josslyn

Immediately I'm me again. Tears start streaming down my face, my vision blurring. I'm choking on my own tears as I gently reach down and touch Oscar's fur. As soon as I place my hand on him he whimpers and attempts to lift his head. He sees me. He knows it's me and he lightly wags his tail a few times, but the energy is draining out of him fast and he's unable to keep wagging his tail for long.

'O-Oscar,' I stutter with a wobbly smile as I gently lift his body into my arms. He licks my hand. 'It's me boy. It's me. I'm sorry I've been away for so long, but I'm here now. It's okay, I'm here.'

I adjust my position so he's cradled in my arms like a baby. I can feel blood running down my arms and soaking the ground around me. I start to cry hard again, unable to control it. My body shakes as my tears mix with his blood. I bury my face into his soft fur and breathe him in.

Josslyn, do something. You are a vet are you not? Save him.

Alicia's voice startles me.

I-I ... there's ... there's nothing I can do. I think his lungs have been punctured and they're filling up with blood. He's haemorrhaging ... I can't ... I can't save him ...

I feel so helpless and I know Alicia feels the same way. I sit and cry, allowing the tears to flow.

Goodbye Oscar. I am sorry.

Alicia's words make me cry harder. I stare down at Oscar's trembling body. His eyes are closed, but his tail is ever so softly moving, as if he is trying to wag it. He's in a lot of pain, but I know he's happy because I'm here with him. I watch as his tail wags for the very last time and I feel his body grow still in my arms.

I lift my head up to the sky and scream at the top of my lungs.

I don't know how long I sit and clutch his lifeless body, but suddenly I can hear footsteps and a man's voice shouting from somewhere in the distance.

'Alexis! Where are you?'

I can barely focus on what's happening because I feel as if I'm in a dream and everything is moving in slow motion. I feel so numb and nothing, besides the dead body of my dog, is registering in my brain. Ben bursts onto the scene and stops in his tracks when he sees me, gasping in horror. He lunges forward to help, but I look up and shout at him.

'Go away! Leave me alone!'

Ben stops. 'Alexis, what's happened? ... I'm ... I don't ... I'm so sorry. What can I do?'

'Go back and tell everyone to leave,' I sob. 'I don't want anyone here anymore. Tell them all to fucking leave!'

'Yes, of course.' Ben backs away a few steps, clearly unable to draw his eyes away from the horrifying scene. There is blood everywhere and I'm covered in it.

Oscar is dead ... and I am officially broken.

However long it is later, I lift my head and look around me. It's now almost completely dark, but the moon's light is ensuring I can still see my surroundings. The blood around me looks like black tar in the dark and it's no longer warm, but turning cold against my skin. I barely have the energy to stand, but I stagger to my feet without letting go of my precious dog.

At that moment I start to think a little more clearly. Numerous thoughts and feelings begin to worm their way into my mind. This was no vicious animal attack. He didn't fall and break a leg, nor did he get hit by a car. Oscar was stabbed, brutally murdered ... by a human and left here for me to find. The white-hot rage starts to build up inside me and I grit my teeth in fury as I stumble back the way I came.

Alicia ... are you there?

Yes, I am here.

I'm going to find him and I'm going to kill him.

Yes ... I know.

We do not need to speak his name to know who we're talking about. This is our punishment for not revealing ourselves to him, for not coming forwards, for trying to run away.

This is my fault. I should have listened to you rather than try and leave.

I don't reply to Alicia. I'm too tired and angry to play the blame game. The only person who needs to pay for this is him ... and I will find him ... and I will have my revenge even if it's the last thing I ever do. Call it a cliché if you will … but I'm fucking serious.

When I appear at the bottom of the courtyard I see that the wine bar is empty and the lights are off, but there is a single light on in my villa, so I make my way slowly up to it. Ben is standing in the doorway. He doesn't say a word, but stands aside to let me pass. He follows me into the living room area where a towel has been laid out on the floor with a plastic bag on top. I collapse to the floor and gently lower Oscar's body onto the black plastic, but I don't get to my feet. I stay kneeling at his side, my shoulders hunched, my head down. I feel Ben kneel beside me.

'I couldn't just leave you here alone.'

I nod my thanks as I feel fresh tears burning in my eyes. His kindness makes me feel even worse, but I can't bring myself to tell him to leave. I'm unable to speak as I feel wave after wave of pure emotion rush over me – absolute anger and then inconsolable heartbreak. Ben places a hand on my shoulder and I unintentionally flinch away.

'I'm so sorry. W-what happened?'

I lift my head and slowly turn to look at Ben. His face is full of genuine concern and even if I wanted him to leave (which surprisingly I don't) I know he wouldn't leave me alone in this state.

'I … I don't know.'

I do know. I have to lie to him. I can't bring him into this whole fucked up situation because he wouldn't understand. My life is fucked up – I'm fucked up. I can't fuck up his life too. Despite what Alicia says I do trust him, but not enough to tell him the truth, not right now anyway.

'Okay. What do you need me to do? I'll do anything, just tell me what to do.'

'I need to wrap him in something – his blanket. I need his blanket.'

Ben immediately stands. 'Where is it? I'll get it.'

'In his bed under the bar.'

'Stay there. I'll be right back.'

Ben leaves me alone with the tiny body. Blood is no longer flowing from him, but it's now starting to clot and become sticky. My legs, arms, face and hair are caked in it. I look like a survivor at the end of a horror movie apart from one thing – none of it is my blood.

I force myself to my feet, my limbs feeling heavy, and it's a constant effort to keep myself from collapsing. I head for the corner of the kitchen where I know Alicia keeps alcohol; there's no gin, but there is a bottle of white wine.

Alicia, I swear to God if you tell me not to drink right now I may just explode.

Actually, I was going to recommend it.

I grab the bottle and unscrew the lid, skip the glass and drink several large gulps straight from the bottle. The liquid burns my throat, but I don't feel the usual warm, happy sensation come over me. Yes, okay, I'll admit it. Maybe I do have a drinking problem. I don't give a fuck right now. I feel nothing. I'm cold now that the blood has turned to ice against my skin. I leave Oscar laying in the middle of the floor and take my wine to the open front door and look out across my property.

He was here. He is still here.

I know.

The knife is under the pillow.

No, it's not the time. I need to deal with Oscar first.

What are you going to do with him?

I don't know yet.

The truth is I can't focus on anything at the moment. I can't look into the future because I'm not even sure how to survive the night.

You think I'm overreacting, don't you? He was just a dog to you.

Of course not.

Don't lie to me, Alicia. You were going to abandon him. You didn't care about him. You never cared about him.

That is not true.

Warm tears start streaming down my cheeks again. How many tears can a person actually produce until they run dry? I gulp down more wine, but it tastes like acid in my mouth. It makes me feel physically sick.

At that moment Ben turns up holding Oscar's blanket. My mum made it for him when I first adopted him and he has slept on it every night since. It's a patchwork blanket made of all my old clothes I used to wear as a child. I think my mum originally wanted to make it for my future child, but thanks to my insistence about never having babies she decided to make it for Oscar instead. He was my baby – my fur baby.

'Thanks,' I say as I take the blanket.

Ben spies the bottle in my hand, but says nothing about it. If he did I probably would've hit him across the head with it.

I lay the blanket out and then gently lift the body onto it, folding in the corners and safely cocooning him inside.

'Should we bury him?' asks Ben.

'No. Not yet ... I can't leave him here. I want him cremated, but I don't know of any facilities in the area that do that.'

'I think there's a vet practice that does that near here. I'm not sure. In the meantime why don't we put him in the freezer until you decide.'

The thought of putting Oscar in a freezer horrifies me, but it's the only option I have right now. I can't bury him and lay him to rest until I have taken my revenge. I don't know how long it will take. I don't care if it takes years (actually I do, but I'm attempting to be dramatic) – I will have my revenge.

'I still need to know what happened, Alexis. Dogs don't just get stabbed to death for no reason.'

I sigh and close my eyes. 'It's complicated. I can't tell you everything, please respect that.'

'Okay, I respect that, but please just tell me what you can. Maybe I can help.'

I stare down at my dead dog and drink more wine. I have demolished almost half the bottle already and can feel the familiar numbness that comes with drinking alcohol too fast.

'Someone murdered him. This person has information about me and they killed Oscar to try and force me into coming forward to confront them.'

'What sort of information?'

'I can't tell you, but it's ... not good.'

'And did it work? Are you going to confront them?'

'You better fucking believe I am,' I hiss through gritted teeth.

'But if this person killed Oscar ... they must be close by. It must be someone who lives around here. Let's check the cameras, maybe they're on there. Maybe it's not who you think it is. How do you know that it's definitely this person?'

'Oh, I know it's them.'

'Alexis ... you're scaring me. You've always had an evil look in your eye, but now you're ... different. You look positively psychotic. I think we should call the police and—'

'No!' I turn and grab Ben's shirt collar. He's at least a foot taller than I am and clearly much bigger and stronger, but I grab him with enough force to send him stumbling backwards slightly. 'You're not to say a word to anyone about this, do you hear me? Not a single fucking word.'

Ben nods quickly and I release him. 'Okay,' he says and then takes a deep breath. 'So what happens now?'

'Now you go home and leave me to deal with this.'

'Absolutely not. I'm in on this now. I can't let you deal with this by yourself. You're clearly not thinking straight and you're upset and you've almost finished a bottle of wine in less than fifteen minutes. What kind of man would I be if I just left you?'

I can hear Alicia muttering under her breath. She clearly doesn't want him here, but I do, even though I'd just told him to leave. I don't trust myself. I feel like I might explode. It's possibly safer for me if he is here, not that I need him to protect me from anyone – more that I need him to protect me from myself. I'm not in the right frame of mind.

'Okay, fine, you can stay,' I say at last. 'But don't ask any more questions.'

'Deal, but can I suggest something?'

'What?'

'I think you should take a shower. I'll stay here with Oscar.'

I take a deep breath as I look down at myself caked in blood. The bottle of wine in my hand is also smeared with it and I can taste it in my mouth, metallic and salty.

'Fine, but don't let him out of your sight.'

'I won't, I promise.'

I leave Oscar with Ben and take my wine with me to the en-suite upstairs in my bedroom. I switch on the light and it burns my eyes, forcing me to shield them with my arm. That's when I catch a glimpse of myself in the mirror. It's the first time I've seen myself in this body. I hardly recognise myself. In fact, I'm not myself at all. I'm her – I'm Alicia. Parts of my blonde hair shine bright red under the fluorescent light. My skin is tanned and smooth, yet also smeared with blood, most of it now dry. I'm not Josslyn anymore. I'm changing into a monster. I watch as my eyes grow dark and I can feel Alicia's burning hatred and psychopathic presence stirring. We're the same now. There's only one thing on our minds ... and that is, that between us, we're going to murder Peter Phillips in the most horrific and gruesome way possible – no matter what the cost.

Chapter Nine
Alicia

My eyes are closed. I have no idea where I am or what the time is. Usually, I am up at the crack of dawn, a routine that has been adhered to since I moved here, but today is different. I have no furry alarm clock jumping on me, nor a wet tongue licking my face, asking to be let out for his morning schedule. Something is wrong – where is Oscar?

Then it all comes crashing back to me and I start to remember the horrific events of last night – Oscar went missing, I found the blood spatters, I heard the low whimpering, I found the shaking body and I saw the blood pouring. There was screaming and a flood of anger and then it all ended. Josslyn took over and I was left as a mere bystander while I watched her fall apart and drink herself into unconsciousness. I have never felt so much pain and suffering before. It was excruciating and something I never wish to experience ever again.

There was someone else with Josslyn last night ... Benjamin was there ...

Benjamin.

He already knows too much. I was unable to stop Josslyn from telling him that Oscar was murdered and that there is someone out there who is trying to threaten us. I know this could now jeopardise everything and the last thing I want is for Benjamin to become involved in something that does not concern him in any way.

I attempt to open my eyes, but even my eyelids appear to scream in pain as I peel them open. This has got to be the worst hangover Josslyn has ever put us through, but I do not blame her. She wanted to feel something other than the gut-wrenching pain of losing Oscar. I can understand that, but what I cannot understand is why I can feel a large, warm body laying behind me, spooning me. A thick, tanned forearm is laying across me, the weight of it pinning me against the bed. I shift my body to look behind me and see Benjamin laying next to me, his eyes closed, his breathing shallow.

Oh Josslyn, what have you done now?

She does not answer.

I am unable to remember a lot about last night. Sometime after Josslyn finished the first bottle of wine I started to fade away into ... wherever it is Josslyn and I go. I remember that she took a shower and washed off the blood that stained her skin. She scrubbed until she could not hold the sponge any longer and collapsed in the shower. Benjamin had attempted to come in and help, but she had shouted at him to leave her alone – she was fine, she said. She turned the water off and sat in the shower with her knees hunched up to her chest, naked, wet and cold for a long time until Benjamin had finally intervened and let himself into the bathroom to assist. He had been a perfect gentleman and handed her a towel to cover herself, although I had noticed his eyes linger for a split second. He is a heterosexual man after all – looking at a naked woman is hard-wired into his DNA. Benjamin helped her get warm and dry and changed into some clean clothes. By this point the alcohol in her system had rendered her almost incapable of functioning normally. Josslyn and Benjamin returned downstairs where Oscar was still laying wrapped in his blanket. They placed him in the lower drawer of the freezer and Josslyn began to drink more. That is all I can recall.

Now I am the one who has woken up to the mother of all hangovers and must deal with the consequences ... and Benjamin.

Gingerly, I lift his arm and slide off the side of the bed. I must inform you now that I do not conduct the ritual foot-tapping and counting that Josslyn used to do. I always found it extremely counterintuitive. There is nothing else that Josslyn does that has any OCD tendencies and I have no idea where that habit originated.

Benjamin and I are fully clothed so I can safely assume that he and Josslyn did not engage in sexual intercourse, but I am not surprised. No man in his right mind would (or should) take advantage of a highly intoxicated woman when she has just had her heart broken into pieces. If he had done so then I would immediately kick him out, but as it happens, I leave him to sleep.

My head has its own throbbing heartbeat and my mouth feels like sandpaper. There is no usual glass of water by my bed, so I carefully rise to my feet and head downstairs to the kitchen. The morning sun beams in through the windows and causes my eyes to go temporarily blind. I shield them as I pour myself a glass of water and down it in one go. I immediately realise my mistake. My stomach rejects the water and I hurl it back up into the sink. I take a moment and regain my composure, breathing in as deeply as I can without feeling the urge to vomit again.

I hear a noise behind me and turn to look over my shoulder. Benjamin is standing in the middle of the lounge area, his hair roughed up from sleep.

'I take it you need some painkillers? I found them in your bathroom drawer.' He holds his hand out and hands me a packet of paracetamol.

I take them with a frown, feeling too nauseous to tell him that he should not be going through my drawers even if it is to help me out. I pop two into my mouth and swallow them with a gulp of water, praying that they stay down. My head is swimming. I need to sit down. I stagger towards the sofa and take a seat. Benjamin heads into the kitchen, fills up the kettle and starts making coffee. It is a warm morning, too warm for coffee, but I appreciate the gesture so I allow him to continue. He turns to me as he waits for the water to boil.

'So ... I would ask how you're feeling this morning, but I think that would be a pretty stupid question, right?'

'Right ...' My voice is croaky and sounds like I have smoked a whole packet of cigarettes. 'What happened last night? I mean, I know what happened ...' I glance at the freezer, '... but I do not remember a lot after we put Oscar in the freezer.'

'Well, you told me to get you another bottle of wine from the bar, which I did. You then proceeded to drink that wine and then vomited several times. I helped clean you up. You then came on to me and tried to kiss me, which I declined because you'd just been sick and also I don't take advantage of drunk girls. Then you invited me into your bed, cried for about an hour in my arms and then you passed out. I thought I'd better stay with you in case you choked on your own vomit in your sleep.'

'I apologise.'

'No need to apologise, I understand. I once had to look after my younger sister who decided to experiment with vodka for the first time and I had to try and hide her from our parents. I've seen worse ... believe me.'

I manage a weak smile. 'Thank you ... for looking after me ... and not taking advantage. You have already gone up in my estimations of the average male.'

Benjamin raises his eyebrows at me. 'You're welcome.' He then begins to make the coffee, leaving me on the sofa.

I glance around the spacious room. It feels strange not having Oscar here, begging for food or jumping up for a cuddle. Usually I would have taken him for his walk by now and fed him his breakfast, but his lead is still hanging up by the door, his food bowl laying empty on the floor, never to be used again. I never realised just how big a part he played in my life. There were times I would think of him as an inconvenience and only a day ago I had been more than happy to give him away and leave him so that I could explore the world independently. What a difference a day makes. One day you take something for granted and the next they are gone, leaving a gaping hole in your life.

'While you were passed out last night I took the liberty of checking your security cameras to see if I could catch the person who did it.'

It takes a few moments for my brain to click into gear. 'You went through my phone?' Maybe he did take advantage of me after all, just not sexually.

'You asked me to do it. You told me your password, but then you passed out.'

I narrow my eyes at him, making a mental note to change my password as soon as I can. Again, I resist the urge to argue with him because my head is not in the right frame of mind.

Benjamin hands me a freshly brewed coffee. I take it willingly and breathe in the warm aroma, but it turns my stomach and I grimace as I place the cup beside me on the side table. My stomach is not ready for coffee at the moment. I have a feeling it is going to be a long, painful day.

'What did you find?' I ask him.

'Nothing out of the ordinary. Whoever the person was they managed to avoid all of your security cameras. Maybe they were able to draw Oscar out of the bar. Is it someone he's met before and trusts, do you think?'

The thought makes a lump form in my throat. Poor faithful Oscar. He loved almost everyone and then he got brutally attacked by a man he thought he knew and trusted. The burning hot rage is back inside me, but I push it down. It is not time to unleash it yet. I must think clearly and rationally and make a plan of action. I cannot sit and do nothing.

'I do not know,' I say quietly.

'But you said you know who it is ...'

'I do.'

Benjamin sighs as he takes a seat on the chair by the window which looks out over the courtyard. He stares out for a few moments, seemingly looking at nothing in particular.

'So ... what happens now?' he asks.

I close my eyes. 'Now I must go.'

'I assume you aren't going wherever you were meant to be going before.'

'No. My plans have now changed.'

'So where are you going?'

I do not answer. I merely stare at him.

'You'd hold up pretty well under torture, you know that?' I find that a very odd and disturbing thing to say, but I do not react as he continues. 'Alexis, I know you're not a big fan of sharing or talking ... but last night I saw a different side of you and, despite what you might think, you need my help. I'm in on this now ... whatever this is. Please let me help you. I have to go home to Cambridge for a few days to check on my mum, but I can still help in any way I can.'

I tilt my head slightly, remembering that he had told Josslyn he grew up in Cambridge, but at the time I had assumed he was lying. The fact that he was telling the truth is unsettling.

'You are going back to Cambridge ... in England.' A statement rather than a question from myself.

'Yes, just for a few days I think, I'm not sure yet. My mum lives alone in our family home and she's been taken to hospital for observations after she fell down the stairs. She's okay, but I feel I ought to go and see her. I haven't been back home since I moved out here over a year ago ... why are you staring at me like that?'

The whole time he had been talking I had been staring and clearly it was making him uncomfortable, but my hungover brain was struggling to make sense of the facts. I needed to fly back to the United Kingdom and then get to Cambridge. Benjamin also needed to go to Cambridge ... at the exact same time as me. It did not add up and it was far too suspicious for my liking. I do not believe in coincidences ... you know that.

'That is where I am going,' I reply with a frown.

'Well, you did tell me that you were from there so that doesn't surprise me. I told you the other night I grew up in Cambridge ... we can go together, you can stay with me at my mum's house, unless you want to go home to your parents, and I can be there for you while you ... do whatever it is you have to do.'

I open my mouth to protest, but then I abruptly close it. I have no words. I should be shouting at him, kicking him out of my house and telling him to fuck off and leave me alone, but I do not. Maybe it is Josslyn rubbing off on me or maybe it is this mighty hangover, but I feel myself drawn to Benjamin. Of course, I cannot allow him to get involved because if he knew who I really was then he would not understand, but for the meantime he may be useful to me. I do require a place to stay while I am in Cambridge. He will be busy looking after his sick mother and I will be busy hunting down my prey.

'Fine,' I say. 'I want to leave today.'

'I'll book the flight and text you the details.'

'You do not have my number.'

'I put my number in your phone last night and then used your phone to call mine so I got it.'

I narrow my eyes at him again.

'You don't remember asking me to do that, do you?'

'No.'

'You asked me for my number and you couldn't remember yours.'

'Right.'

I am going to kill Josslyn for this.

Benjamin leaves an hour later to go and pack and sort out the logistics and I am left alone, finally. The painkillers have kicked in and are easing my headache, but the tight feeling across my chest is still there, as is the nausea. After a hot shower I do begin to feel better and am able to eat a slice of toast without throwing it back up. While I am packing my small suitcase Josslyn surfaces.

Oh my God, what's going on? Why do I feel like I've been run over?

This is nothing. A couple of hours ago I could not even keep water down. You are lucky.

Sorry ... what happened? I mean, I know what happened ...

The end of her sentence hangs in the air, neither of us wanting to finish it.

What do you remember from last night?

I drank ... a lot. Ben was here. Oh shit, Ben! What happened?

We woke up spooning in bed.

Oh God—

Do not worry. Nothing happened, but he did look through our phone. He said you told him to do it. Is that true?

I don't remember that.

I think there is a lot you do not remember. Allow me to fill you in. Benjamin and I are flying back to the United Kingdom and then travelling to Cambridge. His mother is sick and I am staying with him while I search for Peter.

Wait ... his mum lives in Cambridge?

Yes.

He was telling the truth?

I believe so.

Don't you think that's a bit—

Coincidental? Suspicious?

Well ... yeah. I'm not sure whether to trust him.

I feel the same way.

But he's nice, right? I like him. I think we should give him a chance. He certainly seems to like us.

I still believe it is you he likes, not me.

I'm sure he'll warm to you eventually.

I continue to pack some necessary items. There is still the unanswered topic of conversation floating in the air, something I know we both need to discuss. *Oscar.* However, neither of us wish to talk about his death, so I am relieved when Josslyn begins to reminisce instead.

Do you remember when we first got him? He was so tiny and helpless and cute.

I remember. In fact, I told you specifically not to adopt him and to take him to the animal rescue shelter down the road.

I can hear Josslyn laughing in my head, but then she grows quiet. The story of how Oscar came to be in our lives is one I have not recalled for a while.

Let me tell the story. You come across as a bit of an asshole in it and besides, I tell it better.

As you wish.

Chapter Ten
Josslyn

I'd only opened Joss Pets a few weeks ago and I was still finding my feet. I hadn't hired any help yet and to be honest I'd not had many patients sign up, but I was hopeful. I'd sent out a bunch of flyers around the area and was praying that word of mouth would eventually spread. It was a quiet morning and I'd only had one patient attend my walk-in clinic so far – an elderly black Labrador called Vincent who needed a check-up.

I was typing up his notes on the computer when the bell rang above the door, but it wasn't the bell that alerted me. It was the high-pitched yapping of the tiny Jack Russell puppy, which was squirming in its owner's arms.

The man who was holding the puppy was really tall and exceptionally muscular. He had on a tight t-shirt, which showed off his bulging biceps and his chest. His head was shaved and black, menacing tattoos seemed to cover most of his exposed skin. The puppy looked miniscule compared to him and he was holding him in one hand, like a small bag of sugar.

'You!' shouted the man.

I immediately jumped in my chair. 'Can I help you?' I squeaked. Inside I was screaming *dear God, please don't hurt me!*

'You like dogs?'

'Errr—'

'Of course you do, you're a vet for Christ's sake. Congratulations, he's yours.'

The man then proceeded to lean across the reception desk and practically throw the puppy at me. Luckily, I was fairly good at catching. The wiggling ball of fluff tried his hardest to escape from my hands, but I held tight, clutching him to my chest.

'Excuse me,' I said with a laugh. 'What the hell are you talking about? Do you need to book him in for his injections and a check-up?'

'Nope. I'm giving him to you free of charge before I toss him in a bag and throw him off a bridge.'

I gasped in horror. 'What the hell is wrong with you! You can't do that!'

'He keeps fucking barking. All night long. I can't stand it.'

'He's a puppy. He probably misses his mum and brothers and sisters.'

'Yeah well, I need my sleep. You want him or not?'

'I ... I'm not – I mean, I guess ...'

There is absolutely no way in hell you are adopting that dog.

Oh come on Alicia ... look at him! I can't let this man throw him off a bridge. What kind of vet would I be ... in fact, what kind of person would I be if I let that happen?

Tell him to take it to the animal rescue shelter down the road. Dogs are leeches. They constantly need care and attention and by the sounds of it this one is a troublemaker. They are better off without humans. I do not like dogs.

You don't like any living thing.

My point exactly. Get rid of it.

I sighed as I looked down at the tiny animal in my arms. He suddenly started licking me all over my face and I heard Alicia inwardly groan. I think that was the moment she knew that I wouldn't be able to give him up. He was mine now.

'I'll take him,' I told the man. 'Does he have a name?'

'Dickhead sums him up pretty well.'

'I'm not calling him dickhead.'

'Call him whatever the hell you want.' He turned to leave.

'Wait! Do you have anything for him ... a collar or some food?'

'Nope.' The man stormed out of the door and slammed it shut.

This is a mistake. Mark my words ... one day you will realise that this animal was not worth saving, nor worth the hassle.

How can you say that!

I quickly covered the puppy's ears (even though I knew full well that he couldn't hear Alicia's voice because she was inside my head). I then placed the puppy down on the floor and watched him as he scurried around, sniffing everything he could find. He didn't seem afraid of anything and even started barking at the fake plant pot in the corner.

What shall we call him?

He certainly looks like a dickhead to me.

I rolled my eyes.

We will not be calling him anything because he is not staying. Take him to the animal shelter.

No, he's staying. Shut up, Alicia. You're not the boss of me. He needs a name.

He also needs food, a collar, a bed and about fifteen other items, none of which you have right now.

You're right.

The puppy squatted in the middle of the floor and had the longest pee in history.

Fucking perfect.

I cleaned up the enormous puddle and then closed the practice for the afternoon (it's not like I had any patients coming in) and went to the nearest pet shop to buy everything I needed. I bought way too much stuff, which I put on one of my credit cards, and about a dozen puppy toys, but I wanted to spoil him.

That night I was eating cold pizza with the puppy on my lap. I was watching the Academy Awards for no reason other than I was bored and there was nothing else on. I watched as some famous director I'd never heard of won an Oscar for Best Director for a film I knew nothing about. I still hadn't come up with a name for the little guy. I'd been calling him *puppy* all day. He'd been so naughty and had peed about six times in my flat already. Not having a garden was definitely an inconvenience. He'd also decided that my sofa was a delicious chew toy, despite having plenty of *actual* toys to gnaw on.

What about Oscar?

Huh?

The name.

I glanced down at the puppy snoozing peacefully on my lap.

'Oscar,' I said quietly as I stroked his fur. He responded by wagging his tail happily in his sleep. And that was that – his name was Oscar.

I don't mind admitting that Oscar had arrived at the perfect time in my life. I'd been having a hard time and had recently survived through many dark days, but having a tiny, helpless soul to look after really gave me a new lease of life as well as a reason to get up in the mornings. He brought me out of my slump and I thanked him every day for that.

Without him there's already a massive, gaping hole in my life and in my heart and the only way I know how to plug it is to punish the person responsible for taking him away from me. It's the only reason I have left. I don't know what I'm going to do afterwards, but I can't think about that. Now that Oscar is gone I have no one ...

That is not true. You have me. You always have me.

Yes, but I'm the voice inside *your* head. I don't technically exist. Josslyn doesn't exist. What's the point of even being here anymore? Mum and Dad are gone, now so is Oscar.

There is always a point to living.

I'd hardly call what I'm doing *living.* What do you have to live for Alicia? What keeps you going?

Right now it is the thought of strangling Peter until his eyes pop out of his head or slicing his throat open and watching the blood drain from his body.

Thank you.

What for?

For wanting to get revenge as much as I do. You were adamant that you were leaving Oscar behind. You said you didn't care about him, but you do. I don't think you would have left even if last night hadn't have happened.

I do care about him ... I did care. I looked after him last year when he became ill.

He got sick?

Yes. You were still ... gone ... at the time.

Can you tell me the story? I like hearing stories about him. It's better than facing reality right now.

Fine, but let me take over because you are ridiculously slow at packing and we are on a tight schedule.

I admit I'd been fumbling around the bedroom for clothes while I'd been telling the story, but hadn't actually packed a single thing. My head was also starting to hurt. I was still getting used to being in control, but it was exhausting, especially after last night.

Chapter Eleven

Alicia

I begin to fold up some items of clothing and place them in the suitcase as I recount the story of when Oscar was unwell.

I had only just moved out to Tuscany with him and he and I were still adapting to life without Josslyn. I could tell that he knew she was gone and he seemed cold and distant towards me at times. He very rarely came and sat on my lap and he growled at me several times when I raised my voice at him. It was also while lockdown was still happening, so he was unable to see or interact with anyone else. We were clearly getting under each other's skin. On more than one occasion I had threatened to leave him to fend for himself on the streets.

We went on many walks together, but one day he must have eaten something that did not agree with him because he vomited several times upon returning to the villa. For the rest of that day he refused his food, stopped drinking water and started to become dehydrated. He laid in his bed, softly moaning for hours. Luckily, I remembered some of Josslyn's vet training, but I did not have the required medication to hand. However, I researched his symptoms online and discovered he would quite possibly recover within a few days.

I made him plain chicken and rice and filled a small syringe with water. I sat by his bed on the floor and offered him the food by hand. He ate only one or two small bites and licked a few drops of water from the syringe. I stayed with him all day and all night, waking up the next morning having fallen asleep in an awkward position, but when I woke Oscar was curled up beside me on the floor. He seemed to recover quickly after that and drained a full bowl of water.

After that day he always slept on the bed with me and was much more friendly. We became ... friends.

I finish my story as I close the lid to my suitcase.

Awww, that's so sweet. I don't care what you say ... you do have a heart, even if it's dried up and black in places.

I do not respond to her comment.

Yes, I did care for Oscar in my own way, but I would have left him with Benjamin. He would have been safe and happy, but now he is gone ... and someone will pay the ultimate price for taking him away from us.

Benjamin arrives two hours later in a taxi with a small suitcase as hand luggage. He loads mine into the boot and we get into the back of the car. I stare out of the window at my villa as we drive away, not knowing if or when I will return. I *have* to return. I cannot leave Oscar in the freezer. It feels disrespectful to leave him there, but I know it is for the best. I have contacted the estate agent and taken the villa off the market for the time being until I know what is happening with it. I also still have the security app on my phone so I can check on the estate while I am away.

Benjamin attempts to engage in dull conversation as the taxi driver takes us to Pisa International Airport, but I am in no mood to even feign interest in talking. He eventually takes the hint and we fall into a natural silence. As the Tuscan countryside races by I am drawn to a single thought: Peter was within touching distance last night. Maybe he had been watching as Josslyn cried over the body of her dog as he died in her arms. What kind of sick asshole is he? I knew he was sick – he admitted to being in love with his sister after all – but to murder an innocent dog ... who knows how twisted his mind really is. The worst thing is he teaches young boys and is regarded as a hero. He needs to be eradicated from this earth and that is my one and only goal right now.

The flight into London Stansted takes roughly two and a half hours. I am finally feeling more human now that the hangover has worn off, however tiredness has taken over and I fall asleep within minutes of take-off. Despite this only being the second time I have flown in an aircraft I find the experience soothing. Josslyn, on the other hand, nearly had a full-blown meltdown inside my head as we raced up the runaway and took off. It was her first (conscious) experience of flying and it was safe to say that she was not a fan.

I dream of blood, animal corpses coming to life and hooded figures. I can feel a presence watching me in my dream. It is following me down a narrow path, which stretches out into the distance forever. I cannot run fast enough. The hooded figure towers over me, grabs me and begins to shake my body vigorously. My head lolls back and forth like a rag doll and I cannot breathe—

I wake with a start and prepare myself for a fight, shocking an air stewardess who stumbles backwards as I shove her away from me.

'I'm so sorry Ma'am, but we're about to land. I need you to put your seatbelt on.' She scurries away, leaving me to catch my breath.

That is when I see a figure in a dark hood ahead of me standing in the narrow corridor of the plane. I blink and then they are gone, vanishing into thin air.

'Are you okay?' asks Benjamin.

'Yes. I am fine.'

'Did you sleep well?'

'I slept ... that is enough for now.'

While Benjamin and I wait for our suitcases by the rotating baggage carousel I find myself attempting to search for the figure in the dark hood. I am unsure if they were real or a figment of my imagination. Real or not I see a man wearing a black jumper with a hood ahead and I immediately start scoping him out, watching and judging his every movement. I cannot see his face, but he is the correct height and build. He starts walking away in the direction of the exit, a hefty black rucksack slung over his shoulder.

Without giving it a second thought I leave Benjamin and begin to follow him. He was on the plane, I know he was. He cannot hide from me. The man is walking fast, as if he is in a hurry or attempting to flee. That is when he glances over his shoulder and catches sight of me.

It is him.

I start running, my gaze focused directly ahead. I bump into a unsuspecting pedestrian who gets in my way, so I shove them aside and continue the chase. I launch myself at him and tackle him to the ground. We land hard as he starts flinging his arms around in a panic. I grab him by his jumper and pull back my fist ready to strike ... and that is when I see his scared, white face. He has his hands held up in a defensive manner, shaking slightly.

'P-Please, take whatever you want lady,' he stutters.

It is not him.

'Put your hands on your head and stand up slowly!' says a sharp voice from behind me.

I angrily shove the innocent stranger away from me and comply with the request. An airport security guard grabs me and holds my hands behind my back while another helps the man to his feet.

'What's going on here?' asks the man who is holding me.

'Ask her! She suddenly started chasing me. I don't even know who the hell she is.' The man is out of breath and still shaking.

Everyone is staring at me – the man in the black hood, the two guards and about two dozen people in the vicinity. Benjamin has also caught up and is mouthing the words 'what the fuck?' at me.

I think you need to calm down, Alicia. We can't draw attention to ourselves.

I made a mistake.

You think!

'You're going to have to come with us, Ma'am,' says the guard who is still holding me, his grip getting tighter by the minute.

Benjamin steps forward. 'Excuse me. I'm sorry. She's my friend. She's had a rough few days.'

'Sir, that's no excuse for assaulting an innocent pedestrian.'

'I know, but ...'

'He has a weapon,' I interject.

Then all eyes turn on the man in the black hood, whose jaw drops open in shock. He points a finger at me and starts stepping backwards.

'You're fucking crazy lady! I don't have a weapon!'

The guard lets go of me and both guards approach the man, who is holding up his hands again while continuing to back away.

'Stop right there!' yells one of the guards.

The man suddenly turns on his heels and starts running at full speed. Benjamin and I watch as the guards jump on him and tackle him to the ground and then they lead him away. I am left alone and even get a round of applause from the audience, who then all get back to their own business.

'What the fuck was that about?' asks Benjamin.

'I told you ... he had a weapon.'

I'll give you this, Alicia ... you're one hell of a good liar.

Benjamin and I catch the train to Cambridge. I keep seeing men in black hoods everywhere. I feel I may be losing my mind.

I think it's a little too late for that.

You saw him. It was definitely him at the airport.

Maybe you saw what you wanted to see.

I hate to admit that maybe Josslyn is correct. I had acted irrationally and without any thought to the consequences, the way I always react. This time I need to be smart. I cannot just walk up to him and kill him. I must plan this murder. When I killed Daniel and Alicia I did it without thinking and in the spur of the moment. That had been foolish and I had been careless. I must learn from my previous mistakes.

This time you have me on your side. We can work together, but you have to let me take control. I have to be the one who finishes him.

What? You are not a murderer, Josslyn. I am.

Josslyn no longer exists. I can do whatever the hell I want.

We shall talk about this later.

No, let's talk about this now. We need to be on the same page. We can't be fighting with each other. We both want the same thing and that's to see Peter dead.

Yes, and I shall kill him.

No, I'm going to kill him.

I close my eyes and count slowly to ten. Sisters are so infuriating.

'Are you okay?' Benjamin's voice jolts me back to reality.

The train judders to a halt at the next station and dozens of people exit and board the train. I hate crowds.

'Yes.'

'It's just ... well, you're acting really weird. I know Oscar's death must be hard—'

'Do not tell me how I should be feeling.'

'Okay, I'm sorry. Have you told your parents that you're home? I bet they're going to be happy to see you.'

'I do not have any parents.'

Benjamin frowns. 'I-I thought—'

'You thought wrong.'

Give him a break. He's just trying to help and be nice.

I sigh inwardly, then turn to Benjamin who looks like he has been slapped across the face. 'I apologise,' I say slowly. 'The truth is my parents died a long time ago.'

'Oh God, Alexis, I'm so sorry. I didn't know ... do you have any brothers or sisters?'

'No.'

Ouch, that hurts.

'I'm so sorry,' he repeats.

Benjamin gently places a hand over mine which is currently resting on my knee. I stare down at our hands touching and resist the urge to pull away. I hate the feeling of someone touching me, especially without my permission. It feels so alien and wrong to have someone show compassion towards me. This man does not know the true me. If he did he would not be here acting like he cares, but as I look down at our hands I notice a warm, calming sensation wash over me, and it feels ... pleasant, but I do not like it. My mind automatically recalls the kiss we shared not long ago, how his lips felt against mine, how strong his hands were as he pulled me close to him. He wanted me and I had wanted him, but only for a moment; a weak moment. My heart leaps as if it has been jolted with an electrical current and that is the moment I pull my hand out from under his and shift uneasily in my seat.

The skies have turned dark and grey by the time we arrive at Benjamin's mother's house. I already find myself missing the warmth of the Tuscan sun. He reminds me that she is in hospital for a few days for observation so we have the house to ourselves, a sentiment that concerns rather than excites me. His family home is situated only a fifteen-minute taxi ride from the train station. Despite me not enquiring about the details he proceeds to tell me anyway. His father passed away several years ago from a sudden heart attack and his mother has lived here alone ever since. Her health has deteriorated in recent months and she fell down the stairs two days ago; however, she is not severely injured. Benjamin says he will visit her in the morning.

The house itself is semi-detached and feels very claustrophobic as I step across the threshold. The walls appear to squeeze closer and closer and every room is cluttered with possessions collected over years and years of a family living within them. I immediately spy several framed photographs of a young Benjamin, which adorn the walls and are propped up on numerous shelves and cabinets. One photo in particular catches my eye – Benjamin at roughly twelve years of age and wearing metal braces across his teeth and a backwards multi-coloured cap. Before I can stop myself a crack of a smile appears across my face.

'Sorry about all the mess. My mum hasn't wanted to throw anything away or sell it since my dad died. I keep on and on at her to de-clutter this house.'

'Do not apologise. It is ...'

'Go on, you can say it.'

'... Homely,' I finish.

Benjamin smiles at me. 'Yeah, I guess it is. I'll quickly go and make up the guest room for you. Make yourself at home.' He sprints up the stairs two at a time, something he has clearly done thousands of times before.

I am left alone standing in the hallway.

Let's snoop around.

I agree with Josslyn and begin to peer into each room of the downstairs layout. It may be over-crowded with furniture and objects, but it is relatively tidy and clean. The lounge is large and has a three-seater sofa, a two-seater and an over-sized armchair all crammed into it, circled around an old fireplace, which does not appear to have been used for several years. There is an ancient television in one corner, which must be at least twenty years old, back before flat-screens were invented. The kitchen is small and has numerous cupboards and shelves, all laden with random kitchen utensils and cooking instruments.

I head back into the lounge and spy another picture of Benjamin in a university cap and gown, holding a certificate from the University College London. I lean closer and can just about make out the title of his degree – Politics and Law.

Why the hell is he working in a delicatessen in Tuscany when he has a degree like that?

I do not know.

Mid-life crisis?

He is our age.

So ... you ran off to Tuscany and opened a wine bar.

Touché.

I straighten up just as Benjamin walks in the room.

'The guest room's all made up for you. It's the first room on the right at the top of the stairs. I've laid out clean towels. The bathroom's at the end of the hall. You want some food? I make a mean toastie. You haven't eaten all day, you must be starving.'

'Sure,' I say as I walk past him and head upstairs. To be perfectly honest I could brutally kill someone for a greasy toastie right now.

I join Benjamin after I have showered and changed my clothes. He has made two large ham and cheese toasties and two cups of tea. Mine is slightly stronger than I prefer, but I accept it graciously. I sit on the two-seater sofa and he sits in the armchair while we eat.

'It's weird being home,' he says as he glances around the room. 'I haven't been back here for so long.'

Ask him why he's working as a butcher.

'Why did you leave the United Kingdom and move to Tuscany to become a butcher?'

'I wanted a break from real life. My job was becoming stressful. My dad had passed away. I'd just broken up with my long-term girlfriend—'

Oooh, ask him about her next.

'—and I just wanted some peace and quiet. I worked in a butcher's shop part-time throughout university, so I'd picked up some skills. Then lockdown happened and I couldn't go home for a while, but I grew to like it out there ... and then you came along.' He stops and smiles at me. 'I remember coming to your wine bar and coming to your rescue. My friend was being an asshole.'

'You did not come to my rescue.'

'Well ... I tried anyway. I guess you're the type of woman that doesn't need anyone to rescue her. Then later you just happened to walk into the shop one day and ask for some sausages.'

'I remember.'

'I found myself not wanting to leave in a hurry after that.'

I immediately sense the awkward tension in the air and change the topic of conversation.

'What happened with your girlfriend?'

Benjamin smiles at my attempt to change the subject, but politely obliges me. 'She cheated on me. We'd been together since university. It's where we met.'

What's her name?

'What was her name?'

'Claire. She was amazing and so beautiful and clever. At the time I thought she was the one.'

I roll my eyes and take a bite from my toastie, revelling in the moment as the deliciously warm cheese hits my taste buds.

'You don't believe in *the one*?'

'No. There are literally billions of people on this earth. The concept that there is only one person you are suited to be with forever is ludicrous. The odds of meeting them would be astronomical.'

Benjamin smiles again. 'What about you? Have you ever had a long-term boyfriend?'

How are we suddenly talking about us? Oooh, he's good.

I sigh. 'Unfortunately, yes.'

'Tell me about him.'

'Why?'

'I'm curious.'

Um ... this is dangerous territory.

Agreed.

'I do not wish to discuss my previous relationships with you. All men are assholes. The end.'

'Ouch. Whoever he was did a number on you ...'

'What is that supposed to mean?'

'He obviously hurt you and now you've got your guard up, which explains why you don't want us to be anything more than friends.'

'Or maybe it means I am not attracted to you.'

Benjamin coolly smiles as he stands up and takes my empty plate. 'You're good at hiding your feelings Alexis, but you're not *that* good. When I kissed you ... you could have stopped me, but you didn't.'

I watch him as he walks into the kitchen.

He has a nice butt, don't you think?

I roll my eyes again.

Benjamin walks back into the lounge.

'I did not stop you because I was blind-sided and it was over so quickly I did not have time to respond.'

'Right,' he says.

I attempt to steer the conversation back to him. 'So this ... Claire ... why did she cheat on you?'

'So I can't ask you about your relationship, but you can ask me about mine?'

'Okay then, do not tell me.'

There are a few seconds of silence which I fill by taking sips of my tea. Silence does not make me nervous or uncomfortable. I can sit in silence with another person all day without flinching. Benjamin takes a seat in the armchair and lets out a long sigh, clearly not as accustomed to the quiet as I am.

'I don't know why she cheated on me. It just happened. I was going to propose to her, but on the night I was going to pop the question she beat me to it and told me that she cheated on me with some guy from work.'

'I am sorry ... I suppose women can be assholes too.'

Benjamin smiles. 'Not all of them.'

He has no idea. A small part of me actually feels sorry for him.

Chapter Twelve
Alicia

That night I do not sleep well, despite feeling exhausted, as if I have been awake for a week straight. I feel as if my mind is on high alert, expecting something or someone to jump out at me any second to attack. I toss and turn constantly, wondering if I will ever feel normal and safe again. Peter is plaguing every aspect of my life, even my dreams. It is time I confront him once and for all.

We need to make a plan. We can't just wander up to him and say, 'hey asshole, remember me?' and then stab him. Let's think about this.

Josslyn is correct. It is too dangerous and risky to show our true intentions too soon.

Maybe we should stalk him for a while. Do you think he knows we're here in the UK?

Almost certainly. He is not stupid.

But he can't watch us all the time and know our every move. He has a job, a life ... unless he's somehow installed a GPS tracker on us ...

I automatically glance at my phone on the table beside the bed.

No, surely not ...

Maybe let's get rid of that phone and buy a burner phone. Just in case.

Agreed.

Although when we get the new phone we should download the security app again so we can keep an eye on the villa, you know, to check up on the place to make sure Oscar's still ... I mean, I guess he isn't going anywhere, but ...

Yes. Fine.

It is not like I text or call a lot of people anyway. I pick up the phone, open the back, remove the SIM card and snap it in half. I leave the phone off just to err on the side of caution. If he had somehow installed a tracking system in it, it would be too late now anyway. He knows I am here.

So ... what shall we do first ... about Peter I mean.

I say we make ourselves known to him right away. I do not want him to think I am afraid of him. We will go and pay him a visit at work, somewhere he cannot draw attention to himself or cause a scene. He will need to be on his best behaviour in order to keep his cover.

And then what?

We threaten him. I want him to be afraid. I want him to know that we mean business and that he has gone too far this time and we will not leave him alone until he is dead.

He won't scare easy.

I can be very scary.

You don't have to tell me that, but I'd like to talk to him too.

I do not think that is a good idea. You are still fairly weak Josslyn. You cannot take over for very long. It may exhaust you.

Then let me practise slowly. Little by little let me build up my tolerance and strength over the next few days.

That may do the opposite of what you intend. It may make you weaker.

Can I at least try?

Fine.

Starting now?

Fine ... just ... do not get drunk. I do not wish to suffer through another hangover. It is only eight o'clock in the morning and be careful what you say around Benjamin.

Okay fine, no alcohol ... I'll be careful.

Good because we need to be level-headed and focused.

Okay, agreed.

I close my eyes, take a deep breath and I am gone.

Chapter Thirteen
Josslyn

The light burns my eyes and it takes me a few seconds to work out what's going on. I don't think I'll ever get used to this ... this ... body switching thing. It's like something out of a movie. Actually, technically, it's a mind switching thing since there's only one body involved. I miss being able to see things through my own eyes and feel things with my own fingers, smell things, hear things. I really appreciate that Alicia is allowing me to take over now, even if it's only for a little while. I didn't think I'd be able to do it, but I think if I practise a bit each day I'll be able to get stronger and be able to take over for longer. It might make me weaker, but it's a chance I'm willing to take. I don't know how much time I have left.

Just remember ... it is my body, not yours.

Yeah, yeah, I get it.

I can smell coffee so I get out of bed (remembering to touch my feet to the floor and count to five ... some things never change), get dressed and head downstairs. Ben is in the kitchen making pancakes. I have a strange case of déjà vu from when Peter cooked breakfast for me, but Ben isn't Peter. Ben is different ... he's ...

'Morning,' he says when he sees me.

'Hey,' I reply.

Okay, so I may have just been fantasising about him being naked. Oh God, he's seen me naked in the shower! And he obviously looked because ... well all men look, don't they? Unless they're gay of course, but I'm almost positively certain that Ben's not gay ...

'Listen, about last night, I didn't mean to pry into your relationship,' he says as he expertly flips a pancake.

'That's okay, I don't mind.'

I certainly do mind.

'Okay, cool, well just so you know ... whatever asshole hurt you, it's his loss.'

I think of Daniel and then I think of Peter. Both men were obsessed with me and now one of them is dead and the other is threatening me ... I can really pick them, huh?

'Thanks ... and Claire, your ex ... it's her loss too.'

Ben just smiles as he slides the cooked pancake onto a plate. 'I told my mum I'd visit her first thing this morning, so I hope you don't mind, but I'll have to leave you for a few hours. What are you doing this morning?'

Confronting a crazy stalker and plotting his demise.

'Um ... I thought I'd just take a walk. I haven't been back to Cambridge for so long.'

'What about this person you need to see? I still don't know what's going on, but if you need help I'd be happy to help you later on when I get back.'

'No thanks. I mean, I'm not sure how I'm going to handle it yet. In fact, I don't even know if they still live in the area.'

Ben frowns at me. I can almost see the cogs turning and whirling around in his head. He has so many burning questions I can practically see them trying to escape out of his mouth. I remember Alicia's words to me – I must be careful what I say. I wish he weren't involved as much as he is. The last thing I want is to drag him into my mess.

'Just text me if you need anything,' he says.

'Actually ... I'm changing my phone.'

'Why?'

'No reason. I mean ... it broke.' Ah, shit, maybe I shouldn't have told him that. Now I look suspicious and slightly stupid. 'I mean, the contract is nearly up, so I thought I'd get a new phone.'

'So which is it? Did it break or is the contract nearly up?'

'Both.' Shit ... I'm so bad at making stuff up on the spot.

No argument from me on that one.

'Oh, okay. Well ... will you let me know your new number?'

'Sure.'

Or not.

'Pancakes?'

'Yes please!'

I greedily scoff three pancakes which I drown in maple syrup and then slurp my coffee. Ben keeps throwing quick glances at me. It's almost as if he knows that there are two people in this body. Alicia and I are so different, not only in the way we talk, but also in our mannerisms. It's so difficult to hide, but if he does suspect anything (as if he'd really guess the truth – it's impossible) he doesn't mention it and I'm grateful he doesn't. Maybe he thinks I have some sort of personality disorder or I'm bipolar. Let's be honest ... it would make more sense.

I push my plate away when I'm finished and sigh happily. 'Thanks for the pancakes. They were amazing, best pancakes I've ever had.'

'No problem. Pancakes are my speciality.'

'I can tell.'

Ben keeps looking at me, thinking I haven't noticed. Then I realise that I didn't put on a bra this morning and I'm wearing a white t-shirt. It's not like he can clearly see my nipples, but it is sort of cold in here ...

Fuck.

I start backing away from him.

'I'll just go and finish getting dressed,' I say.

Oh my God, I'm so embarrassed right now. I turn my back on him, but then a wave of curiosity washes over me and I coyly glance over my shoulder at him.

'Did you really see me naked the other night when I was drunk in the shower?'

'Yep.'

'How much did you see exactly?'

Ben smiles as he takes a bite of his pancake. 'A lot.'

Fuck.

'And?'

'And I really like your tattoos ... especially the lips on your ass.'

Okay, he's definitely *not* gay.

I wrestle with my mouth to stop from beaming a smile at him. I scurry upstairs and put on a bra, now unsure if my nipples are erect because I'm chilly or turned on.

Ben gives me a spare key so I can come and go as I please and then orders a taxi to take him to the hospital. I really want to snoop around his house some more, but think better of it. I'm only being nosey and I have more important things to do ... like pay my stalker a visit.

I have now been myself for almost half an hour, but I can feel myself slipping. The other night when Oscar ... *died* ... I'd taken over for a few hours, but it had exhausted me. I'll attempt to hold on for as long as I can.

It's a weekday, so I make the assumption that Peter will be at work. The taxi driver drops me outside Lampton Boarding School for Boys and I tell him to keep the change.

It's a big, posh school with huge metal gates blocking the entrance. I'm not even sure if I'll be allowed in. It looks like you need a security pass and vetting clearance just to gain access to the grounds. Surely I can't just ask if I can walk around the gardens. How am I supposed to find him? I know he teaches history, so that's a good place to start, but where the hell is the history building? I'm so out of my depth and have no idea what I'm doing, but I must try ...

I press the intercom by the gate and wait for a response. A high-pitched female voice erupts from the small box speaker.

'Hello, Lampton Boarding School for Boys, how can I help?'

'Err ... hi ... err ... I was wondering if I could come in and have a look around? I'm thinking of enrolling my son next year—'

'Have you got an appointment?'

'Err ... well, no, but—'

'I'm sorry, but no one is allowed in without an appointment.'

'Okay ... can I make an appointment?'

'All appointments must be made via the online booking system.'

'Err ...' Shit, I'm out of options and responses. 'Okay, um ... do you happen to know if Peter Phillips is working today? He's a friend of mine.'

'I cannot discuss the whereabouts of our teachers I'm afraid.'

'Why not?'

'For security reasons.'

'Right ... well, it's really important I speak to him today.'

'I thought you wanted to look around for your son?'

'Well, yeah, I do, but ... Peter's a friend of mine and he said it was okay to just drop by.'

'I'll have to clear it with him first.'

'No! I mean, no, don't do that. That's okay. Sorry to waste your time.'

I immediately turn and start scurrying away like a naughty child that's just been caught doing something they shouldn't. Wow, I really suck at this. Now the lady will probably tell Peter about the weird woman at the intercom and my whole cover will be blown. I don't want him to know I'm arriving and have prior warning. I want to walk straight into him and see the look on his face.

How about you let me handle this?

Urrgg, fine! I'm getting tired anyway.

Chapter Fourteen

Alicia

I straighten myself out and glance back at the school. One way or another I am getting through those gates to look Peter in the eyes. There is no point in denying the fact that he knows I am here. He may even know I am outside the school gates thanks to Josslyn's major fuck up just now, but there is only one way to find out.

I approach the intercom again and press the button.

'Hello, Lampton Boarding School for Boys, how can I help?'

'I am here to see Peter Phillips. My name is Alexis Grey.'

'Just one second ... yes, Miss Grey, Mr Phillips is expecting you. He's in building 3A in the History department. Do you need directions?'

'I do not.'

'Come on in.'

The gates buzz open.

What the actual fuck! She didn't even question if you were the same person as just now. We have the same voice for fuck's sake.

No, you sounded like a nervous liar. It is all about confidence. Have you learnt nothing from me over the past two and a half decades?

I've learnt that you're one hell of a liar.

Exactly, and that is because I am confident in my voice projection.

So ... after all that, Peter knows we're here.

Evidently.

So he is still stalking us?

I am not sure how he is doing it, but we need to be aware that wherever we go we are not safe. He may even know that we are staying with Benjamin, which means he is not safe either.

What should we do?

Leave it to me.

I follow the signs towards building 3A. The school grounds are very large and immaculately kept, barely a blade of grass out of place. I can smell freshly cut grass and hear the faint hum of a lawnmower from somewhere, quite possibly a sit-on mower as the grounds are far too large to be cut by a push-along. The whole estate screams *expensive* and no doubt the pupils who attend here must have very wealthy parents.

Building 3A looms ahead of me, surrounded by huge beds of multi-coloured flowers and greenery. On either side of the front entrance there are bushes cut into the shape of horses rearing up on their hide legs. Whoever the groundskeeper is, he is very talented.

My heart rate begins to speed up as I walk in the direction of the History department, following the well-placed signs. The thought of laying my eyes on the man who murdered Oscar in cold blood is beginning to excite and terrify me. On the outside I am calm and in control, but on the inside I can feel Josslyn's nerves and anger rattling through my body. It is disturbing. I do not like feeling so out of control.

I enter the halls of the History department and begin searching for his office, or maybe he is teaching in one of the classrooms. My eyes are wide, scouring everything I see. There are other teachers and many students roaming about. It is at the top of the hour so I can only assume that lessons have ended and everyone is heading for their next one.

Then I see him.

I slowly walk forwards a few paces, locking eyes with him, but he is only a photograph. He smiles at me whilst holding a trophy in his hand. I lean in towards the photo, which is surrounded by a black and gold frame. Underneath is a plaque that reads 'Teacher of the Year 2020 - Professor Peter Phillips'. The glass protecting the picture is spotless and the closer I get the more I see my own reflection rather than the photograph.

Then I see him.

This time it is his reflection in the glass of the frame. He is standing behind me, a coy smile across his lips.

'Hello Alicia ... or should I call you Alexis now?'

Surprisingly, I am not afraid. My heart rate does not increase further and I am not shaking. His dark, deep voice is familiar and somewhat soothing. Despite my previous trepidation about seeing him, I find myself focused, my mind steady.

I slowly back away from his photo and turn to face him.

He looks good – too good. Without meaning to my mind flashes with visions of his naked body on top of me, underneath me, inside of me, all around me. I can almost smell the hot sweat, taste his skin and feel his touch. His hair is still slightly overdue for a cut, his chin neatly shaven. The jeans, shirt and tie he is wearing accentuate his masculine figure perfectly. He is carrying a small locked briefcase, which no doubt holds his teaching notes ... or something much more sinister. There is a noticeable difference to him though, one which would be easily missed to the untrained eye – and that is indeed what is different about him – his eyes. They are no longer soft and caring, like they had pretended to be when I first met him. Now they are the eyes of a mad individual, a liar ... a murderer, a complete psychopath. I should know, for I am also all of those things.

'Hello Peter,' I say calmly. 'You may call me Alicia.'

'I do like the name Alexis though. It's ... sexy.'

I stare at him. I *hate* that word.

'I'm glad to see you got my message,' he adds.

The urge to lunge forward and beat him to a bloody pulp, choke the life out of him, kick him, spit on him ... anything ... overwhelms me for a second. Josslyn is seething. Her rage is something I have never experienced from her before and it is difficult to control. I am fighting with all my energy to stay rooted to the spot. I must not attack him. This is not the right time. I clench my fists into tight balls at my side and he notices and smiles.

'What's the matter Alicia ... aren't you glad to see me?'

'Not even a little bit.'

Peter raises one eyebrow. 'Well I'm glad to see you. In fact, I'm always glad to see you ... I like the new hair by the way and the new look. It's very ... sexy.' Again with that fucking *word.* 'You look amazing, but then, you always did, even when you were Josslyn. I miss her. You must miss her too.'

Oh my God ... he doesn't know I'm back ...

Or maybe he does and is an exceptionally good liar like me.

'How does it feel to have that body all to yourself now?' he asks.

'I would not know,' I respond, my face deadpan.

Peter's fake smile falters. 'What do you mean? ... Josslyn ... is she back?'

I answer by raising my eyebrows and folding my arms across my chest. 'Let me just say that if she were in control right now ... you would be in a considerable amount of pain.'

Peter joyously laughs and steps towards me. 'Josslyn! You came back to me!'

Fuck me, he's even more deluded than I remember.

This time I smile, straightening my posture so I am an inch or so taller. He is still almost a foot taller, but I do not back down even when he steps to within a few inches of me. His face is close enough to mine that I can smell his minty breath. His soulless eyes stare straight through me, but mine stare right back at him. It is him and me. Neither one of us is backing down, but suddenly I get accidentally bumped from behind by a student who is in a rush to get to his next class. I stumble into Peter's rock-hard body and he grabs me to stop me from losing balance. I immediately shake him off as forcefully as I can, not wanting his hands on me for even a second longer than they need to be.

'Relax Josslyn, baby, I'm not going to hurt you. I'd never hurt you, you must know that.'

'Shut up you deluded asshole. I am not Josslyn and I do not believe a word you say, but you had better believe me when I say this ... I will hurt you in the most inhumane way possible. I will make you wish that you were dead. In fact, I promise you that one day soon I will make you beg me to kill you. I will make you suffer, mark my words.'

Peter laughs at me. 'Josslyn would never allow it.'

Then I smile slightly because I can hear Josslyn laughing in my head. 'Trust me, she is onboard with the idea.'

'Let me talk to her.'

'No.'

It's okay Alicia, I want to talk to him. Just for a minute. I'm strong enough for this.

Remember, it is all about confidence.

Don't worry, I'm ready for him.

I close my eyes and allow her to take over.

Chapter Fifteen
Josslyn

I open my eyes and stare into the face of the man who murdered my sweet Oscar. The fury is almost too much to bear. I know that this isn't the time to lose control. I have visions of grabbing his fucking Teacher of the Year picture on the wall and smashing him over the head with it. Then I see myself pick up a shard of broken glass and stab him in the neck over and over as blood spurts out in forceful bursts. I then watch as he sinks to the ground, clutching his throat, his hand reaching for my arm, but losing grip because of the amount of blood. He then collapses on the ground, twitching and jerking until the last beat of his heart stops and his blood slowly drains out onto the floor into a glorious puddle of crimson liquid.

'Josslyn.' His voice is soft, different than when he was speaking to Alicia. He once told me that he loved me, but the thought alone makes me feel sick.

'Peter,' I respond, my voice not faltering, amazingly.

'I'm so glad you're still here. I thought you were gone forever. I've missed you so much. I've never stopped loving you.' He reaches out his right hand and attempts to stroke my hair. 'I had no idea you were back, otherwise I would have come for you.'

I recoil in disgust. 'Don't touch me or I swear I'll scream this building down.'

'Please, don't be like this. We can have a second chance now.'

'I didn't come here to hear you whine. I came here to tell you that I'm back and that I'm going to kill you. I don't care how long it takes. I'll bide my time if I have to, but I will kill you Peter. I just wanted you to know that.'

'You're not a murderer. Alicia is the murderer. It's her that needs to pay for what she's done to Daniel and my sister. I don't blame you for any of it. She's been manipulating you all this time. She's turned you into something you're not.'

'Why'd you kill Oscar?' I snap.

Peter's lip twitches slightly and he looks startled. 'W-what? I-I didn't kill Oscar. What are you talking about?'

I shove a pointed finger right up in his face. 'Don't you fucking give me that bullshit! I know it was you.'

'I swear on my life I didn't kill him. I can't believe he's dead. I'm so sorry.'

Do not buy his lies. Remain strong, Josslyn.

'Y-you're lying. You said just now that you were glad to see I'd got your message.'

Peter frowns. 'Yeah, I meant the news report interview I did about finding Daniel's body. That was my message.'

'You threatened me. You said bad things would happen if I didn't come forward.'

'Yeah ... it was a threat Josslyn, but it wasn't directed at you. It was directed at Alicia. I didn't know you still existed. I'd never hurt you or anyone you loved, especially not a helpless dog. What kind of monster do you think I am? I needed Alicia to see that I was serious so that's why I did the interview. I want her to pay for what she's done, but now I know that you're back, well ... things can be different now. We can be together again. I need you in my life. I can't live without you.'

I stumble backwards a few steps. I'm losing grip. I can feel myself slipping away, but I need to stay strong. I can't let go yet.

Peter reaches for me, but I yank my arm away. 'Get away from me!' I scream. 'You're a liar. You're a fucking liar! You killed my dog, you stalked me for years. I'm going to kill you even if it's the last thing I do ...'

And then in a flash I'm gone.

Chapter Sixteen
Alicia

When I regain control I am on the ground. Josslyn did well to hold on as long as she did, but she is still weak. Peter is standing over me as numerous confused people hurry past whilst straining their necks to try and get a good look at the drama unfolding in the halls.

'Alicia, get up and stop making a scene,' spits Peter angrily. He knows I am back.

I look up at him and utter the next four words in the most calm and hate-filled voice I can muster, through gritted teeth.

'I ... will ... end ... you.'

Within seconds a security guard turns up and asks Peter if there is a problem, to which he replies that there is not. At least two dozen students and half as many teachers have stopped to watch the show. Peter has donned his disguise of being a mild-mannered teacher and reassures everyone that there is nothing to see, that I am merely an old friend who has received some bad news. One by one the bystanders start to disperse when they realise that nothing of interest is happening anymore, although a few young boys snap some pictures of the scene on their phones.

This has not gone at all to plan. Why does Peter have such a knack of completely destroying me, getting inside my head and twisting things to make out like I am the bad guy and he is the good guy? This is all wrong. I know he is lying.

I slowly get to my feet, never breaking eye contact with him.

'I'm sorry Alicia, but either you accept that Josslyn and I are destined to be together or you back off and leave me alone. Your choice. I only want Josslyn back, that's all. What's it going to be?'

'You are deluded.'

Peter grins. 'Fine, then both of you will pay for your mistakes. You'll regret this.'

'I believe it is you who will regret it.'

And with that I turn and walk away. I do not look back.

I arrive back at Benjamin's to an empty house. I feel utterly deflated and beaten and I do not like it. Whenever I feel invincible, like nothing could get me down or make me doubt myself, then along comes Peter and smashes me to pieces.

I'm sorry Alicia. I shouldn't have fallen apart like that. I couldn't help it. He gets to me.

Do not apologise. I should not have put you in that situation.

What he said about Oscar, that he didn't kill him ... he sounded so calm. He's a very convincing liar, kind of like ...

Me.

Well ... yes, but you're different.

How? How are Peter and I any different? I lied to you for most of your life. I tricked you into having yourself removed so that I could take full control of this body. I lied to you Josslyn, just like he is doing now.

Josslyn does not answer me. It appears that we have a lot to think about and discuss. That is why Peter riles me up so badly. We are the same in so many ways. In fact, I am worse because I have killed two people and he has not (as far as I am aware). He is a pathological liar, as am I. He is a deranged psychopath who is obsessed with another human being. I am a psychopath who is now obsessed with ending his life. The similarities are endless. In another life we would be perfect for each other or would even be classed as friends because friends share common interests and likes. However, there is only one thing that interests me ... and that is to see Peter suffer and die as painfully as possible.

I take a quick shower because his hands have touched my skin and I need him to be gone. I also find that water calms me, whether it be cold or hot. This has always been the case. The feeling of it pouring onto my face and then trickling down my body reminds me that no matter how dirty I feel or become, no matter what bad things I may do, I can always rectify them and become clean again. I feel that by destroying Peter I can wash away my own sins. I killed Daniel and Alicia. That will never change. I do not regret it, but I do regret the *way* that I did it. I could have been more careful. Now Daniel is back to haunt me and Peter is using him against me. Peter wants Josslyn all to himself. He does not want me. He cannot have her because she is mine and I am a very possessive person.

I'm not your property you know.

No, but you are a part of me and I belong to this body.

I know, but I'm just saying—

Josslyn is cut short because we suddenly hear the front door open. Benjamin has returned.

'Alexis?' he calls out.

'Yes, I am here,' I respond.

I hear him climbing the stairs with heavy footsteps. He knocks lightly on the guest bedroom door and peers round at me. I am sitting on the bed after having just changed my clothes, my hair still wet from the shower.

'Hi,' he says. 'How was your morning?'

'Eventful. How is your mother?'

'She is well in herself, thank you, although she's still very unsteady on her feet. She actually has severely injured her leg so they're keeping her in hospital a bit longer because of the risk of blood clots ... or something like that.'

'I am sorry to hear that.'

Benjamin smiles. 'Thanks.'

'It must be a very worrying time for you, especially since you have no other family around.'

'I have my sister, but we don't speak much these days ... actually, we don't speak at all.'

'Where is she?'

'To be perfectly honest, I haven't the faintest idea. The last I heard she was in India and that was over a year ago.'

Ask him what happened between them?

'What happened between you two?'

Benjamin pauses and takes a deep breath. 'You know, if we're going to start reminiscing about our childhoods and talking about family issues and whatnot I suggest we do it in a place where they serve alcohol. Want to join me for a drink at my local?'

'It is barely two in the afternoon.'

'And that's a problem because ...?'

Oh my God say yes, I'm dying for a drink.

Have you learnt nothing from previous experiences with alcohol while being around Benjamin? You are not to be trusted.

Pleeeaaassseee ...

'Fine, but just one drink.'

Yes!

I may live to regret this ... again.

Benjamin and I walk for approximately ten minutes through the Cambridge streets until we stop outside a quaint pub with a thatched roof. To be perfectly honest the building looks as if it belongs in the countryside in a tiny remote village, but instead it is situated almost directly in the centre of a busy city. Despite the oddly located building it is very homely and welcoming as we step inside. Everything is wooden, the furniture, the walls, the floors and the beams above our heads. The ceiling is low so Benjamin has to bend down in several places to avoid hitting his head. There is a black and white cat stretched out on the bar sunning itself in a faint sliver of sunlight which is beaming through a nearby window ... oh shit. I hate cats. Actually ... they hate me, as you are perfectly aware.

Benjamin approaches the bar and the woman behind it suddenly gasps and shrieks like a banshee.

'Oh my God! Ben! Is that really you?' The young, attractive barmaid quickly shuffles out from behind the bar and throws her arms around Benjamin's neck.

Err ... possibly an ex-girlfriend of his?

Unlikely.

Why?

Because he told us that he had a bad breakup with his ex.

People can have more than one ex-partner.

I still say no.

Wanna bet?

Excuse me?

If she turns out to be an ex-girlfriend then I get to take over for a few minutes so I can enjoy a glass of wine, and if she isn't an ex then you can sit there and drink your glass of water or whatever it is you're going to order.

This is such a ridiculous idea. Why would I bet on something like that?

To have a bit of fun ... come on, Alicia ... live a little.

I roll my eyes.

Fine. Deal.

We mentally shake hands, sealing our pact.

The two of them eventually break apart and Benjamin finally realises I am still standing next to him.

'I'm sorry, Jasmine this is Alexis ... Alexis this is Jasmine.'

Jasmine eventually wrenches her gaze away from Benjamin and clamps her eyes on me. She gives me the once over and raises one perfectly plucked eyebrow. Her hair is peroxide blonde at the roots and dip-dyed electric blue on the ends, a startling look, but one she manages to pull off together with her excess of black eyeliner. Her breasts are almost bulging out of her strappy top, which is clearly two sizes too small. I assume she must do well in tips and possibly explains why there are many men in the bar and hardly any women.

'Nice to meet you,' she coos at me.

Did you see the way she looked at us?

'Likewise,' I say back.

We give each other cold smiles.

'I'll be right back Ben. I just have to finish serving a customer and then I'll grab your drink orders.'

'No rush, thanks Jazz.'

They share a knowing smile and then Jasmine goes back behind the counter and finishes serving a male customer who is clearly trying his best to flirt with her. Benjamin and I are left standing by the bar. There is a weird silence.

I've just had a strange thought ... do you think he's brought us here to try and make us jealous?

Quite possibly, but the joke is on him because I do not get jealous.

Well I do, and that cow had better watch herself.

I mentally roll my eyes again.

'So ...' I say, realising I have a bet to win. 'Jasmine is ...?'

'Jazz is an ex-girlfriend of mine.'

Ha! Pay up bitch!

Fuck.

'I assume she is not the one you were going to propose to?'

Benjamin laughs. 'Oh God no! Jazz and I were over pretty quick, but we remained friends.'

'I can see that.'

'What would you like to drink? My treat.'

Pinot grigo please.

'A pinot grigio, thank you.'

Large.

'Make it a large,' I add.

Benjamin smiles. 'Is there any other measurement wine comes in?'

I like him.

Suddenly, the cat, who has got up to stretch, catches sight of me, immediately hisses and scurries away, knocking over a pint of beer in the process. It seems that some things never change.

I close my eyes and allow Josslyn to take over.

Chapter Seventeen

Josslyn

After ordering our drinks (where Jazz and Ben swap a few flirty comments and touches – although it was mainly her that was touching him) we take our seats outside in the beer garden under a sun umbrella, but I intentionally angle my chair so I'm sitting in direct sunlight. Is there anything better than sitting in a pub garden on a summer’s day drinking a glass of wine? I aim my face at the warmth of the sun, close my eyes and breathe in the aromas. I can smell salty chips and earthy beers. I can hear happy chatter and conversations. For a second I forget about my own troubles and just enjoy the moment. I open my eyes and realise that Ben has been watching me with an amused smile.

'What?' I ask him.

'Nothing,' he replies before taking a small sip of his frothy beer. 'You're just cute when you're happy. Something comes over you and you're different somehow. You'll have to tell me the reason for that one day.'

'There's nothing to tell really.' Only that I actually share this body with my psychotic identical twin and I'm actually some form of ... *tumour* (for want of a better word right now) ... and we constantly switch positions and he doesn't have the faintest idea. 'So ... you were going to tell me about your sister,' I say, desperate to change the subject.

'Right ... but only if you tell me something about your childhood afterwards.'

'Um ... okay.' Where would I even start with that?

Ben takes a large gulp and begins. His voice is calm, smooth and deep and it sends me into a very relaxed and happy state, even though what he is saying is truly awful.

'Her name is Laura. She's three years younger than me. She was always the rebel out of the two of us. I was always covering for her, making excuses and lying to our parents. I told you that she once got so drunk I had to hide her from them until she was sober. That was when she was fourteen. Don't ask me how she got hold of a bottle of vodka at that age ... She got worse when she started university. I know she slept around, got wasted every night, even did drugs, but then ... well she dropped out of university and ran off with this random bloke who was twice her age. I think he was a lecturer at another campus, but I can't be sure. Obviously I disagreed with this, but she was adamant that they were in love. She disappeared for nearly a year. I didn't know where she was or if she was even alive. It was torture. I tried to track her down, but had no luck.

'Then, ten months after she left she turns up at my door, no money, no possessions except for the clothes on her back and tells me she made a mistake. She asks for my help. I'm so relieved that she's alive that I don't even have to think about it for a second. I help her out. I offer her my place to stay, I get her a job interview, I buy her new clothes and everything she needs. Everything is going fine until ... I see her getting into a dodgy-looking car. I don't see the driver, but I follow them to a rundown part of town. She has a load of cash on her and she hands it over to a drug dealer. That's when I confront her. I get beaten to a pulp by the druggie and his gang and they then all take off with the wad of cash.

'She tells me that she's sorry. I realise that she's a drug addict and she admits to selling my Rolex that my dad gave me for my twenty-first birthday. That's where all the money came from. I snap. I tell her I'm done with helping her anymore. She tries to guilt me into giving her more money so she can travel somewhere to start a new life. I tell her to fuck off ... and that's what she does. She sent me a postcard from India a year ago saying that she's *sorry, but she has to stay away* and I haven't heard from her since.'

Ben drains half his beer, leans back in his chair and inhales deeply.

'Shit,' I whisper. I wish I was one of those people who always know the right thing to say, but what do you say to a story like that?

'Yeah,' he replies.

'I-I'm sorry. Does she know that your dad died?'

'Nope.'

'Shit.'

'Yeah.'

I take a big gulp of wine. 'And I thought Alicia was bad.'

Oh mother fucking fuck shit! Oops!

'Who's Alicia?'

You idiot!

'She's um ... she's ...' Oh God, what have I done? My defences are down and I'm not thinking clearly. Damn you alcohol! Okay, so I've only had a few sips, so I can't blame the wine. I can't lie. I can't tell the truth. Maybe I can reveal a mixture of the two. 'She's ... my sister.'

Stop talking right now.

Ben raises his eyebrows. 'I thought you said you didn't have a sister?'

'I ... I don't. I mean, not anymore. She died.'

Ben lowers his glass away from his lips. 'I-I'm so sorry ...'

'It's fine. She died a long time ago, but she was a troublemaker too, quite possibly evil and psychotic.'

Ben smiles. 'Older or younger?'

'Err ... older.'

There's a long silence while we take a drink, which is then interrupted by Jazz who saunters over with a phony smile on her overly made-up face. Her skirt is way too short. God, she's such a whore—

'Hi guys! Can I get you another drink?'

Ben looks at me. 'Another?'

'I better not.' Dear God I just can't be trusted with alcohol right now.

'I'll have one more. Thanks Jazz.'

She winks and beams a smile at him before walking away, her hips swaying from side to side in an effort to keep Ben's gaze on her ass, but he almost immediately turns back to me. Clearly the tight skirt squeezed over a tight ass isn't enough to hold his attention. A part of me is slightly smug about this.

'I guess we both have a few skeletons in our closets,' says Ben.

'You could say that.'

'So ... what other secrets are you hiding from me?'

'I think that's pretty much it,' I say with a smile.

Ben takes a drink. 'You know, you're really easy to talk to ... some of the time, but other times you're a bit ...'

'A bit what?'

'Serious.'

I shrug. 'What can I say? I get a drink in my hand and I loosen up, although maybe I was a bit too loose the other night ... sorry about that.'

'I told you that you don't have to apologise.'

I sigh happily, thinking that I wish there was a way I could stay here talking to Ben forever and not have to face the real world, not have to disappear into this body. I wish there was a way I could stay with him forever ...

'So you still owe me a story from your childhood. I told you about Laura.'

'And I told you about Alicia.'

'All I know is that you had an older sister who died and that she was slightly evil. That's not enough compared to what I told you.'

I shrug. 'That's all I've got.'

'What about your early childhood? What were your parents like?'

I do not approve of all these probing questions.

'Same as any other parents really.'

'Right ...' Ben frowns at me. 'You're a hard woman to read Alexis.'

'So you've told me. I'm sorry, I just find it difficult to talk about my sister.'

'Of course, I'm sorry ... maybe it's too soon in our relationship—'

I choke on my wine.

'—I mean friendship,' he corrects.

We share a laugh.

'Will you promise me something?' he asks.

'Depends.'

He smiles. 'One day, if and when you feel comfortable enough ... will you tell me about Alicia?'

I take a deep breath. 'Sure,' I say. 'Maybe.'

'Maybe's good enough for me.'

Chapter Eighteen

Alicia

I am gliding across the ground like a ghost and I am wearing a black hood, which partially covers my face. I do not know where I am exactly, but there is a young woman in front of me. She is screaming and running as fast as she can, briefly glancing back, catching sight of me, screaming again and running. This scene continues to repeat itself. I am getting closer to my prey. The woman is of no significance to me. She is merely an object, but one I wish to devour. I am even closer now, within touching distance. I reach out my hand, which is covered with blood, but the hand is not mine – it is a male hand, strong and with slightly hairy knuckles and wrinkles. I recoil in shock. Who am I? The woman is still screaming and fleeing before me. She is cornered.

'Please!' she begs. 'Please, no! Stop! I beg you!'

I do not acknowledge her scared and pleading voice. Tears are streaming from her eyes as she crouches to the floor in sheer terror. I loom over her. I do not speak as I grab her hair, force her to the ground, pull down her trousers and underwear and—

I jerk awake, covered in sweat. It is light outside. I glance at my watch which reads 05:30 a.m. I slowly lean back against the pillow and study my hands. They are my hands, feminine and nicely manicured. That was a slightly odd and terrifying dream. I was not myself, but I felt like I was in the body of a man and he was about to ... I shudder in disgust. Rape is something I whole-heartedly despise and disagree with. Even I have my limits and when it comes to a man dominating and violating a woman it boils my blood, as it should with anyone.

I push the covers off and wander downstairs in my cotton shorts and loose top. It is early, but I know I will not be able to go back to sleep after that dream. I make myself a cup of tea, switch the television onto BBC News (ensuring it is not too loud so I do not disturb Benjamin) and take a seat in the over-sized armchair. The lady doing the weather is just finishing off her segment. Apparently, it is going to be warm and sunny for the remainder of the week with a few possible showers overnight. Then the news starts and the first broadcast shakes me to my core. I grip my mug, my whole body tense.

'New evidence has come to light in the case of the murder of Daniel Russell, whose body was found last week in a rubbish tip near Cambridge. He was stabbed twenty-six times with a knife. Experts have discovered that due to the depth of the stab wounds it was quite possibly a woman who dealt the fatal blows. A few hairs not belonging to the victim have been found on his body and these, according to DNA experts, belong to a woman also. After speaking with Daniel's parents the police have discovered that he had an ex-girlfriend called Josslyn Reynolds, who is now wanted for questioning by the police. However, Josslyn Reynolds has not been seen for over a year and both her parents are dead. She has no siblings, but if anyone does know her whereabouts they are strongly encouraged to come forward and provide whatever details they can.'

At this point the television screen shows a photo of Josslyn and Daniel taken while they had been dating, no doubt provided by his parents. The screen zooms in on Josslyn's face.

Holy mother of God!

That bastard must have planted evidence on the body.

No offence, Alicia, but it's not as if you were particularly careful when you stabbed him twenty-odd times. You could have easily left behind some hair.

Possibly ... we need to be even more careful now. We cannot go out in public anymore.

Cos that's not going to look suspicious to Ben ... how else are we going to kill Peter? I mean, I know we look different now compared to when that picture was taken, but having blonde hair and less body fat isn't exactly the best disguise in the world.

He is forcing our hand. He must have known this would happen. He is testing us again. He wants to see how far we will go.

Or maybe he thinks that he can save me by swooping in and saving the day. My face is now all over the news. He thinks I'm going to go running back to him for help. He needs to go. We need to kill him before I'm spotted, otherwise we'll lose the chance. I don't care what happens to me. I just want him dead, so I never have to worry about him hurting anyone I care about ever again.

At that precise moment Benjamin enters the room, bleary eyed and half-dressed. Josslyn's face is still on the screen so I hastily switch the television off before he catches sight of it. He does not appear to notice.

We can't let Ben find out about this.

Agreed.

Benjamin shuffles the rest of the way into the room and rubs his eyes. He yawns and stretches, his muscles flexing in the morning light. However, I am far too distracted to notice properly. My face is plastered all over the morning news in thousands of homes across the country. It would not take Benjamin long to recognise the slightly rounder, dark-haired woman as me. I know I need to act fast with regards to Peter, but I need a plan. I need a way of getting to him ... or maybe I need to let him get to me first. Maybe I need to let him make the first move ...

'You're up early,' Benjamin says.

'I apologise if I woke you.'

'It's fine. Unfortunately in this house sound travels and the walls are really thin. I don't know about you, but I need a coffee.'

I hold my mug of tea up to show that I do not require coffee. He nods and heads towards the kitchen, scuffing his feet as if he cannot be bothered to lift them. I stare blankly at the television screen for a few minutes until Benjamin comes back into the lounge with a steaming cup and lays on the sofa, spreading his entire body across it.

'So I messaged my best mate last night to see if he was available for a catch up. We're meeting for a drink tonight. Why don't you come? I can introduce you. I met his sister who was in one of my classes at university. I thought she was cute, not that anything happened with her, but Phil and I became best friends. I haven't seen him since I left.'

'Thank you, but no. I assume you will want to catch up with masculine topics so I would only be getting in the way.'

Benjamin hides a small laugh behind his coffee cup. 'Masculine topics? I assume I'm talking to the formal and serious side of you now ...'

'Excuse me?'

'I told you ... you have two different sides to your personality. One is fun, relaxed and open and that's usually when you have a drink in your hand, and the other is ... formal and, to be perfectly honest, slightly scary at times.' I glare at him without blinking. 'Ah, you see ... scary!' He points at me, yet looks highly amused.

I look away, unwilling to engage him in this particular conversation. He knows far too much already.

Benjamin takes a sip. 'Come on ... just come with me. We can all get drunk and have a right laugh. What else are you doing tonight?'

'I do not know yet.'

'Okay, well if you find yourself with nothing to do, then we'll be at the same pub we went to yesterday from eight onwards.'

'Fine.'

'I'm going back to visit my mum today. I'll probably be gone most of the day.'

'Fine.'

The conversation grinds to a halt and we are left in silence once again.

'Are you okay? You look a bit shaken.'

'I am fine.'

'You know, as a man I'm taught to understand that when a woman says she's *fine* it means she's not really *fine.'*

I glare at him again and sigh. This man is infuriating. Why must he constantly question me and attempt to connect with me?

Maybe because he likes you?

He likes you, not me. He finds me scary.

Maybe he likes both of us, which is, granted, slightly weird, but he doesn't know that we're two different people. He seems to think we have a split personality, but I don't think he dislikes you.

And that is a problem.

Why?

We cannot allow him to get to close to us. He already knows about Alicia and—

Oh come on, he knows nothing! I merely let her name slip, that's all, and he thinks she's dead ... which I guess technically she is, but ... it's not like he knows the details.

Josslyn, we cannot allow people to get close to us. We have each other. That is enough.

But what about when I'm gone? You'll be all on your own. Maybe it's time you start thinking about what will happen in the future—

'Alexis? What's going on right now?' Benjamin's voice disrupts my thoughts.

Sometimes I forget that when Josslyn and I talk it is in my head and not out loud, so if I am with another person all they see is me staring blankly and not speaking.

Benjamin appears slightly confused.

'I apologise. I was just thinking.'

Benjamin raises his eyebrows. 'How I'd love to read your mind, just for one day.'

Trust me Benjamin, you would not be able to handle it.

You've got that right.

'Well, I'm gonna get dressed and go for a quick run before I see my mum. Did you get a new phone by the way?'

Oh shit, we forgot to do that yesterday!

'No, I will do it today.' I still have not turned mine on since I switched it off and destroyed the SIM card. The freedom of not having a phone is very cathartic.

'Okay, cool.'

Benjamin heads towards the stairs which are opposite the front door to the house. I watch him bend down to pick something up from the doormat. He then walks back into the lounge holding an envelope with a frown on his face.

'You have a letter.'

'Excuse me?'

Benjamin holds out the white envelope. I take it with apprehension. It has my name on the front. Only my name, no address.

'Who knows you're here?' asks Benjamin. 'It must have been hand delivered.'

'I am not sure.'

'That's a bit creepy if you ask me ... who's it from?'

I know exactly who it is from.

He's found us. How did he find us so fast? It's like he's watching our every move. How's he doing this?

I can sense the fear in Josslyn's voice, but I do not respond to her as I am aware that I have not answered Benjamin's question.

'I am not sure.'

'Is it the person who you think killed Oscar? They're playing games with you Alexis. I think you should report this to the police. If you haven't told anyone that you're staying here, then it means this person has been watching you. I'm not sure how I feel about leaving you alone for the rest of the day.'

'Do not be ridiculous. I can look after myself. Now go for a run and go and visit your mother. She needs you. I do not.'

'But—'

'Go!'

'There's that scary voice again ... okay, fine, I'll go, just promise me that you'll be careful.'

'I will.'

I wait until I hear a door slam upstairs before I carefully peel open the envelope. I have no idea what to expect: a threatening note, a photograph of Oscar when he was stabbed ... several options float through my head, but I certainly am not expecting this:

Miss Alexis Grey
You are cordially invited to the
Teachers' and Faculty Members' Ball
at Lampton School for Boys
on Monday the 26th of July at 8 p.m.
You are the guest of Peter Phillips
Black tie is mandatory

I reread it again to ensure my eyes had not deceived me the first time.

Wait ... he's inviting us to a black-tie ball? Why?

He wants us to come to him. He is baiting us ... again.

But we aren't going ... right?

I believe we possibly should consider it.

What? Why?

He wishes to try and catch us off guard, ensure we do what he wants. Maybe we should let him, lull him into a false sense of security.

But ... it could be dangerous.

I am counting on it.

I don't understand what you're planning, Alicia.

Leave it to me.

Unfortunately for me, Benjamin has other ideas and upon returning back downstairs he explains that he is not comfortable with leaving me alone all day now that I appear to have some crazy stalker (if only he knew the truth). He insists that I accompany him to the hospital to visit his mother and no matter how hard I try I am unable to persuade him otherwise. I even use my scary eyes and voice, but he takes his stand, which I cannot fault him for.

Benjamin even convinces me to go for a morning run with him. I don a vest and a cap, which I pull low over my face to shield myself from view. I usually like to run alone, but I take him up on his offer, grateful for the opportunity to exercise. I have not exercised in a few days and I can feel my body becoming twitchy and agitated. It feels good to run again, to blow away the cobwebs, as it were. The early morning breeze is cool and soothing and as my lungs fill with fresh air I am momentarily in my own element and world.

We run side by side where the footpaths allow. He leads me through the narrow streets until we reach a more rural area. He is surprisingly fit, however I quickly realise that he is holding back for my benefit. We reach the local park, which has open fields and plenty of paths, which are already scattered with morning runners. I immediately take off sprinting, not to get away from Benjamin, but to initiate a competition. He accepts and is soon racing alongside me. We turn and smile at each other and push forwards, getting faster and faster. I am aiming for the single tree in the field ahead, a solo target. I am nearing my maximum capacity for speed when I finally reach the tree. Benjamin is merely seconds behind me, puffing and panting. He bends over and rests his hands on his thighs, sucking in deep breaths. I place my hands behind my head and stand up tall, doing the same.

'G-good r-race!' he says. 'But I let you w-win.'

'T-then you are weak.'

We both smile at each other while we continue to catch our breaths. Despite knowing the risks I find myself enjoying his company.

Later that morning we visit his mother in hospital where I am completely out of my comfort zone. Josslyn and I have never liked hospitals. I also realise that I am required to be nice to little old ladies (so Josslyn tells me) so I am on my best behaviour.

Benjamin's mother is very frail and can barely stand by herself, but she is extremely stubborn and refuses help to get back and forth to the bathroom. She uses a walking frame. The second she lays eyes on me she starts questioning who I am, how I know her son, how old I am, where I live, among other things. I politely give my answers, using every last ounce of civil conversation I can muster. Benjamin just stands there with an amused smile on his face, knowing for a fact that I am putting on a nice act just for her.

After an hour of being interrogated I leave Benjamin with his mother to talk and go in search of a shop that sells food, promising him that I will not be longer than half an hour. I am not expecting a lot of choice, considering the shop is located within a hospital, but I eat the ham and cheese sandwich hungrily. I pick up a takeaway coffee for Benjamin.

On my slow walk back to him and his mother I stop and watch the news channel on a waiting room television. I have been careful to keep my head down while walking around and have donned my capped hat again, the same one I used while out running. To be perfectly honest the thought of being recognised does not cross my mind until I see my face flash up on the screen again. The broadcast repeats the exact news story as this morning.

I don't think I'll ever get used to seeing my face on the news.

I pull the cap slightly lower over my forehead. I watch as my broadcast finishes and then another one starts—

'Another woman has come forward today saying that she was attacked and raped by a hooded man almost thirty years ago. The police are therefore branding this man a serial rapist and it is possible that he's been attacking his victims for nearly three decades, putting his age approximately in his fifties. The police are urging anyone who has suffered an attack of this nature to come forward so that they can begin to piece together the evidence and a timeline. They still have no prime suspects.'

I am unable to hear the rest of the news story because two nurses walk by, talking loudly. On the screen is a black and white artist's sketch of what the man looks like as described by several of his victims. The man is tall and broad. Only the bottom half of his face can be seen from under the dark hood. His chin is covered in rough stubble, his jaw sharp and solid. There are fine lines and wrinkles around the corners of his mouth.

Who is this guy? Why are you having dreams about him?

I do not think they are necessarily about him in particular.

It's sure a weird coincidence.

Indeed.

I leave the television area and head back to Benjamin who is standing outside his mother's private room, leaning against the wall. He looks up when he sees me.

'Hey, I was getting worried.'

I hand him a paper coffee cup. 'I am hardly going to be attacked in a hospital.'

'You think whoever this person is would attack you?'

'It is a possibility.'

'I really wish you'd tell me what's going on. Some person kills your dog in another country and then follows you back to the UK and posts a letter through my door addressed to you ... it's fucking weird Alexis.'

'I will handle it.'

'Can't you let me help you? I know you don't want to tell the police, but I'm honestly worried for your safety.'

I do not reply immediately. I merely stare past him at a man who is wearing a black hoodie and is walking towards us. The man casually strolls past without giving either one of us a glance. I find myself not only on the lookout for Peter, but also a man in his fifties wearing a black hood.

'Will you please come with me tonight to meet my friend? I wouldn't feel right leaving you alone at my house. He's perfectly nice, honest.'

I roll my eyes and clench my jaw. 'Fine.'

We eventually leave the hospital and head back to Benjamin's house, however on the way I stop by a phone store and buy a cheap pay-as-you-go phone. I swap numbers with Benjamin because he insists on it. I am certain that Peter knows my whereabouts at all times, despite turning off my original phone, but at least there is no way he can now track my new one.

I cannot shake Benjamin. He is becoming an annoyance. How am I supposed to plan and kill Peter when I have my own bodyguard constantly following me? I plan to sneak out of the house bright and early tomorrow morning to get away from him, just for a while. I do not care what he thinks, but first I must get through this tedious meeting with his friend.

We arrive at the pub at eight o'clock exactly. Jasmine immediately stops what she is doing and makes another highly inappropriate fuss over Benjamin, throwing me dirty looks in the process. Benjamin, I admit, looks good tonight. He is wearing jeans and a fitted, black, long-sleeved, v-necked top, showing off a small amount of chest hair. He has rolled the sleeves up slightly, as it is a warm evening. I am wearing high-waist jeans and a white strap top tucked into them. I even applied some makeup for no other reason than I felt like it.

And you wanted to look better than you did the other day when Jazz first saw us.

I do not care what that bitch thinks.

Well, whatever reason you did it for, it seems to be working. She keeps glaring at us.

By the way ... you will not be making an appearance tonight. I will have one drink and that is all. End of discussion.

Uhh, you're so boring.

Benjamin orders our drinks and then scans the seating area, presumably looking for his friend.

'Ah, there he is ... come on.'

We start walking towards a corner of the room where there is a man sitting at a table for four with his back to us. He has dark hair that is slightly long and wispy and is wearing a checked shirt.

'Phil!'

The man turns in his seat and smiles as he sees us ...

Oh my fucking God ...

It is him.

It is Peter.

Chapter Nineteen
Alicia

I feel as if I have been smashed in the chest with a brick ... repeatedly. I cannot breathe, the air around me appears to have vanished and been replaced by tiny shards of glass. I attempt to swallow, but a large lump has formed in my throat and I am unable to do anything. My body wishes to react in shock, but I am fighting the urge with all my might. I ... must ... not ... react.

I breathe in and out slowly through my nose, hoping to steady my breathing as I watch Benjamin and Peter give each other a manly hug and a slap on the back. They laugh, bump fists and generally act like teenagers while I stand rooted to the spot a few feet away, not sure whether to turn and run or stand my ground. I do not know what to think, but I quickly gather that Benjamin clearly does not have a clue that his best friend and I know each other ...

I-I don't understand what's going on right now. Alicia ... this feels wrong. What the hell is happening?

Just ... let me handle this.

Ben and Peter ... Peter and Ben ... I don't ... I ...

Josslyn is clearly too shocked to form proper thoughts and words. I do not blame her. I am having a hard time contemplating everything myself. My mind races with the possibilities of what this means, but before I can form a complete thought in my head Benjamin has turned to me and is introducing me to Peter.

'Phil, this is Alexis, the girl I told you about. Alexis, this is Phil, my best friend from university.'

Benjamin steps aside while the two of us move towards each other. Peter is smiling and he holds out his hand for me to shake it.

'Nice to meet you, Alexis. Benny's told me all about you, and by the way, my name's actually Peter, but Benny's always called me Phil cos my last name is Phillips.'

My bottom lip starts to tremble, but I bite it hard. He is enjoying watching me fall apart. He knows exactly what he is doing. I hate being caught off guard, but yet again, Peter has managed to do exactly that. I slowly extend my hand and we shake. I grip his hand tight and we lock hold for a few seconds before breaking apart quite forcefully.

'Hello,' I manage to say.

I wish my body would hurry up and get over the shock soon because I do not intend to be portrayed as the victim any longer.

My mind suddenly flashes back to the first time Josslyn met Peter at his house. He told her that his best friend, Benny, had set him up on a blind date that night. I feel so foolish. The signs have been there all along, but once again Peter has managed to completely blind-side me. I despise him more now than I ever thought possible. I want to grab the beer bottle on the nearest table and smash him over the head with it, watch as he crumples to the floor. Then I want to stab him in the face with the jagged edges and destroy his handsome features as the flesh peels off his skull.

'Yeah, sorry, I just always call him Phil. It's a name that's just stuck around,' says Benjamin with a laugh. He moves to the table and pulls out a chair for me. 'Shall we?'

Peter and I continue to stare at each other.

'Ladies first,' he says as he steps to the side to allow me to pass.

I grit my teeth. 'Thank you ... *Peter*.' I will not call him Phil for that is not his true name.

We take our seats. Peter sits opposite Benjamin and I. We are face to face, merely a few feet from each other. I listen quietly while the men start a conversation with each other.

'Wow, Benny Boy you look great man! Nice tan.'

'Ha, thanks. You're not looking too bad yourself, although your taste in clothes is still awful.'

'Well, what can I say, I like a checked shirt. The ladies still dig it.' Peter winks at me and I feel my blood start to boil. 'By the way I heard about your mum, how is she?' he asks Benjamin solemnly. I find it fascinating that he can go from amusing to serious in the blink of an eye.

'She's doing better each day thanks. She should be able to come home in a day or two,' answers Benjamin, taking a sip of his beer.

I am twirling my wine glass round and round on the table in front of me. I have not touched a drop yet. I continue to glare at Peter across the table, wishing I had the power to make his head explode and watch as tiny pieces of his brain stick to the walls and ceiling.

'Ah, that's great to hear. So you said you got back a few days ago? How long are you sticking around for?'

'I'm not sure yet.' Benjamin turns to me. 'Alexis and I have a few things to sort out first.'

Peter leans forward in his chair. 'Oh yeah? What sort of things are they then?' He directs the question specifically at me.

I take a deep breath, my initial shock finally fading to acceptance. It is time to destroy this man and put him back in his place.

'I came back to correct some wrongs in my life.'

'That sounds serious.'

'It is.'

'And Benny's helping you?' He raises an eyebrow at his friend.

'Actually, Alexis is quite secretive. She won't tell me the ins and outs, but I intend to help in any way I can.'

'Well ... good luck with that.' Peter grins and downs the remainder of his pint in one go. He slams it on the table and motions for Jasmine to approach. 'Another of the same for me ... Benny, you'd better catch up mate.' He nods at Benjamin's almost full pint glass. Benjamin immediately downs the entire contents. 'And another for Benny. Alexis?'

We both look at my wine glass which has remained untouched. There is no way I am going to be bullied into downing a large glass of wine.

I agree. We can't afford to get drunk right now.

'Nothing for me,' I say.

'Coming right up.' Jasmine heads back to the bar.

Peter spreads his arms wide and rests one on the back of the empty neighbouring chair. 'So ... tell me about you two ... how'd you meet? Benny's told me lots about you.'

Benjamin coughs and shakes his head. 'I haven't told you that much ... I haven't I swear. Phil likes to tease me,' he says to me, clearly slightly embarrassed by his friend.

I am unsure whether to believe him or not. What exactly has he told Peter about me? Has Benjamin been spying on me too?

Let's not jump to conclusions just yet, Alicia.

I take Josslyn's warning on board, but my defences are certainly on high alert. I cannot trust anyone and that is exactly what I have been saying from day one.

'I'd rather ask how you and Benjamin met,' I say.

I do not wish for this conversation to be solely about myself. Peter deserves some of the attention – the more I can deflect on him the better. He may stumble and say something that he should not. If Benjamin is unaware of the whole story then Peter will not want his friend to find out right now, not like this.

Benjamin takes this one. 'I told Alexis very briefly the main gist of the story earlier, but I'll happily fill in the blanks ...' He glances at Peter for approval. Peter nods and Benjamin begins his story.

'So basically I met him through his sister, Alicia. We were in the same class at uni. I thought she was mega hot, so I sat next to her and struck up a conversation. We hit it off and we found ourselves sitting next to each other in that same class for a few weeks. Then one day I saw her talking to this asshole in the corridor outside the classroom. She introduces us and I find myself utterly relieved when it's revealed he's her brother. Anyway, the next time I meet the guy I get his name wrong and call him Phil. I assume it's because my subconscious remembered his surname, but not his first name. The name stuck and he's been Phil ever since. Things fizzled out with Alicia unfortunately, but me and Phil seemed to become friends somehow ... and the rest is history. We became best friends on a wine tour ... that's why I have a fondness for Cannonau di Sardegna. We drank rather a lot of it that day. Oh, wow! I've just realised that you both had a sister called Alicia ... how weird is that?' Benjamin frowns and appears to be deep in thought for a few seconds.

I watch his expression, wondering if he will work it out and put two and two together, but it appears that he is clueless about everything. Or he is an exceptionally good actor and liar. It is not definite about what he knows.

Peter raises his eyebrows at me. 'You had a sister called Alicia too? What a small world we live in. Unfortunately my sister disappeared. What happened to yours?' Peter is speaking as casually as we would have been discussing the weather or asking about each other's hobbies.

I stare at him, my teeth clenched. My jaw is aching from attempting to hold back the spiel of abuse I want to throw at him.

'She died,' I reply bluntly.

'I'm so sorry to hear that.' He does not ask how, as he probably is aware how rude that would sound to Benjamin, so instead he leans across the table towards me and gently places a hand over my arm. I resist the urge to wrench my hand away, but I cannot hide the small flinch as I feel his warm hand against my skin. 'My deepest sympathies,' he whispers.

I do not reply, despite knowing that it appears rude of me not to return the compliment.

Benjamin glances at each of us. 'I'm sorry to bring them up. It's just that Alicia was really special and if it weren't for her I would never have met him. He's my best friend.'

I cannot help but think that Benjamin has atrocious taste in friends.

Benjamin continues. 'It's just awful that she disappeared. Phil's never given up hope of finding her. Speaking of which dude, I saw you on the news the other day. You found a body! What the fuck man, you didn't think to call me and tell me?'

Shit ... he did see the news after all.

Evidently so.

Peter shrugs. 'Didn't seem relevant for you to know. Besides, you were in a different country.'

'I still like to keep up to date with what's going on. So are there any new developments in the case of that dead guy ... what was his name? ... Russell something—'

'Daniel Russell,' I correct. Both men turn their heads towards me. 'I also happen to watch the news,' I reply as I stare coldly at Peter. I see his lips twitch slightly, trying to hide a smug smile. I would love to lean across the table, grab the back of his head and smash his face into the wooden table, breaking his nose and causing him intense pain.

'The police are looking for his ex-girlfriend ... I can't remember her name. Alexis, do you remember?'

Let me answer this one.

I really do not think that is—

Josslyn forces her way into my body, something we shall have strong words about later.

Chapter Twenty

Josslyn

I look at Peter and tilt my head slightly. At this point Jazz places the new pints of beer on the table and then saunters off.

'Her name is Josslyn Reynolds.' My words are strong, solid and unwavering. I see the look on his face as he realises it's me he's speaking to now. I finally take hold of my wine glass and drink a few gulps, which seem to soothe my whole body.

'Right, that's it. Josslyn ... Josslyn.' He whispers my name and smirks as he drinks his beer.

'Do they really think she killed him?' asks Ben. 'I mean, wasn't he stabbed like twenty something times? That seems really ... violent.'

'Maybe he had it coming,' I say casually, leaning back in my chair. I think I've got over the shock of seeing him now. Alicia and I are determined to stay focused. Peter won't risk revealing the truth to Ben, I'm sure of it. We have our own little game to play – just the two of us and I don't intend to lose this time.

'Maybe,' replies Ben with a frown.

'You know, she kind of looks like you Alexis, don't you think?' asks Peter.

We glare at each other across the table, neither one of us breaking eye contact. He is dangerously close to having this wine glass shoved in his eye. He's baiting me. He wants me to let down my guard or lose my cool. Ben appears to have noticed the odd tension between us and clears his throat.

'Err ... what are you on about Phil? I saw that news article pop up on my phone earlier and Alexis and that Josslyn girl look nothing alike.' Thank God for small screens on phones. He might think differently if he ever sees the news on a large television screen.

'My mistake,' replies Peter.

'Alexis is ... well she's ... I mean ...' Ben glances at me and blushes bright red. I smile at him, which seems to relax him. 'Sorry, I just mean you're much more attractive, that's all.'

I'm not sure whether to take that as a compliment or an insult. Did he just call me ugly and fat? I mean ... the old me.

'Thanks,' I say. Right, it's time to move on from this awkwardness. A change of subject is definitely in order. 'So, Phil,' I say cheerfully, 'are you seeing anyone? Is there any girl in your life that you just can't live without, that you have to see every single day, or are you still hung up on an ex that you're never going to see ever again?'

There ... that broke the tension ... I have now created a whole new mess of ... something.

Ben sucks in some air and Peter looks as if I've just caught him with his boxers down because he splutters on some beer that he was in the middle of swallowing.

'Sorry, did I say something wrong?' I ask innocently.

'N-no ... not at all. It's just that I've recently got out of a long-term relationship, that's all.'

'Oh, I'm sorry to hear that. What happened?'

Peter speaks slowly. 'We both loved each other, but we just ... didn't ... I mean ...' (It appears that Peter isn't as good at thinking up lies on the spot as he thinks he is.) '... We just grew apart over time. You know how it is.'

'Right, of course.'

'Yeah, his ex was a nutcase,' interjects Ben. 'Didn't she start stalking you at one point? I never met her, but she sounds like a bit of a weird one. You told me once that she broke into your house and moved things around. Like ... who does that!' Ben laughs and shakes his head.

I raise my eyebrows at Peter, who is trying to hide his face behind his beer glass as he gulps it back. I think he's finally beginning to realise that this was a bad idea. He clearly doesn't want Ben to know the truth.

'You were stalked?' I ask, trying my best to sound shocked and horrified. 'Wow, that must have been really scary.'

Peter says nothing for a few seconds. He takes a breath and seems to relax a little. 'Yeah, she was a bit crazy, but she loved me and that's the only thing that matters.'

'You think love is a good enough excuse to stalk someone?'

'Yes.'

A silence hovers in the air. Ben appears oblivious to the new awkwardness. He downs the remainder of his pint.

'Well, I have a bladder the size of a pea, so if you'll both excuse me a moment ... Phil, Alexis ... another round?'

'Sure Benny, another of the same would be great. And maybe grab us some shots, your choice ... just not Tequila, cos, well you know what happened the last time you drank that stuff.'

Oh God, he's trying to get me drunk, knowing full well I'm a liability when I'm hammered.

Ben groans. 'Oh man, you know shots are a bad idea!'

'That's why they're a great idea.'

Ben gets to his feet. 'Alexis, another wine?'

'Actually, can I have a gin and tonic instead please?'

'Of course. Be right back. Be nice to each other.'

Ben walks away towards the men's toilets. Peter and I watch him intently until he's out of sight and then slowly turn our heads to look at each other. We're alone. There aren't that many people in the bar, not in close proximity anyway. I'm staring at him, wondering if I should say something, but I suddenly feel lost for words. He's waiting for me to make the first move, offering me the upper hand. I have a choice now. Do I remain fairly polite and pretend like he's a stranger or do I confront him here and now before Ben comes back? I opt for the latter.

'What's your game *Phil*?'

'What game is that Josslyn?'

'Ben was the only friend that I could depend on and now you've tainted him and I can't trust him. What's going on? It can't be just a random coincidence that Ben met me all the way out in Tuscany. Did you plant him there to spy on me for you?'

Peter laughs out loud, a little too loud for my liking. A few people from way across the bar glance over. He wants people to be aware of us sitting in the corner in case things get ... nasty.

'Wow, that's very presumptuous of you, Josslyn. You think I sent my best friend out to another country to keep an eye on you even though he didn't know that that's what he was doing? Even I'm not that clever and twisted.'

'I whole-heartedly disagree.' I can't help but notice he doesn't actually answer my question.

'So, here's the million-pound question.' Peter leans forward in his chair and across the table towards me. I automatically recoil and lean back as he speaks. 'Will you accept my invitation and go to the ball with me tomorrow night?'

'Why?'

Peter shrugs his shoulders. 'Think of it as one last chance for me to prove my love to you. I'll show you a night you'll never forget, but not Alicia ... I want you. We'll dance, we'll talk, we'll drink—'

'So it's like a date?' I interrupt.

'Exactly.'

This time it's me who laughs loudly. 'You're completely insane, like seriously, you're the most insane and deluded person I've ever met.'

'That didn't sound like a no.'

Oh my God, what's wrong with me? Why am I not saying no? Does that mean I actually want to go with him?

Alicia ... help me out here.

Say yes.

Are you sure about this?

Yes, but say that you cannot guarantee that you will be available for the entire evening. You are still gaining your strength to be able to take over for longer. I can already feel you slipping.

Alicia is right. I am losing my grip.

'Fine,' I say. 'I'll go.'

Peter grins. 'Thank you, Josslyn. It'll be an amazing night, I promise.'

'I might not be able to guarantee that Alicia won't make an appearance. She's the main owner of this body now.'

'I'm sure Alicia will be on her best behaviour.'

We shall see about that.

I'm about to open my mouth to continue to speak when Ben appears beside me with a tray of drinks: two beers, a gin and tonic and six shots of unknown origin.

Oh fuck.

'Sorry I was so long. Jazz kept talking.'

'Man, she still fancies you,' jokes Peter as he starts handing out the drinks across the table. 'You should hit that again!'

'I don't think that's a good idea.' Ben glances at me briefly and smiles.

Peter notices and then I think it dawns on him ... his best friend likes me too. Ben may have alluded to the fact that we weren't dating, but the fact that he likes me is quite plain to see. A shadow of jealously crosses Peter's face and I see his jaw clench.

Uh oh.

I feel as if I'm caught in a love triangle, except I'm not in love with either of them. Well, I mean, if I had to choose then obviously I'd choose Ben because he's ... wait, what am I saying? It just sounded like I said I was in love with Ben, which clearly I'm not. I mean, it's not like I think about him all the time and imagine us spending our lives together or anything ...

I can't trust either of them. Ben's possibly been spying on me for the past year or so. I don't know if he's telling the truth. The smart thing to do would be to get up and run out the door yelling 'call the police!' at the top of my lungs, but I don't.

'So ... what did you two talk about while I was away?' asks Ben.

Peter hands a shot to each of us. 'Actually, I was just mentioning to Alexis that there's this black-tie ball tomorrow night at my school for the teachers and faculty members. I said that I didn't have a date and asked her if she'd like to go with me, and she said yes.' Peter downs the shot and slams it down onto the table.

Ben glances at me as if I'm crazy. 'Really? You're going to a ball with this idiot?'

'Sure, why not?' I down the shot and resist the urge to gag. Yuck! It's Sambuca. I cough and splutter and make a disgusted face. I can't do shots ... ask anyone. Oh God, now I'm making Ben jealous.

'You're invited as well Benny.'

Wait, what?

'We can all go together,' finishes Peter. He's enjoying the game again. What the hell is he thinking? Why would he want his best friend there when we are supposed to be on some magical date night?

Ben looks taken aback for a few seconds. 'Uh, sure, yeah, sounds like fun. I think I have my old tux somewhere at my mum's house.'

'Perfect!'

Okay, what the fuck just happened? How did I end up on a double date with my crazy stalker and his best friend to a black-tie event? What am I thinking? What is *he* thinking?

I need a drink. I reach and grab the other shot. The three of us clink glasses and down the burning fire liquid in one. Bottoms up!

One thing is perfectly clear ... I'm going to need one hell of a dress ... and look absolutely drop-dead gorgeous and sexy as hell while I'm at it.

Chapter Twenty-One
Alicia

Peter and Benjamin continue to buy rounds of shots for us and after six shots I am able to take back control and bring a halt to the proceedings. Josslyn can never seem to say no, despite my frequent attempts to stop her from downing them one after the other. She needs a clear head, but her anger and frustration at Peter is causing her to let her guard down. So I did her a favour and stepped in. Peter appears to notice the change between us. Even though I am considerably inebriated my personality change is clear.

I stand up, my head immediately spinning, and grab the back of my chair.

'Whoa!' says Peter.

Benjamin attempts to help me, but I pull away from him.

'I am fine. I require some fresh air, that is all.'

'I'll come with you—'

'No! I told you I am ... fine.' We share a look. I am aware that we have had this conversation before and he told me that when a woman says she is fine, it never means that she is fine, but he does not question the matter any further. I just require some space to think, to clear my head, to try and sober myself up.

I-I'm sorry. You know how I get when I ... d-drink.

You need help.

I-I'm not an a-alc-coholic ...

I beg to differ.

H-how come you're not ... w-wasted?

I can control myself when I need to.

I feel sick.

As do I.

I quickly excuse myself and briskly walk to the ladies' room and throw up in the toilet, which actually makes me feel a bit better. I splash cold water on my face and take a few sips from the tap. I stare at myself in the mirror, which happens to need a decent clean.

I need to get a grip.

We cannot let this happen again Josslyn. We are putting ourselves at risk. Peter is very intelligent and he knows exactly how to play us. We cannot allow this to happen tomorrow night at the ball. Tomorrow night we are there for one thing and one thing only, and that is to kill Peter. Do you understand? You must not get in my way. I know what I am doing. You cannot ruin this by getting drunk again.

Y-yes, of course. I-I'm with you all the way, I promise. I'm sorry. It w-won't happen again. Can we go home now? And b-by home I mean back to Ben's?

Yes, I believe that is a good idea.

I return to the table where the two men have bought more shots and are lining them up.

'Please may I have your house key Benjamin? I am going back now.'

Benjamin seems to notice my change of tone and immediately digs his key out of his pocket and hands it to me.

'I'll come with you,' he says.

'No, you stay here and catch up with ... Peter. I shall be ... fine.'

Peter stands up and wobbles slightly. 'It was lovely to meet you, Alexis. I'll see you tomorrow night.'

'Yes, you will.'

'Will you text me when you get back to mine okay? I really should come with you,' says Benjamin.

'Please, do not. I will text you. Goodnight, *gentlemen*.'

'Goodnight ... Alexis,' says Peter. 'Good luck.'

I do not question what he means by that statement.

'Goodnight, Alexis,' says Benjamin. His facial expression tells me he is disappointed that I am leaving.

I turn and walk away, my teeth clenched. The sound of Peter's drunken voice makes my stomach churn again. The fresh, cool air of the night hits me like a tonne of bricks. My head spins, my stomach gurgles, but I manage to stop myself from heaving. I steady myself against a nearby brick wall. I am slightly disorientated, but I believe I can remember the way back to Benjamin's house. Josslyn has retreated into the depths of my subconscious, hopefully to have a severe word with herself about how much she has come to rely on alcohol lately, so I am alone with my thoughts as I begin to retrace the path Benjamin and I took to the pub earlier in the evening. It is dark, but I have a general idea of where I am going. Things look vaguely familiar.

Despite it being one o'clock in the morning there are many people milling about, most of them intoxicated like myself, staggering out of clubs and bars, talking too loudly and smoking. I ignore them all and keep my head down. One loud and boisterous man attempts to grab my arm and drag me into the club with him, shouting that he loves me, despite the fact that he has never met me. I grab his wrist and twist it, causing him to release my arm.

'Ow! Fucking crazy bitch!' he shouts. He then spits at me and promptly turns back to his group of friends who all sneer and laugh.

I continue on my way, muttering under my breath that it would be so much easier if I could just kill anyone I wanted who got in my way, like I did with Alicia and Daniel.

Fucking Daniel.

He has caused me nothing but trouble and now, even though he is dead, he is still fucking up my life, as well as Josslyn's. Everything is wrong and things are spiralling out of control.

I am suddenly aware that I am not safe out here on the streets. Fuck. Without meaning to I have let my guard down and forgotten the fact that I (or more appropriately, Josslyn) is wanted for questioning by the police. There is a police car parked on the road across from me, but the officers are nowhere to be seen, possibly inside the nearby club breaking up a fight or dealing with a theft.

I dip into a narrow side alley, attempting to leave the busier streets, in search of a quieter route. I realise that I am not doing a particularly good job at keeping myself hidden. That needs to change, but first I have a job to do. Peter needs to go. He does not deserve to remain on this earth. I have many loose ends to tie up: Daniel, Benjamin, Oscar, but Peter requires my immediate attention and I must focus solely on him. He is dangerous; too dangerous. I do not know how I will deal with Daniel and the DNA found on his body. There is nothing I can do. I killed him. That is the cold, hard truth and the fact is that … wait … I may have killed him, but Peter was the one who disposed of his body. Had he been careful and worn gloves and made one-hundred percent certain that he had not left any of *his* DNA on the body? Mine had been found, but there had been no mention of any foreign male DNA discovered. There was a chance that Peter had been reckless and left a trace of himself somewhere on or near the body. It was a hope I would have to cling on to for now, while I forged my own plan. I would deal with Daniel later, but …

I stop walking because I can hear footsteps behind me. I do not glance over my shoulder, but all my senses appear to heighten simultaneously. I can smell stale smoke and alcohol. The footsteps have stopped, but I can hear shuffling. I continue to keep my eyes focused directly ahead; my peripheral vision working overtime, looking for anything out of the ordinary.

I begin walking again, but I increase my pace without realising it. I am not afraid, but I do not appreciate being followed by someone I cannot see, especially when I am alone in a strange city and clearly not in the right frame of mind. Mistakes can happen too easily when one is under the influence. My immediate thought is that it is Peter or Benjamin or maybe just some other drunken soul trying to find their way home.

Then I hear the footsteps start to get louder and faster – someone is running. I spin round to confront the perpetrator and see a man wearing a black hood launching himself towards me at full speed. I do not run, but I am not quick enough, thanks to my still-intoxicated brain, to dodge out of his way. The hooded man collides with me and we fall to the concrete with a sickening thud. The air is knocked from my lungs as he lands heavily on top of me. My immediate reaction is to defend myself so I start kicking and punching the large man who is pinning me to the ground, but my limbs feel numb and useless. My once sharp self-defence skills are not as effective as they should be in this situation. The man is strong and is attempting to grab my flailing arms and get them under control. I manage to scratch his face with my fingernails, which causes him to yelp in pain. He pulls back and that is when I get a good look at his face underneath his hood.

My attacker is merely a boy, barely twenty I expect, his face showing no signs of old age or a weathered life. Whoever this is ... he is not the hooded man. And now I am angry. How dare this puny excuse for a man attack me! He is not big, he is not terrifying. He is nothing but a pathetic, weak male who thinks he can dominate and take advantage of a drunk woman. I am seething with rage as I bring my knee up right between his legs and deal the fatal blow that all men fear. The boy yelps again and rolls over on the ground next to me, clutching his precious groin area. It is not over. He must pay for what he has done to me. I kick him over and over, in the stomach, the face, the legs. My foot makes contact with his nose and I hear a small snap as it breaks and blood begins to pour out across the ground.

'P-Please! Stop!' he begs. 'I'm sorry!'

I stop and stand over my prey as he lays begging for his life at my feet.

'You are sorry, are you? Tell me, what you are sorry for?' I snap at him. My breathing is erratic. I feel so alive, so powerful and strong. All the effects of the alcohol seem to have evaporated and all that is left is sheer adrenaline pulsing through my veins.

'I-I ... I don't know, I was ... I'm sorry!'

'For what?' I repeat again, taking a step closer to him. I can see the fear in his eyes, which are swimming with tears. 'Say it.'

'I ... I was going to rape you!' he shouts. The word *rape* echoes around the deserted street as my attacker buries his head in his hands.

'Why?' I snap. 'Why would you want to rape a woman?'

'I-I don't know ... I'm sorry.' He starts to weep again and now I am disgusted by him. I do not wish to waste any more time on this hopeless human being. Yes, I should kill him, but I decide against it, knowing I have enough issues to deal with for the moment. I do not need yet another dead body on my hands. For once, I shall show mercy.

I turn to leave and that is when he lunges forwards and grabs both of my ankles, knocking me off balance. I had not been expecting him to attack again and I land hard on the ground once more, banging my forehead on the solid concrete, which stuns me. He is grabbing at my legs, dragging me towards him, attempting to pull my jeans down, but luckily they are too tight.

'Fucking, stupid, fucking bitch!' he spits at me. 'I'm going to make you pay for that. I'm going to rip you open!'

His hands are like claws and dig into the bare areas of my skin. I kick and punch and fight as best as I can. He lands a knuckle across my jaw, which causes my head to spin and my teeth to bite down into my tongue, drawing blood. I spit the blood into his face angrily. He retaliates by slapping me across the cheek. The pain is like red hot fire across my face and I cannot see properly.

I am about to be raped. I know I must do whatever it takes to save myself. I will not be a victim. I do not know how, but somehow I manage to free my right arm and I stretch it out to the side, groping around for any sort of weapon to use against my rapist. He is landing blow after blow into my stomach and ribs, winding me, whilst still attempting to drag my jeans down my legs. The top button has finally given way and they are sliding down my legs, his hands groping and grabbing any part of my anatomy he can find.

I fear I may black out at any moment, but I must keep fighting. I will not surrender. My fingers wrap around an object and, without caring what it is, I use all the strength I have left and smash the object into his skull. He collapses on top of me. I shuffle out from underneath him, stagger to my feet and continue to use the object to finish him off. I am fuelled by pure rage and hatred. Blood is gushing from his head wounds; brain matter is being flung against the brick walls.

I finally stop when I cannot lift my arm any longer. The brick in my hand is saturated with blood, pieces of cranium and brain. I wobble slightly and my legs give way as I trip over my jeans that are pooled around my ankles, the brick tumbling out of my hand and laying to rest a few feet away. I sink to my knees next to my latest victim, his head and face no longer recognisable. I realise in that instant that the killer instinct inside me is still there, as strong as it always has been. When I have something to kill for I am unstoppable, but this should have been Peter. This should not have happened. I should not have had to kill a stupid young man who thought it was acceptable to rape a woman in a dark street at night.

But there will always be these types of men, women ... people. Evil does not discriminate and it will never die out. This evil is inside people and this boy has now paid the ultimate price. I do not feel guilty for taking away his life, but I am fucking annoyed that I have another body to deal with.

I cannot be seen. I must work quickly to leave this area, but I am in no position to dispose of a body. My DNA is everywhere in this crime scene and on his body. There is no escaping that fact. This corpse will be discovered and sooner or later the police will realise that the DNA they will undoubtedly find is the same as that found on Daniel Russell's body. I will be a wanted fugitive. I am a murderer.

I pull my jeans up and attempt to button them, but the button has been flung somewhere.

But it was self-defence.

Josslyn ... I did not realise you were there.

I saw it all Alicia, but I couldn't do anything to help. I couldn't even scream. I tried. I'm sorry. You were going to let him live, you showed him mercy and you turned to leave, but he attacked again and you did what you had to do.

Yes, I did what was necessary to survive.

This wasn't a murder done out of will ... this was done to protect yourself.

No matter what I do this body will be discovered. I cannot dispose of it.

I know ... but maybe there is someone who can ...

I ... what do you ...

And then I realise what Josslyn is trying to say. *Peter.*

No.

But he's got rid of a body for us before—

Are you being fucking serious right now? I am not giving that man any more leverage over us. Yes, he disposed of a body, but he also dug it back up and informed the police. I will not allow him to control us anymore. This is my mess ... and I will deal with it.

Okay, you're right. I'm sorry. I'm not thinking clearly. You're right. What are we going to do?

I continue to kneel in the ever-expanding puddle of warm blood. I am thinking. There is a large pile of black bin bags nearby, along with many ripped and discarded cardboard boxes, as well as a skip a bit further down the street. I must hide the body for now. It will most likely be discovered, but it will take time to examine the remains. I still have time to kill Peter before I am hunted down by the police and the media.

I struggle to my feet, surveying the state of me. My jeans are ripped and dripping with blood, my once white vest top stained forever. My face is still stinging in pain, but the worst pain I feel is in my side. I believe I may have a broken rib. I am unable to draw in a deep breath. I grab the murder weapon and toss it into a nearby cardboard box. Then I grab the black hood and begin shuffling backwards, dragging him towards the skip. He is heavy, but I summon the strength from somewhere within, ignoring the stabbing pain in my rib cage. When I moved Daniel's and Alicia's bodies I had been at full strength, but after being attacked and beaten I have fatigued quickly. I hoist the dead weight onto my shoulders and perform the heaviest squat lift of my life, balancing him on the edge of the skip and then shoving him over the edge. I am near to collapsing again, but Josslyn tells me to keep going, so that is exactly what I do.

I fetch several bundles of rubbish from around the area and stack lots of items on top of the body, ensuring he is completely buried in the skip full of God only knows what. Blood is still saturating and staining the ground around me, but then, as if on cue, it begins to rain, heavy, thick droplets, diluting the thick puddles. I stand and stare up at the dark sky, allowing the cool water to soothe my weary body. I feel renewed, as if it is a sign that I am moving along the right path.

I use what there is available in the dark street to mop up the blood, which is now being washed away by the torrent of rain. I am drenched, my top now stained pink and almost see-through, my white lace bra easily seen through the thin fabric. My hair is sticking to my face, my makeup running down my cheeks and smearing under my eyes as I finish my work. The scene around me is clean to the naked eye, but upon closer inspection the secrets will no doubt begin to reveal themselves.

It is time to leave.

As it turns out I am not far from Benjamin's house and he has not returned home from the pub yet as the building is in darkness when I finally arrive. I let myself in. It has not stopped raining since it started half an hour ago and I am now starting to shiver due to the shock and the cold.

I remove my shoes before entering the house and slowly make my way up the stairs to the bathroom, stopping on the landing as I notice a photograph in a frame that I had glanced at briefly before, but had not recognised the young man standing next to the young Benjamin – Peter. They are of university age each holding a set of golf clubs and smiling. It is unmistakably Peter, the same brown hair, the same flirtatious smile. I cannot help but wonder if he had been a sadistic stalker back then too. In fact, when had it all started? Had it begun with Alicia or did he stalk women before he began stalking her? The fact that the sick bastard was in love with his own sister (adopted or not) was enough to tell me there was something wrong with him, even back then.

I waste no more time staring at the photograph. Benjamin could arrive home at any second and I cannot allow him to see me covered in blood and bruises. I peel my sodden clothes off, being careful not to drip diluted blood over the tiled floor of the bathroom. I rinse them as best as I can in the sink and wipe away any remaining stains. My rib is painful to touch and there is already a faint bluish outline of a bruise starting to form around the area. There are a few scratches on my arms from his fingernails (which means my skin cells are embedded in his nails) and my lip is cut and starting to swell at the right corner. Other than that I am decent shape, although I feel as if I have been run over by an armoured tank. It should be easy enough to hide the injuries from Benjamin, although the cut lip might be difficult to explain. I shall merely convince him that I bumped into a door because I was inebriated. The slightly black eye can be covered with makeup.

The steaming shower water helps wash away the remaining stains, dirt and sweat. The alcohol has all but faded from my system, leaving me with a slightly dry mouth and the beginnings of a headache. I drink a glass of water before I crawl into the guest bed, but I do not sleep. How can I? I may feel no emotion, but the fact of the matter is – a man attempted to rape me and I killed him. I know I should feel guilt, remorse, anger ... yet I do not feel anything. I feel empty inside and very much alone.

I'm here. You're not alone, Alicia.

How do you feel? You suffered through that attack ... tell me what I should be feeling right now.

I was scared, really scared, but also I was angry. Now I feel ... I feel ... empty.

As do I.

Neither of us attempt to continue our conversation for we do not know what else to say. We have been through an experience that no woman (or anyone for that matter) should ever have to endure. We just lay in bed, staring up at the ceiling.

We hear Benjamin return home a little after three in the morning. He is exceptionally noisy as he stumbles up the stairs. I pretend to be asleep as I hear him knock on my door. It creaks open and then closes. I never texted him to say I had arrived home safely. He must have been worried. That is when I glance at my phone and see that he has left me seven texts and two voicemails. I read and listen to them all in order.

00:34 – Hey, you get home okay? Ben x

00:43 – Let me know you're back safe. Ben x

00:50 – 'Hey, just checking in to make sure you got back to mine okay. I'm sorry, I should have come with you. It was stupid of me to let you walk back by yourself. I apologise. Please just give me a text so I know you're okay.'

01:05 – Alexis, hope you're okay. Text me x

01:30 – I've just come back home and you're not here. Where are you? I'm worried x

01:35 – 'Alexis, you're not at home. Where are you? Call me!'

01:58 – Please Alexis, where are you? Please just text me so I know you're safe. I'm going out to look for you x

02:15 – Look, I know you're not my girlfriend or anything, but I really care about you and now I'm worried you've been abducted or something, or you've got lost and are wandering about the city. It's not safe, not with your stalker out there. Where are you? x

02:30 – I'm going to check back at home and if you're not there I'm calling the police.

My phone pings a new text.

03:05 – Sweet dreams x

I roll my eyes and clutch my phone to my chest, as it buzzes again.

03:06 – There had better be a damn good reason as to why you didn't text me back! x

Yes, there is a good reason, but he will never know because I shall never tell him.

I suddenly find myself needing human interaction and contact. I cannot explain the reason why. I have just been attacked by a vile man, yet my body is now craving the touch of a man who I know cares for me. I know it will cause further issues, but I do not care. My mind is made up. I cautiously get out of bed (I am only wearing an over-sized t-shirt) and walk across the landing to Benjamin's room. I knock lightly and enter without waiting for a reply. He is already in bed and he sits up when he sees me. The room is dark, but the moonlight is enough to be able to see that he is topless.

'Alexis ... are you ... is something wrong?'

'Do not speak,' I say as I walk towards him.

I sit on the edge of the bed and, without pausing to think, lean across and kiss him, hot and heavy. His body responds immediately and he begins to run his fingers through my damp hair and starts to remove my t-shirt.

'No,' I say. There is a chance he may see my injuries. He understands my reluctance to remove my top and merely nods. He respects my decision.

Our bodies entwine together perfectly. He tastes of liquorice (the Sambuca) and his hair is still damp from the rain. His hands touch and feel every part of my body and I have to suppress the urge to flinch when he puts pressure on my rib cage, but the pain is nothing compared to the waves of pleasure I experience and eventually we collapse into each other's arms, completely spent, and I finally sleep, a dreamless sleep.

I am gone before he wakes up.

I am making coffee when he appears downstairs at nearly midday. I have showered and washed off any trace of him, like it never happened.

'Hey,' he says.

I do not look up or acknowledge his presence.

'So ... can I speak now?'

'Not if it is about what happened last night between us.'

'But ...' he begins and then sighs as I shoot him my evil glare. 'Okay, fine ... why didn't you text me back last night? I was really worried. I was close to calling the police.'

'My phone battery died and I got lost on the way back, but I eventually stopped and asked for directions.'

'And that's all?'

'Yes.'

'Are you sure?' I stare at him. 'Okay, fine! Just stop giving me those evil eyes.'

I turn my attention back to the coffee machine.

'I require a dress for tonight. Where is the best place to purchase one?' I ask bluntly.

'Err ... probably the main high street. I can take you there.'

'Fine.' I finish making the coffee, place his cup in front of him, grab mine and turn to leave. He suddenly grabs my arm.

'Wait ... we need to talk about what happened.'

We lock eyes. 'I do not know what you are talking about.'

'Really ... you're just going to deny that it happened? I'll remind you Alexis that it was *you* who came into *my* room last night. You clearly wanted something from me.'

'I got what I wanted.'

'And that's all it was for you ... just sex.'

'Yes.'

Benjamin lets go of my arm. 'Why do you do this? Why do you keep pushing me away all the time just as I'm about to get close to understanding you a bit more?'

'To protect you.'

'Protect me from what? Getting hurt? I'm a big boy, I can take care of myself.'

'Then why are we still talking about this?'

Benjamin slams his hand down on the countertop in clear frustration. I do not react or even flinch. 'Damn it, Alexis! You're the most infuriating woman I've ever met. Phil was right—'

This piques my attention and interest. 'What did he say?'

'He said that you're quite possibly trouble and that you'd break my heart, that you weren't worth the risk and that I needed to leave you for someone else to deal with.'

I will admit that Peter has a clever way with words.

'Maybe *Phil* is right,' I say with a shrug.

'Or maybe he's wrong ... maybe you are worth the risk.' Benjamin frowns and I realise that he has just noticed my cut lip. 'What happened?' He attempts to touch my sore mouth.

I immediately turn and start walking away and this time he does not stop me.

'I walked into a fucking door!' I yell at him as I climb the stairs.

You can deny it all you like, Alicia.

Deny what?

You like him.

That is not true. You are the one who likes him.

Um ... I'm pretty sure it was your idea to climb into bed with him last night and have mind blowing sex. Don't worry ... I didn't pry ... mostly.

I merely required human company and reassurance, that was all.

That's very ... normal of you.

Shut up.

I'm just saying it's perfectly natural to need comfort after the ordeal that you went through last night. I don't blame you. Alicia, our lives are fucked up, like seriously fucked up. Ben's a nice guy.

What are you saying?

As I've said before, maybe you should start to think about the future, about when I'm gone for good. You need someone in your life and Ben cares about you.

Josslyn, let me get one thing perfectly clear. Just because I had sexual intercourse with Benjamin it does not mean I have feelings for him. I do not get *feelings.* I sometimes require sexual release, as do most people, and Benjamin was there and he did not turn me down. We cannot be in a relationship. I cannot be in a relationship because I do not have feelings for him. I would only end up hurting him and that is the last thing I want to do.

I think it's a bit late for that.

He said it himself. He is a big boy. He will adjust.

Also, I'd just like to point out that you saying you don't want to hurt him means that you do care about his feelings in some way.

I do not reply.

It was pretty great though, right?

What was pretty great?

The sex.

It was satisfactory.

Josslyn laughs in my head and then moves on.

So ... what's the plan?

Buy a dress, attend the ball with Peter and Benjamin, find a way to get Peter alone, kill him, then flee the country.

Great plan.

Chapter Twenty-Two

Alicia

I stare at myself in the full-length mirror in the guest bedroom. I barely recognise myself. The dress I bought earlier this afternoon is perfectly stunning; black, floor-length with a thigh-high split and flattering. It clings to my curves in all the right places, emphasising my small waist. The fabric is sparkly and the top half of the dress is asymmetrical with only one long sleeve (I specifically chose this dress for that reason so my right arm would be covered to hide the cuts and bruises) and the other side has no shoulder strap. The neckline of the dress is modest and not too revealing. I am wearing strappy black high heels, which have a small band of sparkly gemstones across the ankle strap. My hair is freshly washed and pinned up into a neat up-do with a few loose strands of hair falling on either side of my face. Due to the wonders of makeup I have managed to hide my black eye and cut lip. My eyes are framed by brown and beige coloured eyeshadow and layers of black mascara coat my long lashes.

We look hot!

I turn sideways and admire my own figure.

Indeed, we do.

Please can I have a turn tonight? I've never been to a ball before.

We are there to kill Peter, not enjoy ourselves.

I know, but it's not like we're going to kill him straight away. We've got a plan. We just need to stick to it.

And the plan requires us to stay focused, which means no excessive drinking.

Yeah, okay, I get it. I feel like you're turning into my mum.

I turn as I hear a knock on the door.

'Enter.'

Benjamin pokes his head around the side of the door, catches sight of me and his mouth falls open. He opens the door the rest of the way and stands in the doorway staring.

'Wow ... you look ... wow.'

I nod my thanks. He is wearing a black tuxedo, the collar of the jacket made of smooth black satin, which shimmers when the light touches it. His shirt is crisp and white with tiny black buttons, set off by a satin bow tie, expertly tied. The ensemble fits him perfectly, outlining his masculine figure. His hair is smooth and combed neatly into place. I am unable to ignore the fluttering in my stomach as I lay my eyes on him.

Wow ... he scrubs up well too!

Indeed.

I think I may be in love with him a little bit.

'Well, would you look at us,' says Benjamin, beaming. 'Who would have thought we'd be off to a ball together.'

I press my lips closed and pick up my small black clutch bag, containing my essentials items; phone and lip-gloss. I contemplated earlier about taking a small knife (just in case), but decided against it as I expect there to be security at the school. I walk past him to the door.

'Shall we?' I ask.

'We shall,' he replies.

Benjamin and I arrive at the school at ten minutes past eight. A taxi drops us off outside and we walk the rest of the way up to the main building. I am unaccustomed to walking in heels and the pain due to my broken rib is causing me difficulty in walking. Benjamin appears to notice and offers me his arm for support. I take it without saying thank you, slightly annoyed with myself that I require his assistance. I am not at my full strength and I am restricted in movement due to this dress and footwear.

We enter the grand ballroom (after being thoroughly searched by two security guards) and the decoration is beyond spectacular. My eyes are immediately drawn to the large crystal chandelier dangling from the beautifully moulded ceiling. It is larger than an average-sized automobile. There are dozens of exquisitely laid tables on either side of the room, each set with polished silverware, crystal clear champagne flutes and enormous flower arrangements, giving off a sweet, summery scent. Waiters mill around the room in white suits, topping up empty glasses with Moët & Chandon champagne. An attentive waiter immediately hands us a full flute of champagne, which we take and sample. It is cool, crisp and delicious.

'Wow, who knew boarding schools had so much money to spend on lavish parties,' says Benjamin, as he scans the room, possibly looking for Peter.

I do not respond because I have already spotted him. He is walking towards us and is staring directly at me, his eyes locked with mine. He licks his lips as he stops in front of me. Benjamin is saying hello to his friend, but Peter completely ignores him, only looking at me.

'Alexis ... you look ... wow.' Then he breaks eye contact and glances down at my arm, which is entwined with Benjamin's. His face darkens, his eyes glare at his friend.

'Allow me,' he says as he takes my hand and pulls me away from Benjamin, who is left looking like he has just had his favourite toy taken away. 'Let me show you around ... Benny, you coming?'

'Uh, yeah, sure.'

There is clearly some underlying tension between the men, but neither one of them decide that this is the moment to confront it. It may be that something else went on between them last night when I left the bar.

Peter is also wearing a black tuxedo with a shimmering satin collar, but his shirt is black. In fact, everything he is wearing is black; his shirt, his bowtie, his shoes, his heart. It suits him, in more ways than one.

The touch of his hand makes an eerie shiver run up my spine. He keeps a tight grip on it as he leads me around the room, pointing out where the facilities are and explaining how the evening will run. There is a sit-down dinner, followed by a few speeches and the presenting of awards, one of which he will be given, then dancing later on in the evening. He tells me that he wishes to introduce me to everyone and explains to Benjamin that he will point out the single, attractive women for him. Benjamin replies with an eyebrow raise and a nod. It appears that Peter wishes to get rid of Benjamin as soon as possible, which raises the question of why he invited him in the first place if his goal was to have me all to himself for the evening. I sense that Peter's plan is a devious one, but I must allow him to think he is in control for the time being. It will not be easy, but it is what must happen.

We are eventually shown to our seats. I am placed on Peter's right-hand side and Benjamin sits on his left, away from me. The food is brought out table by table; starter, main, dessert, each plate perfectly presented. I find myself feeling awkward and uncomfortable. Neither Josslyn nor I have ever been good at dealing with social occasions and despite her previous excitement of attending the ball she is now glad that she does not have to do the talking.

I'll just observe for now.

Bitch.

Let me know when the dancing starts.

Benjamin and Peter have been talking a lot, mostly about sports, and I sit quietly listening to them. The man sitting next to me attempts to engage in conversation, but I merely provide him with one words answers. He gets the hint within minutes and now has his back slightly turned to me and is talking to the other woman next to him instead. I keep staring at the steak knife on the table in front of me, wishing I could plunge it into Peter's neck and watch as his blood soaks into the crisp, white tablecloth, spreading across it like a slow-moving stream.

Peter disrupts my dark thoughts. 'You look sensational tonight, Josslyn,' he whispers for only me to hear.

'I am not Josslyn.'

Peter grins. 'Well, you both look sensational.'

I do not reply. I gaze straight ahead.

The dinner is drawing to a close and the microphone is being set up at the head of the room ready for the speeches. Benjamin has left the table to use the facilities.

'I'd like some time alone with Josslyn before the night is over,' says Peter softly.

I ignore his request. 'Why did you invite Benjamin?' I ask bluntly.

'I like a bit of competition.'

'Well, I am afraid you have already lost.'

'What do you mean?' I allow the silence to hang in the air. It speaks a thousand words. 'Wait ... have you ... did you?'

'Last night. It appears that your warning to him about me did not work as well as you had hoped.'

Peter clenches his teeth together and balls his fists. He wants to hurt me, but I know I have already hurt him more than I ever could physically.

'How could you do this to me? I thought we loved each other Josslyn. I love you. Why would you do this to me?'

I roll my eyes at him, unable to even dignify that with a response. Peter then relaxes slightly and smiles.

'Wait, I get it ... it wasn't Josslyn who slept with Benny. It was you ... Josslyn still loves me.'

Right, that's it. Let me finish him off.

Remember the plan.

Yes, I remember the plan. Chill out.

I close my eyes and sink into the abyss as Josslyn emerges.

Chapter Twenty-Three
Josslyn

It feels good to be me again ... well, I guess I'm not actually *me* anymore, but you know what I mean. It feels good to be ... *real.* I don't think I'll ever get used to being second in command.

The first thing I do is take a gulp of champagne because I've been looking forward to tasting it all night. Oh my God, it's so damn good, so tingly, cool and refreshing, but I must remember not to drink too much. Tonight isn't about me, it's about him ... and right now he's staring at me waiting for an answer.

'Hi Peter,' I say with a fake smile. 'It's me.'

'Josslyn! It's really you! Tell me the truth right now. You didn't sleep with Benny, did you? Please tell me it was Alicia.'

'No, it wasn't me.'

I feel a slight pang of ... jealousy? Is that what I feel? Am I jealous that Alicia had sex with Ben first? I know ... I get it ... it's weird. Don't judge me. I miss sex, like any normal warm-blooded human being would. Technically, we're the same person, but it was her he was touching and kissing and ... okay, yeah, I'm definitely jealous, but I don't hold it against her. She'd been through a lot last night. I don't really remember a lot of it, thankfully.

'You do love me though, don't you?'

'Love's a strong word ...'

Peter's face drops. 'Right, of course. You still need time to adjust.'

'Err ... yeah.'

That's the fucking understatement of the century.

Even being this close to him is making my skin crawl and my insides churn. I really dread the idea of seducing him, but it's all part of the plan. I need to get him alone and make him drop his guard and that means making him think I actually like him, which I quite clearly don't ... like, at all! God, he's so needy. I hate needy men.

Ben returns seconds later and takes a seat. We make eye contact and my stomach does a weird flip. This is so weird. I think I do like him, but he slept with Alicia, not me. Alicia is adamant that she doesn't like him (even though I know she does), which means we fancy the same guy, which is just ... fucking wrong. All of this is fucking wrong and—

'Welcome ladies and gentlemen—'

My interest in the speeches wanes quickly and I find myself drinking a full glass of champagne within minutes. And now I need to pee. I go to stand up, but Peter grabs my arm and yanks me back to my seat, which actually really fucking hurts because of my broken rib. Oh, yeah, I forgot about the broken rib ... until just this second.

Ouch!

I wince and bite my lip to stop myself from yelping like a dog.

'Sit down, Josslyn.' An order, not a request.

I'm so angry I want to explode. I stare at the side of his head while he watches the speeches. I wish I had the ability to make his head blow up like a balloon and then pop.

Ben notices me glaring at his friend and gives me a *what are you doing?* look, to which I respond with an *I'm bored* shrug. He then gives a *let's get some fresh air* head tilt and I provide him with a *hell yes* head nod.

Ben and I stand at the same time and Peter realises that he can't control both of us, however he does scowl at Ben, who quickly says, 'Don't worry, we'll be back in time for your speech and award mate.'

'Excuse us,' I whisper in Peter's ear.

Take that, asshole!

Ben leads me through the corridors and out into the courtyard where there are a few people having a smoke. It fills the air and causes me to cough. Seems like there are some people who can't be bothered to listen to the speeches either.

'Can I ask you a question?' asks Ben.

'I'm pretty sure you just asked me one, but you can ask me another if you want.'

Ben smiles. 'What do you think of Phil?'

I raise my eyebrows. I hadn't been expecting such a loaded question. How long has he got exactly?

'Why?' I ask, my voice full of trepidation.

'Well, call me crazy, but I get the impression that there's some sort of tension between you two and I can't for the life of me figure out why. So ... what do you think of him? Be honest.'

'He's, um ... nice.'

'Nice.'

'Right, yeah ... nice.' The word floats about in the air and loses all meaning within seconds. 'Okay, fine, I find him a bit ... intense,' I add.

'Intense.'

'Are you just going to repeat everything I say?'

Ben smiles. 'Okay, fine, he's nice and intense. I get it.'

'What are you really asking me, Ben?'

'Nothing, forget it.'

But I can't forget it. Does Ben sense how dangerous and psychotic Peter really is? Has he always known? Is this all just a massive cover-up and Ben's in on the whole thing? I shouldn't trust Ben. Every fibre in my body is telling me I shouldn't, but I do ... and I think Alicia does too in her own weird way. Ben is being fooled by his best friend, there's no doubt about that.

Now is not the time to tell him.

I know, but I feel sorry for him.

Well, stop it. There is no time for pity.

Alicia ... always the voice of reason.

Ben and I continue the general chit-chat for a few minutes and that's when I realise that I really do need a pee now. I excuse myself and go in search of the ladies' room. I find it, do my business (with some difficultly with a broken rib and this dress, which may as well be a straight-jacket), patch up my makeup and then return to the ballroom where I join Peter at the table. Ben has also returned to his seat.

'And now ladies and gentlemen I'd like to present The Outstanding Achievement Award to our wonderful Teacher of the Year ... Professor Peter Phillips!'

The entire room erupts into clapping and cheering as Peter makes his way to the makeshift stage, lapping up the praise as he does so. I notice that every woman in the room is zeroing in on him, smiling and hoping to catch his attention (even the old birds!) Wow ... he's good. He's got every single one of these people fooled and eating out of the palm of his hand.

The older man with the microphone (who I recognise as the head teacher from the news article) shakes hands with Peter and hands him a massive gold trophy.

'Thank you Henry, and thank you everyone for coming tonight. Cheers!' Peter raises his flute and takes a drink, as does the entirety of the room. 'Don't worry, I'll keep this speech short ... a couple of hours should do it, right?' he jokes. Everyone laughs. Dear God, if I have to listen to him for two hours I may just slice my own throat open with the steak knife in front of me.

Henry pats him on the back and takes his seat.

'As you all know, winning the Teacher of the Year award for the sixth time is a dream come true for me, but winning this award on top of that is just ... wow, I'm just lost for words. I truly am. Thank you all so much. I love nothing more than to teach, shape and develop young minds for the future. The young lads at this school are something special and I hope I can continue to do my best for them and help create the next bright spark that will help change the world. My sister, Alicia, always used to tell me that I was special and I hope that wherever she is ... she's proud of me.'

There's a murmur of pity and 'awwws' from everyone in the room. I roll my eyes and Ben notices. He frowns at me, so I quickly look busy by drinking champagne.

'I'm looking forward to continuing my work at this school in the years to come and I hope you can all join me by raising your glass and toasting to the future.'

There's a chorus of 'to the future!' and everyone takes a drink, as they continue to look at Peter with nothing but admiration and respect.

'Oh, and one more thing ...' says Peter, leaning closer to the microphone. 'I'd love to introduce everyone to a very special lady in my life ... my new girlfriend ... Alexis. She's not been in my life for very long, but I feel like I've known her for years. Thank you for being here tonight babe. I love you.'

The room goes dead silent and I suddenly choke on my champagne and spit it all over the table. A random spotlight appears on me and I'm left sitting with my mouth open in pure shock and horror as I listen to bitchy comments from women and congratulatory remarks from the men around the room. People start to slowly clap as Peter makes his way over to me. I can't even bring myself to look at Ben. What must he think of me? What the hell is happening right now?

Peter stops beside me, pulls me to my feet and kisses me and the only thing I want to do is shrink down to the size of an ant and scurry away. Oh God, people are staring at us ... at me. What if someone recognises me?

Just act calm. Do not make a scene.

I think it's a bit late for that!

I force my lips into a smile and thankfully the buzz dies down as the next set of speeches start. Peter keeps hold of my hand the entire time, squeezing it a little too hard. I still haven't looked at Ben.

Finally, after what seems like an eternity, the speeches end and the music starts. Ben immediately leans over to Peter.

'What the fuck was that?'

Peter smiles. 'Calm down man, it's just a ruse to try and stop all the women in the room flocking to me and trying to get me to dance with them all evening. Whenever I go to these things it drives me mad.'

Right, having loads of women pay attention to you must be really irritating. Fuck me, what a pompous, arrogant asshole.

'You don't mind, do you Alexis?' Peter asks me.

'You might have warned me you were going to do that earlier.'

'Sorry, it was a spur of the moment thing.'

'I bet it was,' I mutter.

Ben still looks like he's sucking a sourball. 'Excuse me,' he says and he walks away, back towards the gardens.

He's annoyed, I can tell. I need to fix this. I don't want Ben to think there's anything going on with Peter and me.

'I'll be back in a second ... I need another pee,' I tell Peter. I pull my hand out of his grasp.

'Don't be too long.'

I turn my back on him and roll my eyes. I've been doing that a lot lately, haven't I? I quickly scurry through the throngs of people, desperately searching for Ben. He's out in the same place we were earlier.

'Hey,' I say.

He looks at me sternly. 'What's going on? And don't say nothing because I can tell it's something.'

'It's ... complicated.'

'I bet it is. Care to explain?'

'Not really,' I say.

The evening has grown cooler, but there's a warm breeze in the air, making it just warm enough to tolerate. The sun is setting now, casting beautiful colours across the sky. Ben and I watch the sunset for a while, soaking it in.

'I swear ... I had no idea that he was going to say that or kiss me. There's nothing going on between us. I promise.'

'But there is ... something else ... going on?'

I wait a few moments before I speak. 'Yes, there is *something else* going on, but I can't tell you everything right now. It's not the right time. Do you trust me?'

Ben looks at me, straight in the eyes and my heart does a little flutter. He moves closer to me, but doesn't try and touch me. We hear loud music coming from the ballroom and lots of chatter. The dancing has started. We smile at each other, our bodies close.

'Would you like to dance?' he asks me softly. I realise he hasn't answered my question, but that doesn't seem to matter right now. I assume that he has accepted that I'll eventually tell him the truth and that he must be patient with me. He trusts me.

'I'd love to.'

We are then interrupted by Peter who makes his presence known by clearing his throat loudly. Ben and I move apart unconsciously. Peter reaches out and takes my hand.

'May I have the first dance Alexis?'

I throw a quick glance at Ben. Shit. How's he going to react?

'It's fine,' says Ben with a kind smile. 'I'll have the next one.'

Peter looks pleased with himself and I suddenly feel like I'm standing in the middle of an arena as two alpha males are about to fight to the death.

'I just need to pop to the loo,' I say to Peter, as I pry my hand out of his.

I begin to walk away, casting a look over my shoulder at the men. They have squared up to each other and appear to be having a serious talk, their chests lifted, their body language aggressive. Fuck ... what have I done? I can't hear what they're saying, so I don't even bother trying to overhear them, but whatever it is, it isn't friendly.

I dance with Peter. I dance with Ben. Then I dance with Peter again. It would be a wonderful, magical evening if I wasn't basically being passed around between the men like a rag doll. Okay, maybe that sounds a bit too sexual, like I'm in some sort of steamy threesome, but honestly, I can feel the masculine tension building each time they are both near me. It's time to end this ... now. It's time to put the plan into action.

'Can we go somewhere ... private?' I say to Peter as we slow dance. His eyes widen and his body automatically presses firmly against mine. I resist the urge to shudder as his hand moves to my ass.

'Of course. You just read my mind.'

He takes me by the hand and leads me off the dance floor. I don't know where Ben is. The last time I saw him he was dancing with another woman who Peter had introduced him to. She was cute and friendly and slightly too drunk, but she clung to Ben as if her life depended on it.

I hope you know what you're doing Alicia.

I do.

Peter grabs two flutes of champagne on the way outside, expertly holding them in one hand while pulling me along with the other. Fuck me, my side really fucking hurts right now. We finally make it outside and into a secluded section of the garden, away from prying eyes. The nearest person is out of ear shot.

'Finally, we're alone,' he whispers.

'Uh-huh.'

He hands me a flute, we clink and each take a sip. He leans in close to me and begins to stroke my body with his free hand. He breathes in my scent and kisses me gently on my neck. Every ounce of strength is put into not overreacting and running to safety. The feel of him, his smell, everything about him makes my skin crawl and I feel sick. I take another sip to steady my nerves. My head spins slightly and I wobble. Oh shit, I've had too much champagne. Wait, no I haven't. I've been really fucking good tonight. I've had two glasses over the entire evening. This is my third glass and I've only had two sips. My vision starts to go blurry and the darkness around me seems to creep closer and closer.

'You're mine.'

Peter's voice is the last thing I remember before I pass out.

Chapter Twenty-Four
Alicia

I do not know where I am, but I am not alone. I can hear a man breathing near me, but I cannot see him. I cannot move. My body will not respond as it should. I am sitting on a hard, possibly wooden chair. I can feel that both of my ankles are bound to the chair legs and my wrists are tied together behind the back of the chair. It is an extremely uncomfortable position, so I attempt to adjust my arrangement, but the pain in my side is unbearable and I immediately cease moving, fearing I will cause myself more harm. My restraints are tight, too tight, causing my extremities to feel numb, as if they no longer belong to my body.

Alicia! Alicia! Wake up. Please, wake up!

I rouse at the sound of Josslyn's voice in my head, but I still cannot see for there is a blindfold over my eyes. It is so tight that I cannot even crack open my eyes to catch a glimpse of my surroundings. I am also gagged by some form of damp cloth, which is pushed to the back of my throat, causing my breathing to be fairly shallow.

I am here.

Alicia, I don't know what happened. One second I was with Peter and then ... I was gone.

I believe he may have drugged us.

Fuck. I'm sorry, I didn't mean to screw up the plan. I thought I had everything under control.

This is the plan. You performed perfectly.

What?

I ignore her. I must focus now.

I can hear breathing again, slow, steady breathing. It is very disturbing. I know who the breathing belongs to and I know what perverted thing he is doing. He is enjoying watching me as I sit tied to this chair, helpless and defenceless. He thinks I am afraid. I am not. He is mistaken. The breathing finally slows down and then he grunts, clearly finished with himself. I hear some shuffling. Then he speaks.

'What am I going to do with you, Alicia? You've caused me nothing but trouble. You're a fucking psychopath, so why can't you just leave me the fuck alone and let Josslyn and I be together? I thought I was obsessed with you once. Yes, you're fascinating. You're unique and you always have been. If you were smart you'd accept me for who I am and we could be together, you, me and Josslyn, as one, but you just keep getting in my way. Why is that?'

I do not move or make any attempt to spit out the sodden gag. I cannot see him, but I face forwards in his direction, my breathing shallow, my heartbeat steady. He is about to see how much of a psychopath I truly am.

He continues speaking as I hear him walk around me slowly in a circle, the way I can imagine a predator surrounding its prey, closing in.

'How do I get rid of you once and for all? I know, I can't. That's what's frustrating. You and Josslyn are inseparable. Maybe I can convince you to leave us alone ... would that work Alicia? Is there a way I can convince you to leave us alone?'

I feel him lean his face close to mine, his warm breath tickling my nose. He reaches round behind me and I do not flinch as he grabs hold of my little finger on my left hand and forces it backwards, bending it to almost breaking point.

'Can I torture you? Will torture work for you? Do you even feel afraid? Do you feel pain? Of course you do, you're not indestructible, you're just a normal human being ... that feels nothing ... well, I reckon you'll feel this.'

Peter pushes my little finger backwards and a loud snap, like a twig breaking, fills the room. I exhale harshly, trying not to react at the now searing pain in my finger. Josslyn's screams fill my head. I wish there was a way I could protect her from this torture. There is no way she can actually feel the pain in this body, but we are identical twins, the same person. She feels what I feel. When one of us hurts we both hurt. It has always been that way.

'See ...' says Peter, moving away from me. 'You do feel pain. You are breakable and I will break you, Alicia. I don't care how long it takes. I will find your weakness.'

I inhale deeply through my nose, close to passing out due to the pain and the remnants of whatever drug he made me ingest. I feel dizzy, nauseous, but not afraid. My only thought is that I need to get through whatever he has in store for me … and then finish the job I came here to do.

Yes, I planned for this to happen, but I did not imagine he would torture me to this extent. It appears that Peter has darker tendencies than I originally believed. I am angry at myself for hesitating, for waiting, for biding my time. The psychopath within me had wanted to kill him immediately. I should have let her, but the humanity I have come to realise is inside of me held me back. I will never make that mistake with regards to Peter ever again.

Never again.

I believe that I am still wearing my ball gown because my legs are bare, as is my left arm (the design of the dress). I realise I am cold and I begin to shiver, small goose bumps appearing over my exposed skin. The air is cool and stale, as if no fresh air has been allowed in for days. I can also smell something salty and unpleasant … semen. I do not believe Peter has raped me, but who knows how many times he has masturbated in here while I have been unconscious, perhaps even ejaculating over me … I cannot be certain of this, but I cannot put anything past him. The thought and smell makes me want to gag, but I keep my composure.

If I had to make an educated guess I would say I am located in a sealed room, possibly a basement, but this is unconfirmed. I cannot remember seeing a basement when I was with Peter in his house a year and a half ago, but the likely outcome is that he has taken me back to familiar territory, somewhere he can control the situation. He thrives on control. He gets off on it … and that was exactly what I had imagined him doing. I needed to get away from prying eyes and ears and he has brought me here ... right where I want him, but first I must survive at any cost.

I wait for his next speech or his next torture element, but it does not come, not for a long time. I do not know how long I wait, but I feel exhausted. The throbbing pain in my finger, as well as my broken rib, is sapping the energy out of me and I am struggling to remain conscious. I fight with all the strength I have, but the darkness eventually comes and takes away the pain.

I wake to the sensation of warm breath on my face. A heavy weight is on my lap. Peter is straddling me, our bodies close. I do not react, even though the pain in my rib is causing me to take short, sharp breaths. Peter begins to release the dark blindfold over my eyes. I am relieved that it is gone, but I do not show it. As he lowers it down our eyes meet, locked together, neither one of us faltering or blinking.

'There you are. You have such beautiful eyes.' He inhales deeply, clearly enjoying this moment. I can feel him hard against me as he straddles me. 'What do you think?'

Peter breaks our eye contact and flicks his eyes around the room, but I do not fall for his trick. I do not stop glaring at him. My eyes speak more than a thousand words ever could. The hatred and anger I feel towards this man is more than I can stand. It radiates out of me like electricity.

I want him to suffer, more than any human could ever withstand.

'Come now Alicia, take a look at my masterpiece ... you're a big part of it. I'll leave you alone to take it all in ... enjoy.'

Peter smiles as he stands and I find I am relieved to have his heavy weight off my lap. He turns his back on me and leaves the room through a door directly in front of me. I do not let my eyes wander or blink until he has disappeared from view.

Then I notice the walls of the room – his *masterpiece*.

All four walls are covered with hundreds and hundreds of photographs, newspaper articles, clippings, scraps of clothing, small items such as teddy bears, hairbrushes and even used tampons in plastic bags. It takes my brain a few seconds to apprehend what my eyes are looking at.

This is a shrine dedicated to all the women he has ever stalked.

Even the door he disappeared through is covered with photographs and paraphernalia. There is not even a slither of wall visible, every inch (even the ceiling I notice as I glance up) is laced with ... evidence of his psychopathic mind. The photographs are all of women, grouped together in their relevant sections with their names across the middle in large printed letters.

Alicia.

Josslyn/Alicia/Alexis.

Rebecca.

Laura.

I cannot turn to see behind me, but I expect there is more of the same. The photographs are taken from afar, mostly, but others are taken up close and personal. He knew all of these women somehow and they knew him, allowed him to get close, too close. The section of wall with my name on is the largest:

Josslyn/Alicia/Alexis.

We are all the same person. He has clearly spent a lot of time gathering details and information on me, long before I even knew about him. There are photographs of Josslyn with her parents, with Oscar, at work, driving her old red car, even ones of her with Daniel. There are photographs of me when I took over Josslyn's body. He was studying me and there are dozens of Post-It Notes and scribbles, noting the differences between Josslyn and I.

I am unable to make a lot of them out, but one I can read says: *She walks differently. She talks differently. Who is this? This isn't my Josslyn.*

Another reads: *She killed Alicia. I know she did. She will pay.*

I let out a low throaty growl, as I scan my eyes over to the area dedicated to Alexis. There is a massive hand-written note which says: *Where is she?*

It appears that when I disappeared to Tuscany he struggled to locate me, as was my plan. Lockdown appeared to have disrupted his plans of tracking me down, as there are many newspaper articles about the virus and notes saying: *Lockdown will ease soon. I will find her.*

Then I notice a picture of Benjamin and he is circled in red pen with the words: *Use him.*

So, it appears that Benjamin really is unaware of his friend's sick and twisted mind.

Benjamin.

I am suddenly curious as to where he is and what has happened to him. Without even meaning to I feel myself concerned for his safety. Peter appears to not only trick and manipulate women, but also men, and his best friend too. There are no further pictures of Benjamin or any other men from what I can see so I presume I can safely state that Peter only stalks women, but uses whoever he needs to get his way.

Like I do.

The thought snaps into my head and I find I do not like it nor want it there, but I cannot ignore it. Peter and I are the same. We are both obsessed, twisted and dangerous and capable of dark, disturbing things. I close my eyes. I no longer want to see the photographs on the walls. I do not wish to see anything but the insides of my own eyelids. I lower my head so my chin is close to my chest. I feel another wave of exhaustion wash over me. I wish for the darkness to swallow me ... and it does once again.

I can hear her voice coming from somewhere far away. It is Josslyn and she is calling my name. My whole body is stiff, sore and frozen, and I am unable to move. I am still bound to the chair. I lift my head ever so slightly; even that tiny movement takes an enormous effort. There she is. I can see her before my eyes. Josslyn is standing directly in front of me. She looks like she did before I physically changed her - brown hair, fuller figure.

I have missed her.

'Alicia, wake up. You have to wake up. We have to finish this.'

Her words are no longer inside my head. She is flesh and blood now, but the rational part of my brain knows that is impossible. She is a hallucination brought on by fatigue and the onslaught of the physical and mental abuse I am withstanding. I do not know how long I have been here. My stomach is rumbling with hunger and my mouth is bone dry. I need to drink water soon or I shall surely die from dehydration before I succumb to my injuries. It is not possible to die from a broken finger and rib, but to die from a lack of water is a severe possibility.

Josslyn lifts my head and looks me in the eyes. *'Keep fighting. You're strong. We can get through this. I'm here.'*

I nod slowly and look around the room. We are still alone. The photographs are still there. I scan the room, searching for anything I can use to help me escape, but the room is empty. There are no windows from what I can see. It is possible that they are covered by the copious amounts of photographs and items, like the door.

I stare at the door, willing Peter to return. Time drags by endlessly, but Josslyn stays with me. She attempts to open it, but her hand floats through the handle like a ghost. She is not real, but at least she is here.

Then the door opens and Peter enters. He is only wearing a pair of faded jeans and nothing else. His torso is tight, tanned and solid and his arms are much more muscular than I remember. He has been training hard, as have I over the past year and a half. Has he been waiting for me, as I have for him? Peter is holding a long, sharp knife and the blade catches the light as it moves. He also has a glass of water in his hand. I watch as Josslyn circles him, her eyes totally transfixed. I have never seen her look that way at anyone before. It was always I who had *the evil stare* as she called it, but Josslyn has changed.

'I thought you might like some water,' says Peter. He walks towards me and stops. 'You can have some water on one condition ... you do not make a sound until I tell you to. Understand?'

I glare at him, unwilling to give him the satisfaction of answering him.

Peter sighs in frustration. 'Do you want to die of dehydration? You've been down here for nearly two days. I don't want to have to deal with your dead body.'

Two days. It feels longer than that.

I reluctantly nod my head slowly to show that I accept his terms and he places the knife on the floor and then gets to work on removing the gag in my mouth. When it is free I cough and open and close my mouth to get my jaw working again. The gag was so tight and stuffed so far into my mouth that eventually I could not feel anything and my jaw stopped trying to fight it and just accepted its fate. It still hurts from where I was punched by that fucking rapist two days ago.

Peter lifts the glass to my mouth. I take small sips, knowing that if I drink too fast I will choke and possibly spill the precious liquid on the floor. I take my time and I swallow every last drop. Peter does not talk while he watches me drink. When I am finished I take as deep a breath as my broken rib and bindings allow, relieved to be free of the gag.

'Now,' says Peter. 'What do you think of my masterpiece?' He spreads his arms out wide, admiring his own work. 'Did you take a good look?'

I open my mouth to speak. It is difficult to force my tongue to work again.

'Y-You are s-sick.'

'You don't like it? Look ... this is you, and this is you, and this one ...' He points to photographs of me over the years. Then he stops at one in particular and unpins it from the wall. 'This is one of my favourites.' He shoves the photograph in my face. It is a picture of Josslyn in bed asleep. She is completely naked and the bed sheets have been pulled down to reveal every bare inch of her body. He must have taken it when they slept together.

'*Oh God, that's so fucking creepy,*' says Josslyn.

I flick my eyes towards her and Peter notices. He spins around to look, but he sees nothing. She is only visible to me.

'What are you looking at?' he demands.

I do not answer him. He leans in close to me, barely half an inch away from my face.

'Tell me,' he growls.

I take the opportunity, pull my head back and head butt him as hard as I can. He recoils, clutching his face. Blood begins to drip from his nose. It appears that I landed a decent blow.

'Fucking bitch,' he mutters, wiping the blood away. 'You'll pay for that.'

I hear Josslyn shout, 'No!' as he smashes the empty glass across my face. It smashes apart, embedding tiny slithers of razor-sharp glass into my skin. I feel trickles of warm blood slide down my face and begin dripping onto my chest. I do not shout out in pain, even though it feels as if my face has been torn off.

'Think carefully, Alicia. I know you want to get out of this alive and to do that I need you to cooperate. Will you do that for me? Will you cooperate and answer my questions?'

'I have nothing to say to you,' I respond slowly.

'Oh, but you will ... you're going to tell me what I want to know one way or another.'

'And what is it you want to know?'

'Where is my sister?' He takes a deep breath. 'I need to know where she's buried. I can't rest or move on until I know. You're the only person who knows where she is and you're going to tell me. I don't want the police to find her one day and take her away from me. I want her body.'

I smile. I feel powerful knowing that I still have a hold over him. He may be a crazy stalker, a master manipulator, a skilled liar, but he is nothing without his sister.

'She was my first obsession,' he says. He walks over to her collection of memorabilia on the wall and begins to study each photograph, gently stroking each one. 'I loved her from the start. I used to sneak into her room at night and sleep next to her. I snipped off strands of her hair. I kept personal things that she'd throw away. She was my everything ... and you took her from me. Tell me where she is.'

'I will never tell you. Killing her may have been wrong but it set her free from you. If I had not killed her she would still be trapped and controlled by you and she would be terrified. God only knows what you will do to her corpse if you find her. She was my sister too ... and I will keep her safe from you, even in death, no matter what the cost. You cannot have her.'

'Why Alicia, it sounds like you do have a heart after all. You do care about others, about Josslyn ... about Oscar.' My face twitches as Peter speaks his name. 'Okay, I can see the problem. Alicia is dead. I can't cause her any further physical pain. Oscar is dead. I cannot hurt him, but there is one person I can hurt physically ... someone who I think you do care about even if you constantly deny it.'

I clench my teeth together to stop them from chattering, not from fear, but from the cold. Peter is topless, but he does not appear to be affected. He has not been in here for two days, starving and in pain. My body is beginning to react all on its own. I cannot control it.

Peter leaves the room and I am left in silence.

Josslyn turns to me. '*What can we do? I don't know what else to do.*'

'There is nothing we can do,' I say aloud. 'We must endure whatever he has planned for us. He will not kill us, I am sure of it. We must hold on.'

'But he's going to torture you ... and it's going to really hurt.' Tears begin to form in Josslyn's eyes and she runs her hands through her hair and then lets out a loud, frustrated scream.

The door opens and Peter enters, dragging the limp body of Benjamin.

Chapter Twenty-Five

Alicia

Benjamin is unconscious, but alive. He has been badly beaten and looks to be in a worse state than myself. He has several deep cuts across his face and arms, all of which are clotted with dried blood. The jacket of his tuxedo has been removed and the once pristine white shirt is filthy and soaked in blood. His shoes are missing and his feet are cut and bleeding. It appears that while I have been left alone in this room Peter has been torturing his best friend in another. The truth about the extent of Peter's evilness is quite startling to witness. This man is a beloved and trusted teacher of children and young men. I can only hope that his warped mind has not evolved enough to target the boys he spends his days teaching. If he had worked at a girls' school then the outcome may have been very different.

Peter dumps Benjamin's body at my feet.

'Now we'll see if you truly do have any emotion in that twisted brain of yours. If you don't tell me where my sister is buried, then I will kill Benny, right in front of you ... slowly.' He stands over the unconscious body holding the knife, waits and watches me.

'I will not tell you.'

'Are you sure about that?'

'Yes.'

'Suit yourself ...'

Peter grabs Benjamin's shirt and drags him so he is lying on his back. He crouches over him and begins to slice down his chest with the blade. The cut is not deep, but it is enough to rouse Benjamin from unconsciousness. He wakes with a start, but he cannot retreat for he is also bound by his hands and feet. Benjamin sees his friend hovering above him and I see the fear return to his eyes, which were once blissfully closed.

'Hi Benny ... miss me?'

Benjamin is not gagged so he is able to speak. 'Get off me! Fucking get off me!' Then he notices me bound to the chair next to him and he begins to panic. 'Alexis! Thank God! He wouldn't tell me where you were. I thought he'd kill you. Are you okay?'

'I am alive,' I respond.

Benjamin's eyes travel up and down my body, taking in my injuries. 'I'll fucking kill you, you asshole!' he screams at Peter. 'Leave her alone. Why are you doing this? What the fuck is wrong with you?'

Peter grins as he handles the large knife in his hands. He twirls it expertly around his fingers and even flips it over and catches it.

'It's a long story, Benny. I'm sure I'll get around to telling you soon, but first things first ... I want this bitch to tell me where my sister is.'

'How the fuck would Alexis know? Alicia killed herself you freak, quite possibly to get away from you by the looks of it. I know I always went along with your stupid idea that she just *disappeared,* but let's face it. She's fucking dead. The sooner you accept that she's gone the sooner you can move the fuck on. She was depressed and lonely and she killed herself.'

'That's where you're wrong, my friend.' Peter points the knife at me. '*She* killed her and buried her somewhere.'

Benjamin frowns and then laughs hysterically. 'You're crazy man! You're fucking crazy!'

I begin to pity Benjamin because he has absolutely no idea about anything. Peter allows the silence to develop. Benjamin looks at me, then at his captive, confusion furrowing his brow.

'Alexis? Is that true? I-I don't ... what's going on?'

Peter suddenly screams and slices the knife across the top of Benjamin's right leg. The blade easily pierces the layer of clothing and several layers of skin. Benjamin shrieks in pain at my feet.

'Tell me!' Peter bellows at me.

'I will not.'

'Tell me!'

Another slice, another scream from Benjamin.

'Never.'

'Alicia, tell him, please!' Josslyn is crying and has her hands partially covering her face as she crouches on the ground. '*Please just tell him. I don't want Ben to die.'*

Peter grabs Benjamin by the hair and holds him tight, pushing the tip of the blade into his neck, blood seeping from the pressure. Benjamin is attempting to struggle, but it is useless. Any large movement would cause the blade to penetrate his throat.

'Tell me ... or I will cut his throat out and you can watch him bleed to death. Let's find out if you truly are a psychopath, Alicia ... who's it going to be? My sister ... or Benjamin? Tell me ... now.'

At the mention of my name Benjamin's eyes grow wide. He is unable to speak because if he does the knife will pierce his Adam's apple, but I can almost see the questions pouring out of him: *Why did he just call you Alicia? Who are you?*

Peter continues and repeats, 'If you truly are a psychopath then you will let him die and if you're not and this is all just an act then you'll save him ... now ... what's it to be? It's your choice. You can save him, or you can let him die. Choose. Now.'

I glance at Benjamin and then at Josslyn. He is a good man and he does not deserve to die. I do not want this. I do not want to be responsible for any more deaths. Alicia is dead. She is safe from Peter's abuse. I will never let Peter escape and find her, so for now, I must choose the logical choice, in order to save another person's life.

'She is buried at the old tree at the farmhouse Josslyn and I grew up in, in the New Forest.'

'My Place?' asks Josslyn. *'You buried her there? Why?'*

Josslyn's question remains unanswered.

I watch as Peter's body relaxes and he drops the knife to his side.

'Thank you, Alicia. Thank you. I guess that means you do have some feelings and emotions after all. Are you sure you're a psycho?' He stands, leaving Benjamin to collapse to the ground.

I watch Peter as he walks over to Alicia's shrine on the wall. He touches a few of her photographs.

'We'll be together again soon,' he whispers. Then he turns sharply to me. 'I want to speak to Josslyn ... now.'

'What the fuck is going on?' screams Benjamin. 'Who the fuck is Josslyn and why do you keep calling her Alicia? Her name is Alexis!'

Peter laughs hysterically. It fills and echoes around the room. 'Oh Benny! I've got so much to tell you. You're never going to believe this. This is going to be so much fun, but I really should set the mood first. Hang on ...' Peter abruptly leaves the room and slams the door.

'What the fuck is he talking about?' shouts Benjamin as soon as the door is closed. He is still lying on the ground at my feet, merely inches away.

'Shut the fuck up and try and untie my legs,' I mutter angrily at him. 'I do not have time to explain.'

Benjamin suddenly realises that we have a slim chance of escape and he wiggles his body around until his hands, which are tied behind his back, are within touching distance of the rope that binds my ankles to the chair. He frantically begins to grasp at the rope, but due to the awkward position he is in he is unable to make any progress in loosening it. This does not deter him though. He shifts his position and tries again.

'Honest to God Alexis, or whoever the hell you are, I'm going to fucking kill Phil the first chance I get.'

'Not if I get to him first. Hurry! He is returning.'

'I can't ... quite ...'

Benjamin has been able to slightly loosen both ropes around my ankles. I can feel the blood flow returning to them after being restricted for so long. Pins and needles flood my feet. It is agony, but I do not move a muscle as Peter barges back into the room, holding a bottle of red wine and a glass. He holds them up high.

'Perfect!' he says.

'Fuck me, he's a bloody lunatic!' says Josslyn with a hysterical laugh. *'He's actually enjoying this!'*

'Now, I would offer you both some wine, but I think with your injuries and the fact you haven't eaten or drunk anything for two days means you might react quite badly.' He unscrews the lid and pours the wine. He takes a drink, his eyes closed and breathes in deeply. 'Perfect,' he says again.

'Phil, what the hell man! I'm your best friend. We grew up together. We lived together at university. I fancied your sister once. We're like family!'

'My name is not Phil!' spits Peter angrily. 'I've always fucking hated that name. Do you know how many times I've wanted to beat your fucking face in whenever you've called me that name? Think yourself lucky that you've even survived this long.'

Benjamin begins to laugh out of sheer confusion and exhaustion. Then he suddenly notices the walls of the room. I assume he was so caught up in seeing me and almost having his throat ripped open that he had not noticed the photographs, until now. His faces drops and he shuffles himself up into a seated position and stares around in astonishment and horror.

'What ... the ... actual ... fuck?'

'Ah, I see you've finally noticed my masterpiece.'

'Your masterpiece? What the ... Is that my sister?' he shouts.

'Indeed it is,' says Peter as he walks to the section of wall where the name *Laura* is displayed. 'She was merely a bit of fun, to hone my skills, but when she moved away it was much harder to keep tabs on her, so I gave up and focused my skills back on Alicia. Laura never meant anything to me, not really, just a practise piece. However, I did track her down eventually ... remember that time I travelled abroad for two months—'

'You son of a bitch! What did you do to her?'

'Calm down Benny. She's fine! At least I assume she is. I don't kill my masterpieces, but I may make an exception for this one ...' He looks at me and slowly smiles. 'Alicia is special you know.'

'Man, I don't know what crazy things are going on inside your head right now, but this is not your sister. This is Alexis and she has ... nothing ...' Benjamin is now beginning to notice the areas labelled Josslyn/Alicia/Alexis and how all of the photographs depict the same woman – me. 'What the hell?' He turns to me. 'Who are you?'

'I think the question you should be asking yourself right now is ... who is your best friend?' I reply solemnly. 'He has lied to you from the start. He lied to me too.'

Benjamin does not break eye contact with me. 'Please can someone explain to me what is going on and how we ended up tied up in my best friend's basement being tortured?'

'Oh, this isn't a basement. I mean, you've been kept in someone else's basement for two days, but this isn't one. It's the spare room at my house, but I've boarded up the windows and soundproofed it as much as possible.'

'You sick fuck! So that's why you've never let me crash in your spare room ... because it's been a fucking shrine to all the women you've been stalking over the years?'

'Exactly!' Peter takes a large gulp of wine. 'I've fooled you for all these years Benny Boy, but you know what's even more incredible ... you've been helping me watch these women the whole time without even realising it. All the times I asked you to keep an eye on my sister in class because I was worried she was getting too much male attention. All the times I asked you where your sister was or if you'd heard from her. The time I told you that you should take a year out and move to Tuscany and check out this new wine bar I'd heard about—'

A horrifying silence fills the room as it slowly dawns on Benjamin that he has been a pawn in his friend's sick game.

'Wait ... you set all that up? That's ridiculous. That wasn't you, that was my plan.'

Peter wags his finger. 'Think about it, Benny Boy. You were trying to get over that bitch of an ex-girlfriend of yours and said you needed some space. I suggested a year abroad would help clear your head. You said it was a great idea and planned to go to America, but I suggested Tuscany because of the spread of the virus in the States being too widespread. You agreed. I said you should check out the wine country and that there was a cute little wine bar called A Slice of Paradise that you just had to try out. I booked the flight for you and I even found you a place to stay. You then met Alexis and when I first messaged you and asked how it was going over there you just couldn't help but mention the attractive woman who ran the wine bar. After that, whenever I asked about her you'd tell me something about her. You had no idea that you were feeding my masterpiece ... my obsession.'

Benjamin's mouth is hanging open in horror. 'I-I don't ... how did you ...?' He stops talking.

Peter turns his attention to me. 'I found you eventually ... Alexis. You may have changed your name, your hair, your body, but I found you eventually. Do you want to know how? Of course you do.'

I stare at him without blinking.

He smiles as he continues. 'I happen to be a member of a Facebook group called Wines of the World, under my false name of course. People often tag new up-and-coming wine bars or different wines they have tasted from around the world on the page. One day I was casually browsing and I saw you ... I'd recognise your face anywhere, even if you did try and fool me with the blonde hair. An old couple had visited your bar and taken a selfie of their trip. You were caught on their camera ... here it is ...' Peter pulls a photograph off the wall and shows it to me.

There I am. The old couple are huddled together, but due to their lack of understanding of how to take a selfie correctly they have mostly taken a photograph of the top of their heads and the scenery behind them. I am in the background, carrying a tray of wine glasses. It is unmistakably me, my skin tanned from the sun, my hair shining bright blonde, but it is me. He found me.

'Then I started researching the bar. You didn't have a Facebook page or a website, but you were listed as a business on *Angloinfo Tuscany*. There were no pictures of you of course, but Alexis Grey was listed as the owner. It didn't take me long to form a plan. I even visited you a few times once lockdown eased a bit. I watched you from afar. I didn't tell Benny that I was there of course. I allowed you to think that you were safe and hidden. I needed to get you to come back home. I couldn't have you so far away from me. I managed to convince Benny to live there for a while, but he wasn't reliable and I couldn't keep an eye on you as closely as I wanted, so I tried to draw you out. I went back and found Daniel's body, informed the police, delivered my message ...'

'You killed Oscar,' I snarl.

'I've already told you I didn't kill him.'

'Wait ... you killed her dog?' Benjamin gasps.

'I did not kill him!' shouts Peter. 'I'm not a fucking dog murderer.'

'No, you're just a creepy stalker who hunts women,' mutters Benjamin. 'Why do you even do it, man? You're a good-looking guy. You've never had any trouble getting women to jump into bed with you. The amount of times you've told me stories of how many women you've slept with ... why do you have to stalk them? I don't get it.'

I take this one. 'Because he always wants what he cannot have. All the women he has stalked have been unattainable to him in some way ... Alicia – his sister, Laura – your sister, Josslyn and myself – I do not know who Rebecca is, however I assume she is also someone you cannot have.'

'Actually, you're wrong Alicia. I mean, you're right about the fact I could never really have Alicia or Laura, but as for you, I could have had you ... I did have you. You threw yourself at me willingly—'

'Wait ... you slept with him?' Benjamin interrupts.

'Oh great, now we're about to have a fucking pissing contest.'

I nod slowly. 'I admit. Yes, Peter and I engaged in sexual intercourse. I was not aware at the time who he was. This happened over a year and a half ago.'

'This is fucking unbelievable. I finally fall in love with a woman and I find out that you've slept with her first.' Benjamin glares at Peter, who suddenly spits out the wine he had been about to swallow.

'Oh my God ... what did he just say?'

'Wait ... you're in love with her?' Peter laughs out loud. 'You can't be in love with her. I'm in love with her. Wait ... who are you in love with?'

Benjamin shakes his head. 'I just told you.'

'No, but ... oh fuck me! You don't know, do you?'

'Know what?'

'She's been lying to you this whole time. This, my friend, is Alicia and Josslyn Reynolds.'

Josslyn is now standing next to me with her arms folded. *'This is going to be fun* ... and *take a lot of explaining.'*

Indeed.

'This isn't how I imagined him finding out.'

There is nothing we can do to stop it now.

Benjamin looks at Peter, but he says nothing else. He begins to back out of the room.

'Why don't I let you two get better acquainted ... oh, and don't bother to try and set yourselves free ... I'm watching you.' He leaves the room, laughing. 'Have fun explaining this one Alicia!' he calls out.

Benjamin and I are left in complete silence. He is still sitting on the floor not far from me. Neither of us can move and neither of us even attempt to move. I do not know what to say to him, so I wait for him to speak first. There is no point in trying to deny anything at this moment. I know that. I must reveal the truth and we must get out of here alive and in order to do that Benjamin must know everything ... the whole truth, whether he chooses to believe it or not.

'So ... let's hear it then ... who's Alicia and Josslyn Reynolds?' he asks me, finally.

'Let's hope he's ready for this,' says Josslyn.

'He will never be ready for this,' I say aloud.

'What?' he asks. 'Who are you talking to?'

'Let me do it. I think he'll understand a bit more if it comes from me. You might scare him.'

'As you wish ... but I will warn you ... you will be in a lot of pain.'

'I can handle it.'

I lower my head, close my eyes and when I open them I am gone. Josslyn opens her eyes and I am standing beside her, invisible, having swapped places.

Chapter Twenty-Six
Josslyn

The pain in my body is unlike anything I've ever experienced. I mean, being inside Alicia's body I can still feel things, but not in the same way as when I'm in control. Nothing could have prepared me for the amount of pain and discomfort I now feel. Okay, maybe I can't handle it. I'm a bit of a wimp. If I ever have kids I'll definitely opt for an epidural ... wait ... what am I saying? Of course I'll never have kids ... let's move on. I'm clearly delirious right now.

I writhe against the ropes tying me to the chair and crack my neck to the left and right, stretching and moving my body as much as possible to try and stimulate blood flow. Ben is staring at me as if I'm crazy. I need to come clean with him and I just think it will sound better coming from me rather than Alicia. She has a way of making things appear worse than they actually are sometimes and she can be quite ... abrupt.

While stretching my neck I see Alicia standing beside me. It's a weird sensation to see your identical twin sister standing next to you, as if she were flesh and blood. Okay, I guess that usually people can see their twins because usually they aren't inside their own body ... so I guess it wouldn't be weird to most people, but I'm not most people. I haven't seen Alicia in so long. I know she's always been inside my head, but I haven't seen her properly since we were children. She used to be my imaginary friend and I could see her as clear as day. Now she's here with me ... while we're being tortured by our crazy stalker. It's slightly surreal. I wish I could hug her, but I know she doesn't do hugs. In fact, neither do I, but if I had to hug someone it would be her.

'Hi Ben,' I say weakly. I'm not surprised when he doesn't respond straight away. He just continues to stare at me. 'So ... I guess I have a lot to tell you, but first I want you to keep an open mind. It's not going to be easy to hear, but I'd rather you hear it from me than anyone else. This isn't how I planned on telling you.'

'Tell me what? Alexis ... what the hell is going on?'

I take a deep breath. 'A few days ago you asked me if I'd tell you about my sister Alicia when I felt comfortable enough ... well, I'm not exactly comfortable about telling you this, but I don't have any other choice. My name's not really Alexis Grey. It's Josslyn Reynolds ... and Alicia. I'm two people. Alicia is my identical twin sister, or at least she would have been had she been born.'

'Wait ... what? You're making no sense.'

'I know, I'm sorry. I'm doing my best here. Just listen. My name is Josslyn. I grew up with a voice in my head who I called Alicia. I assumed at the time that I was either crazy or I had a split personality. I didn't know who or what she was until about a year and a half ago. Alicia is my unborn identical twin sister. She lives as a ... living organism ... inside me, but she tricked me. I had her cut out of me via surgery thinking that she was the … organism, but it turns out it was me …'

'What was you?'

'I'm the … organism, the tumour, whatever. I'm not really the true owner of this body. Alicia is. Alicia took over this body and moved to Tuscany. Then you met her. She changed her name to Alexis in order to hide from Peter because we found out he'd been stalking us for years. I know this is a lot to take in and it sounds completely crazy, but—'

Ben laughs out loud. 'It's fucking ludicrous! You're telling me that you're a—'

'The technical term is a foetus in fetu.'

'A what?'

'A foetus in fetu, a parasitic twin, whatever you want to call it.'

'That's utterly and completely absurd.'

I can't help but feel a little hurt at the way he's taking it. I know it sounds crazy, but a part of me hoped that Ben would understand.

'It's true,' I say slowly.

'Okay … so you're basically a … parasitic twin living in Alexis's body?'

'Yes.'

'And Alexis is actually called … Alicia—'

'Yes.'

'Who is Peter's sister—'

'No. This is where it gets more complicated … Peter has always had an adopted twin sister called Alicia, but she disappeared. She's actually our biological sister too.'

'Wait ... how is that possible?'

'Alicia Phillips and I were separated at birth. We were born as what looked like fraternal twins; that means that we weren't identical, but no one knew about my identical twin inside me. We would have been triplets, had we all been born together.'

Ben takes a deep breath. It wouldn't surprise me if he passes out. He must be in a lot of pain, but hopefully my story is distracting him somewhat.

'Are you okay?' I ask. I can't imagine this shocking news is helping him feel any better. His mind must be like jelly right now.

'Am I okay? Are you kidding me right now? What you're telling me is physically impossible. It's ridiculous! How can you be two people? You must have some sort of personality disorder. Have you ever seen a professional about this ... whatever this is?'

'No, I haven't. I was always afraid they'd do experiments on me and they'd lock me up in a mental institution.'

'Alexis, I really think you should see a professional therapist. You clearly have a personality disorder and for some reason you think that this ... foetus ... thing ... is a real person talking to you inside your head. Do you actually realise how insane that sounds?'

My eyes start brimming with tears and my bottom lip starts quivering, so I bite it to get it to stop and to hold the tears at bay.

'I knew you wouldn't understand,' I say slowly. 'I should have listened to Alicia. I should never have trusted you.'

'Look, I'm sorry ... I just ... I'm trying to understand. Really, I am, but—'

'Alicia isn't just a different personality,' I snap. 'She's real. She's my sister.'

I stare at Ben and he looks back at me for several long seconds.

'Okay,' he finally says. 'Okay ... I believe you. If you say Alicia's real, then she's real.'

I don't believe him, but I smile.

'Thank you, but ... there's more.'

'Of course there is. What more could you possibly tell me that will top that?'

'Alicia's a psychopath.'

Ben stares at me. I think he's searching my face for some sort of clue as to whether I'm lying or not, but my face is serious.

'A psychopath?' he repeats. 'As in a person who feels no empathy nor shows any emotions?'

'Yes. Although, she is gradually learning to show her true feelings. I think we're rubbing off on each other.'

'Right ...'

'You don't believe me, do you?'

'I ... it's just ... it's a hell of a lot of information to receive in the space of two minutes. I really don't know what to believe right now. So you're telling me that all this time I've known you I've actually been talking to a psychopath?'

I nod. 'Yes. Alicia is in charge of our body most of the time. I've only just learnt how to control it for small amounts of time.'

Ben seems to think for a moment and then gasps. 'Oh my God ... my name ... Alicia speaks formally, doesn't she? She calls me Benjamin even though I keep telling her to call me Ben. And you call me Ben and you use contractions when you speak. Alicia doesn't.'

'Yes, that's right.'

'How did I never notice that before? I mean ... I knew there was something ... different ... about you, but I just assumed that maybe you were bipolar or something, which to be honest, still makes more sense than this ... foetus ... in ... whatever.'

I slightly raise my eyebrows and shrug my shoulders. I don't really know what else to say to make him believe me, but there's so much more to tell him and I know we don't have a lot of time. Maybe I should just get it all over with in one go, like pulling off a plaster.

Quick and painless ... quick and painless.

'There's more ...'

'You're kidding me, right?'

'My Alicia killed our sister Alicia Phillips ... and also Daniel Russell.'

'The guy they found at the rubbish dump?' I watch as Ben's face turns from confused to looking as if a light bulb has just lit up above his head. 'Wait ... Josslyn Reynolds ... oh my God, you're wanted for questioning by the police. You killed your ex-boyfriend?'

I wince at the shock in his voice. 'Well technically yes, but it was Alicia, not me.'

Ben stares at me for ten solid seconds, waiting.

'Why are you staring at me like that?'

'Is there anything more you want to tell me?'

'No, I think that's it.'

'Okay, then maybe you want to explain why Phil ... or Peter ... whatever ... why my former best friend has us tied up in his fucking stalker den. I'm still trying to get my head around the fact that he's a psycho. So, let me get this straight – you, or more precisely, the psychotic person inside you, killed Alicia, his sister, who is actually your own twin sister and now he wants to kill you, but yet ... he's also in love with you?'

'It's a long story.'

Ben glances around the room and shrugs his shoulders. 'We've got time.'

I sigh and roll my neck again. Urrgg, all this talking is exhausting and all I want to do is sleep. My rib hurts, my finger hurts, my whole body hurts.

'Peter is clearly a fucking stalker, creepy weirdo, right? Well, like he said, he started with stalking his own sister, however long ago that was, then obviously moved on to stalking other women. Then his sister disappeared and he tracked me down because he thought I had something to do with her disappearance. He then fell in love with me while stalking me, then he found out about my Alicia, but he had no idea who or what she actually was. I found out I had a twin sister called Alicia Phillips and tracked Peter down and we started looking into her disappearance. He lied to me and never let on that he already knew who I was. One thing led to another and I slept with him ... several times ... and then basically the whole truth came out. I told him who my Alicia was and that she killed his sister and eventually I figured out he was my stalker. Alicia then had me cut out of her body and ran away and moved to Tuscany. Peter hasn't stopped looking for her, for us, I assume to take revenge on Alicia, but also to try and convince me to love him ... and now we're here ...'

I take a deep breath, having realised I pretty much hadn't taken a breath during the entire speech. I know I've left some stuff out, but they are only minor details. I'm sure he can fill in the gaps.

Ben is frowning, clearly wrestling with his brain. I can't imagine sleep deprivation, starvation and pain is helping him put all this together.

'So ... Phil is in love with you and wants to kill Alicia?'

'Yeah, pretty much.'

'That's fucked up.'

'Tell me about it.'

'And ... are you in love with him?'

'Of course not!' I snap. 'I'm not fucking crazy. He killed Oscar! Haven't you been listening? He's a freak.' I look up at the ceiling and shout. 'You hear me! You're a freak!' I'm not sure if that's where the camera is located, but I'm sure Peter gets the gist, wherever he is.

Ben lowers his head and stares down at the floor. 'How the hell did I get myself into this mess?'

'I'm so sorry. I didn't want to get you involved. Both me and Alicia tried to warn you and stop you, but you wouldn't listen, but by the sounds of it you've been involved in Peter's plan for a while ... all to get to me.'

Ben looks up slowly and looks me in the eye. 'Of course I didn't listen. I knew there was something weird going on. I couldn't let you deal with whatever it was you were dealing with alone. Your dog got brutally murdered. You were a mess. I had to try and help you, protect you because ... I love you.'

The words hang in the air. Three little words. Yet they almost make no sense to me. When Peter says he loves me it makes me cringe, but when Ben says those words I feel ... something. He surely can't mean it.

'You've been tortured for two days. You're not thinking clearly.'

'Says who?'

'Me! I've just told you that I've been lying to you and that I'm actually two different people and you've just told me that you love me. It makes no sense, like ... which one of us do you love?'

Ben doesn't even pause to think about his answer. 'Both of you.'

I see Alicia raise her eyebrows and fold her arms. She hasn't said a word since I took over. I'm not really sure what she's thinking at the moment because I can't actually hear her thoughts anymore. She's outside of my body, not inside and I'm finding it difficult to adjust.

'How can you love both of us? We're different people in the same body.'

'I fell in love with the neurotic, slightly alcoholic, fun side of you ... and the darker, scary side of you. Yes, okay, so you've just told me that you're actually two people, but ... I didn't know that at the time and I unknowingly fell in love with both of you, although the moment I knew for sure was when you first appeared on our little not-a-date thing. You changed in the blink of an eye and I knew then that I loved you. I can't just suddenly not be in love with one of you just because you've told me that you're two people in the same body. It doesn't work that way.'

'So do you believe me now?'

Ben smiles. 'Yeah, I guess I do.'

I open my mouth to start arguing with him again about the whole *love* thing, but then close it.

Alicia steps forwards. *'May I speak to Benjamin?'*

'Alicia wants to speak to you,' I say.

Ben swallows and nods. 'O-okay.'

'Are you afraid of her?'

'Now I know what she is ... yeah, a little bit.'

Alicia and I share a smile as I close my eyes.

Chapter Twenty-Seven
Alicia

I open my eyes slowly, not enjoying the fact that the unbearable pain is flooding my body again. I am aware that the ropes binding my ankles are slightly looser, but my arms and shoulders are beginning to lose feeling. My broken finger has become numb. I must escape soon, not just for my own sake, but for Benjamin's as well. He is staring up at me with his head slightly titled to one side, studying me, clearly looking for signs that I have changed. There is a part of me that believes he still does not think Josslyn is telling the truth. It is a difficult reality to accept and I am not sure that I fully trust him.

'Hello Benjamin.'

Benjamin jumps slightly, clearly taken aback by my abrupt change of tone. 'Holy crap, that's freaky. Alicia ... could you hear everything that me and Josslyn were just talking about?'

'Yes.'

'So you heard me when I said that I love you.'

'Yes.'

'And do you not have any sort of response to that?'

'No.'

Benjamin sighs. 'Wow, you really are different. I mean, I noticed that there were times when you were ...

different, usually when you, or Josslyn, were drinking, but I never thought, not in a million years—' Benjamin breaks off his sentence and shakes his head. 'You're really a psychopath and have killed people?'

'Yes.'

'And you don't feel any guilt or remorse ... or anything?'

I sigh in slight frustration. 'I killed Daniel because he abused Josslyn. I killed Alicia because she got in my way and threatened to destroy my plan of taking full control of this body. I kill when I have to, not because I necessarily enjoy it.'

'But you do enjoy it a little bit.' A statement, not a question.

'Yes, I will not lie. At the time I enjoyed killing Daniel and Alicia, but I believe I have changed since then. I no longer enjoy killing a person, even if he deserved it at the time.'

Benjamin frowns. 'Why ... who else have you killed?'

'That is not important right now.'

'Um, it kind of fucking is important Alicia!' shouts Benjamin. He then lowers his voice as he continues. 'Look, obviously you're a very ... unique person and I respect that and what I said is true. I do love you, but ... to be perfectly honest I'm not sure I can accept the fact that you've killed people. It's going to take me some time to ... I-I just need to think about it.'

'I do not expect you to accept it. No normal human being should.'

'It's going to take some time, that's all.'

'Well, you may not have much time left because I assume Peter plans to kill you soon.'

Benjamin glances around every corner of the room. 'He's watching us.'

'I am aware.'

'Do you have a plan?'

'Yes.'

'Are you going to tell me the plan?'

'No.'

'Come on Alicia, give the guy something. He's trying,' says Josslyn. She is now pacing around the room like a caged animal, studying the various photographs pinned to the walls.

'I cannot trust him,' I say aloud.

'Who are you talking to? Oh, wait ... Josslyn, of course. So do you have full conversations in your head with each other?'

'Yes, although at the moment she is standing behind you.'

Benjamin jerks his body sideways in fright to look behind him, but there is no one there. 'What are you talking about? I thought she was in your head.'

'Usually she is, but due to my weakened state I believe I am now hallucinating.'

'Shit ... we need to get out of here.' Benjamin is still looking around the room for Josslyn, who is now crouched down next to him.

'He's bleeding pretty bad, Alicia. Whatever your plan is you'd better do it soon.'

I nod my understanding. 'Benjamin, I require you to be quiet and whatever happens next you are not to interfere. Do you understand?'

'What? I can't agree to that.'

'If you truly do love me then you will trust me ... and do as I ask. Promise me.'

'I ... I ... okay. I promise.'

I nod again and inhale as deeply as I am able. 'Peter ... I am ready to talk.' My voice is calm, stern, and I am ready.

'What are you going to do?'

I shoot Benjamin my evil stare, warning him that he has already broken his promise. He shrinks backwards slightly.

Then Peter enters the room and I steel myself, ready for what is to come.

Chapter Twenty-Eight

Alicia

Peter begins to slow clap as he walks towards me. He is still carrying the bottle of wine, but now it is almost empty. He has made a mistake by causing himself to become intoxicated. I can, and shall, use that to my full advantage. He will not be thinking as clearly and rationally as before. His mind will be hazy, but that does not mean that he is not dangerous.

'That was one hell of a show. I really enjoyed it. Poor Benny, you poured your heart out and neither of them returned the favour. Josslyn doesn't love you. She loves me. And Alicia ... well, she doesn't love anyone. She's incapable of love. Isn't that right, Alicia?' He looks at me for an answer, but I do not give him what he wants, so he continues. 'You may have saved his life earlier by telling me where my sister's buried, but let's face it, you don't really care, do you? You don't care about anyone. You're just a hollow husk of a shell. Josslyn is the real woman here, not you. You don't deserve to be in this body. You stole her life and I think it's time you gave it back, don't you?'

'What do you suggest?' I ask calmly.

Peter raises his eyebrows. 'Are you saying you're ready to actually discuss an arrangement?'

'Yes. Tell me exactly what it is you want from me.'

Peter wobbles slightly as he steps closer. 'I want you gone. I want Josslyn back in control of this body ... forever.'

'I am afraid that is not possible. As you know I had her removed. There is still a small piece of her left, but she is weak. She cannot control this body for long. I cannot give you what you want Peter. It is not physically possible.'

Peter sucks on his lip for a few seconds. 'Then what do you suggest? I want Josslyn. I'm not letting you go until I get her back.'

'Then you shall have her. I will relinquish control and allow Josslyn to take over for as long as she is able. It may be a day. It may be a year or more. I cannot tell you how long she has, but I will give you that time with her. I do not have any control over how she reacts or what she does during that time. That will be your problem, but I shall step back. When she disappears for good I shall return and I shall leave and you shall never see me again. That is my deal. Take it or leave it.'

Josslyn is holding her breath. She trusts me. I know she does, so she does not attempt to argue with me, but Benjamin is horrified. I can see it all over his face, but he remains silent.

Peter leans his face close to me. 'How can I trust that you'll keep your word? You're exceptionally good at lying Alicia ... How do I know you're not lying now?'

'You cannot know, but you also cannot take the risk that I may be telling the truth ... can you?'

'What's the catch? Surely you're not just going to hand her over out of the goodness of your heart?'

I smile. I have him hooked and exactly where I want him. He cannot resist Josslyn, even if it means only having her for one day. He is pathetic and weak.

'As we are both very much aware, I have no heart. This is the catch ... you untie me and we fight it out until the end. If you win then you get Josslyn and if I win ... then I will kill you.'

'How will we know who wins the fight?'

'Simple. We fight until either I am unconscious or you are dead.'

'So all I need to do is knock you out.'

'Yes.'

'I could do that right now with you tied to this fucking chair,' he growls.

'Yes, you are correct, but it would be much more satisfactory for you to fight me one on one. I killed your sister. You have been wanting to fight me, to cause me pain, ever since you found out. Now is your chance ... take it.'

Peter and I stare into each other's eyes, neither one of us blinking or backing down. His eyes are bloodshot and glassy – a sign that he has ingested too much alcohol, which is of great benefit to me. I can tell that he is wrestling with his own conscience but thankfully, I am correct about him, and he finally nods.

'Very well. I accept your terms.'

'Alicia ... wait ... you can't ...' begins Benjamin, but Peter lunges at his former friend and kicks him in the face, rendering him unconscious within seconds. At least Benjamin will not get in the way now. It is better that he does not witness this.

Peter grabs his knife and kneels down to cut the ropes free from my ankles, then starts on the ones binding my wrists and around my abdomen.

Finally, all the ropes are cut and my body collapses to the floor in relief, too weak to remain upright on the chair without support. I knew this would happen. It will take time for the blood to pump to my previously restricted limbs. While I wait for what little strength I have left to return I must endure Peter's torrent of abuse against me as best as I can. I doubt he will hold back for Josslyn's sake.

He immediately gets to work on kicking me while I am curled up defenceless on the ground. I clench my jaw together to stop myself from shouting out in pain. My broken rib now appears to have company. I roll over into a foetal position, attempting to protect my wounded body and the most vital organs from sustaining any further damage. Josslyn is hovering nearby, unable to intervene. I cannot let her down. I will not let her down.

Slowly, I can feel my limbs starting to respond to the blood flow. My head is dizzy and I am disorientated, my body weak from days of torture and lack of sustenance. I lift up my head just in time to see Peter's foot collide with my face, breaking my nose. I am not fast enough to respond and block the attack. Again, my heads spins and I can taste blood running down the back of my nose and into my mouth. I gag and spit it out and roll to the side just as another blow comes towards me. This time I am able to dodge it. I react instinctively and grab his ankles, sending him off balance and crashing to the floor. He lands with a heavy thud and a grunt.

I hastily grab onto the chair that has held me captive and use it to drag myself to my feet. I am vaguely aware that I am still wearing my classy evening dress, which is restricting my movement somewhat. I wobble upon standing, attempting to stabilise my footing before Peter gets to his feet. The room around me is fading away and the walls appear to be sliding towards me and then back away. I cannot give in. I will not give in. I am fighting not only for my own life, but for Josslyn's life. I must summon every ounce of strength I have left and every skill I have learnt and dispose of this enemy once and for all. It is now or never. This is the end for him.

I ball up my fists as Peter lunges at me, clutching the knife in his right hand. He swipes fast, but I manage to duck just as I feel the swish of the blade brush past the top of my head. This causes me to lose balance, but I quickly gather myself and throw a punch into Peter's ribcage with my non-broken hand. It makes contact and he is momentarily winded. I immediately use the split second of time and grab the chair, intending to smash him over the head, but he is too fast and runs towards me, tackling me and we both fall to the floor.

I land awkwardly on my side with his heavy weight bearing down from above. I am unable to stop myself from screaming in pain. I involuntarily kick my legs out, hoping one will connect with Peter; it does. He backs away from me to catch his breath and then attacks me again. I land another kick from the floor, this time to his shin and he loses balance, dropping to the ground. Clearly his inebriation is lowering his reaction time. I scurry away from him on my hands and knees. I heard the knife clatter to the floor a few seconds ago, but I cannot find it. My vision is blurry and my eyes are unwilling to focus on anything.

Josslyn is standing in front of me so I crawl over to her. I do not have much time. She bends down to my level and we meet eye to eye.

'You can do this. I know you can. I believe in you ... also, kicking him in the balls wouldn't be seen as a low blow in this situation ... just saying.' She winks at me.

I manage a weak smile as I roll onto my back, exhausted from merely crawling across the floor. I search frantically around the room, but I cannot see anything to use as a weapon, apart from the chair.

I watch as Peter regains himself and picks the knife up off the floor. He is shuffling towards me with a slight limp due to my kick to his shin, his nose is flowing blood which is dripping down his naked torso. The only consolation I have is the fact that I know he will not kill me. He wants Josslyn. His goal is to render me unconscious, whereas mine is to end his life.

'You're a fucking pain in my ass, Alicia. You've taken everything from me!' Peter yells, his voice full of anger and pain, spit flying from his mouth.

I draw in a few short, sharp breaths, still on all fours on the ground. I spy my target just behind Peter – the chair; it is my only hope. I am not strong and able enough to take him down without some form of weapon to assist me. There are coils of broken rope strewn across the floor nearby; these could also be useful, but I aim for the chair as I push myself to my feet and fling my tired body forwards, dodging him as he attempts to grab me.

I collapse into the chair and without a moment's hesitation I lift it up above my head and then slam it down on the floor. The spindly wooden chair disintegrates at its weakest points and a leg is splintered apart from the main body. I grab the makeshift weapon from the floor and point the jagged end at Peter, who laughs.

'You're gonna have to do better than that bitch,' he snarls.

We are standing at opposite ends of the room like two generals ready for battle; just him and me, no one else. I do not answer him because I do not believe in throwing witty comments back and forth during a fight. I require my breath to keep myself conscious, not to talk. Peter has the knife and I have the wooden stake. Metal against wood. Man against woman. Psychopath against psychopath. There is no doubt in my mind that I will not win because there is no alternative.

Peter begins to charge towards me. I ready myself for the intense pain that I am about to endure. He almost reaches me, but the alcohol in his system does its job and he loses concentration and balance for a single moment, which I take advantage of by slashing him with the wooden stake. He howls in pain as it makes contact with his skin. I immediately kick him in the side and follow up with a blow to the side of his head. He goes down. I seize my chance, wedge my knee into his back as he lays face down, grab his hair, pull his head back and then I slam it into the floor. A sickening thud follows and then there is, finally, complete silence.

I wait for him to move, but he does not. He lays still, face down in a small puddle of his own blood and saliva. The knife is still clutched in his hand. I relieve him of it and stand up tall, holding both the knife and the stake in each hand.

I watch as Josslyn walks towards me, a smile across her face.

'Is he alive?'

'For now.'

'Now what?'

A grin spreads across my lips. 'Now we have our fun.'

Josslyn returns my smile.

I fetch the coils of rope and bind Peter's hands and feet in exactly the same way he bound mine. I ensure it is as tight as possible.

Then I grab hold of him and drag him with difficulty until he is leaning propped up against the wall. He is exceptionally heavy, at least twice as heavy as myself. The adrenaline within my body is doing an excellent job of keeping me conscious and focused. His head lolls to one side as he slumps against the wall. Behind him are the pictures of his victims, each one controlled by him no longer. His torrent of abuse is now at an end.

At this moment I hear Benjamin groaning and stirring behind me. I had almost forgotten about him. Now that Peter is subdued I walk slowly over to Benjamin.

'A-Alicia? What's going on? W-what happened?'

'It is over. Peter has been restrained.'

Benjamin glances past me to where Peter is hunched over. I use the knife on the ropes encircling Benjamin's wrists and ankles, relieving him.

'Fuck ... are you okay?' he asks.

'I believe I will live.'

'Is Josslyn okay?'

'I'm fine Ben.'

'Yes.'

Benjamin nods and gingerly gets to his feet once he is free. He rubs at his wrists and stretches his arms above his head, immediately wincing in pain.

'What happened?' he asks me.

'We fought ... I won.'

'That's putting it lightly. Now what do we do?'

'Now you will leave the room and you are not to inform the police.'

'W-what? Of course I'm going to call the police. He needs to be arrested and taken to jail.'

'No,' I respond bluntly.

'No? What do you mean *no*? I'm not letting him get away with what he's done.'

'He will not get away with it.'

Benjamin then realises what I mean. I can see the realisation dawn on his face. 'Alicia ... you can't kill him. That's cold-blooded murder. I know I said I wanted to kill him earlier, but it was just a throw-away comment. I thought you'd changed. I thought you didn't enjoy killing people.'

'I lied ... I am going to thoroughly enjoy ending his miserable life.'

'I won't let you kill him. Josslyn ... do something! You can't let Alicia kill him. It's wrong. You know it is!'

'Tell him that I'm sorry.'

'Josslyn says that she is sorry, but you need to leave ... now. You are no longer a part of this. We shall deal with Peter.'

Benjamin and I square up to each other. I still have both weapons in my hands and I fully intend on using them if necessary.

'Alicia ... listen to me ... I—'

I do not give him a chance to finish his plea. I ram the blunt end of the wooden stake into his forehead, knocking him off balance. He stumbles backwards towards the door. While he is clutching his face I open the door and manoeuvre him through it, forcing him to the floor. He stares up at me, blood dripping from his nose and mouth.

'Don't do this Josslyn!' he screams. I slam the door in his face, locking it. 'Josslyn!' he shouts. 'Alicia!'

It is no use. I can barely hear him now thanks to the soundproofing in this room. I slowly turn around and face my prey, who is beginning to awaken.

'Let's do this,' says Josslyn.

'With pleasure,' I reply.

Chapter Twenty-Nine

Alicia

I glance around at the faces of the women Peter has tormented and stalked over the years, each one blissfully unaware that the man they knew, loved and cared for, had been using them and molesting them from afar.

Alicia – his beloved sister. She had grown up with him by her side. According to her journals he had been her annoying but loving brother, her best friend. Yet he had been in love with her, controlled her, watched her every move and made her fear for her life, which, quite possibly, had aroused him. She was where it had all started for Peter. Maybe Alicia really was his one true passion and I took her away from him. In a way, I saved her. She is safe now, buried beneath the earth, never to be controlled by him ever again. She can finally rest in peace.

Laura – his best friend's sister. Apparently merely used to keep his stalker skills sharp, a play-thing, his toy. A human life used only for his amusement, control and arousal. I expect he enjoyed the irony of defiling his best friend's sister as well as his own. Now she has disappeared – or has she? I am not aware that Peter has ever physically injured any of these women, but I do believe that he is capable of anything. Whether she has disappeared or is dead she is safe from him now.

Rebecca - the stranger. I do not recognise her face, but it cannot be a coincidence that she is adorning his walls. Who is she? By the looks of the photographs and his scribbled notes he has stopped watching her recently because she has disappeared as well. For the past year his sole focus has been on Alexis/Josslyn/Alicia – me. Whoever she is, she is safe for now, but the fact that she is one of his victims intrigues me. There must be a reason why.

I scan the wall with my name on it. Alicia Phillips may have been his first obsession, but I am definitely his most prized possession. He has meticulously tracked my every move for over five years, ever since he found out about me. I read a few of his notes, some of which are typed out on paper and pinned next to photographs; one of Josslyn's parents and one of Oscar:

Josslyn is afraid to leave the safety and comfort of her home. She's close to her parents. She will never leave them as long as they are alive. Amanda and Ronald Reynolds are very caring parents, but they aren't her real family. Do they know about Alicia? Do they know who Josslyn truly is?

Josslyn loves Oscar. She rescued him when he was a puppy. He never leaves her side - <u>problem</u>. Josslyn is devoted to him. Alicia is not.

I let out a low grumble, feeling it rumbling throughout my body as I squeeze my fists together, ignoring the throbbing pain in my broken finger. I turn towards Peter who has been watching me as I have been reading and studying his work. He has a smile across his face, seemingly unfazed that he is tightly bound and beaten.

'Tell me the truth,' he says. 'You're quietly impressed by all this, aren't you?'

'Impressed is not the word I would use.'

'But you are. You're impressed that I've been able to get away with it for so long, to remain undetected. I even fooled you Alicia, remember?'

'I was never fooled by you. From the start I had my suspicions about you. I just did not know why I had them. I always knew there was something ... off about you.'

Peter laughs. 'You were distracted by my wit and charm and good looks, right?' I scowl at him, but do not reply. 'It's okay, Alicia. All the women fall for me, for my charm. It's why I can get so close to them. It's why they trust me.'

'I never trusted you.'

'You have never trusted anyone.'

I fiddle with the sharp, shiny blade in my hand, feeling the cool metal between my fingers. I stare at my reflection. I am focused. I imagine plunging it directly into Peter's heart, stopping only when the tip hits the ground below him.

'You can't kill me,' says Peter slowly. 'There are too many unanswered questions. Without me, you'll never find out the answers.'

'You clearly do not know the lengths I will go to in order to learn the truth.'

We stare at each other for several seconds.

'I want to talk to Josslyn.'

'Not yet. I have not finished with you. She will have her turn with you soon.'

'Josslyn won't let you hurt me.'

'That is where you are wrong.'

I kneel down next to him and slowly drag the sharp point of the blade across his toned torso. It does not pierce the skin. I imagine it merely tickles him. He stirs slightly and I see him struggle against the ropes.

Without any further warning I stab the knife into the top of his thigh, not too hard, but enough for about an inch to disappear into his flesh. Peter shouts out in pain as I remove the tip and stab him again, this time in the other leg, slightly deeper.

Next, I place the knife on the floor beside me, grab his little finger on his left hand and thrust it backwards, snapping it. A blood-curdling scream erupts from his mouth, but then he takes a few deep breaths and composes himself, glaring at me the entire time.

'Y-you don't scare me, Alicia.'

'Are you quite sure about that?'

I grab the knife, stand and walk slowly over to Rebecca's wall.

'Who is she?' I ask calmly.

She has long, dark hair and brown eyes, approximately in her late twenties or early thirties. Her body is petite and dainty, but she has a strong, determined look about her.

Peter laughs again. 'She's no one. A new target to fill the time.'

'You are lying. Who is she?'

'She's a fucking whore, that's who she is,' he spits.

I spin around and glare at Peter. 'Who is she?' I say again.

Peter merely grins. 'I still have all the control. Let's face it, I always will because I know more about you than you will ever realise. I've been doing a bit of digging and what I've found is extremely interesting. If you kill me then you'll never know.'

I begin to walk towards him. 'I believe I can take that risk.'

'Are you sure about that?'

'You have no control,' I tell him.

'You may be holding the knife ... but I'll always be able to control you.'

I stand beside him, pressing the sharp blade against his ear, then with one swift movement I slice half of his ear off. It falls to the ground as he screams again. Blood runs down the side of his head in thick streams, coating every surface it touches.

'Did you not hear me correctly Peter?' I whisper into his complete and functioning ear. 'You ... have ... no ... control.'

I stab him again, this time deep into his stomach. Thick, red blood oozes out of the wound, pooling around him. I kneel down in his blood and slowly twist the knife further into his body. He is whimpering and spluttering, but his eyes are glued to mine the entire time.

'P-Please,' he begs. 'Don't.'

'Don't what? Kill you?'

'I know about your childhood ... about what really happened to you,' he stutters.

'What are you talking about?'

Peter smiles, blood dripping from his mouth. 'You don't remember, but I can help you remember.'

'*What's he talking about?'* asks Josslyn.

I do not respond directly to her, but to Peter instead. 'Explain yourself.'

'Your parents ... they lied to you.'

'I already know that.'

'Josslyn is already aware of the fact that Amanda and Ronald lied to her and that she was adopted.'

'No ... they lied about something else too. Everyone's been lying to you.'

A silence fills the room as Josslyn and I glance at each other. We both know how manipulative Peter is and that he can lie as easily as I can. He could very well be making this up in order to prolong his life. The one thing I do know for certain is that I am not leaving this room until Peter is dead.

'I do not believe you,' I whisper.

'Fine ... you don't believe me, but I bet you'll believe this ... I know who The Hooded Man is,' he stutters.

I cease twisting the knife, but do not remove it. I had not been expecting him to mention The Hooded Man, the rapist from the news. It is impossible that he knows I have been having dreams about him and seeing him randomly. He has captured my interest and I despise myself for it. His spiel regarding Josslyn's parents can wait ... but this is important.

'The Hooded Man is a serial rapist who has been raping women for possibly decades. He has nothing to do with me,' I say.

'And yet you're interested in him. You watch him on the news. You were attacked the other night by a man in a black hood ... and you killed him.'

'How do you know that?'

Peter manages to grin through his pain, coughing and spluttering again as more blood seeps out of his dying body. 'You forget, Alicia ... I know ... *everything*.'

'Tell me ... *now*.'

Another grin. As he speaks his voice is raspy and he is stuttering over almost every word.

'I will tell you, but only because I want to see the look on your face when I do. I know people, dangerous people. There's an online chat room where we go and talk and show off our masterpieces. I am a god to them. My masterpiece has won me awards. I have even been teaching a student of mine. I caught him one day watching a female tutor. He'd sketched her and I looked through his notebook. He'd been watching her for months. I told him I could help him hone his skills. I showed him the online chat room. It was a risk, but he didn't report me.

'I began to teach him outside of the classroom. He wanted to show the others what he could do. He wanted to rape a woman to show them that he was worthy. I helped him. I told him that for his first rape it couldn't be just any random woman. I've never raped a woman, but I have slept with my conquests, except for my sister, but I never raped them. I always had their consent. I told him about you and I could tell that he wanted you more than anything, but I told him not to rape Josslyn, only you. He made sure it was you. I told him where to find you and said I was only in the pub around the corner if he needed my help. When he didn't respond I feared you may have been too much for him. He was only a kid. I found him ... and I cleaned up after your mess. You're fucking welcome by the way.'

Peter coughs and spews up a fountain of blood. The ground beneath us is sodden and sticky, the smell of blood is wafting around us. I feel nauseous, but not because of the smell or the sight. Peter is more evil than I could ever have imagined. Not only has he subjected his victims to his abuse, but he has also been teaching a young boy to objectify and rape women. Now that boy is dead because of him ... and me.

'You see the things I do for you? Even though I fucking hate your guts I still look out for you because of Josslyn.'

'Look out for me? You sent a young boy to rape me!'

'He was eighteen.'

'I do not give a fuck how old he was. You have been showing off your victims to members of an online group and teaching boys to rape women. Who else is part of this group?'

'The Hooded Man.' Peter coughs up more blood. 'He's our leader. He started the group years ago as a way for rapists, murderers and stalkers to meet and share stories.'

'Have you ever met him?'

'No. We don't meet in person, not ever. Michael was the only one I met ... because I introduced him to the group, but thanks to you he's now dead.'

'What is the group called? Who else is part of it? What is The Hooded Man's real name?'

Peter laughs and coughs up yet more blood and stammers as he continues. 'I'm not telling you anything else, but I will tell you this. The Hooded Man is after you now. They all are. I told them what you did to my Alicia and who you are and if you kill me they will all come after you ... do you really want that?'

I lean my face close to his. 'Bring ... it ... on.'

'You'll regret this.'

'Doubtful.'

'Let me do it. It's time.'

'This is where I say goodbye Peter ... my job is done. Just know this ... I won and you failed. I have control ... always.'

I close my eyes and take Josslyn's place standing over the fading body of Peter, as she leans in closer to him.

Chapter Thirty
Josslyn

I can taste blood in my mouth, metallic and salty. The smell is almost overwhelming, but knowing that the majority of the blood belongs to Peter allows me to ignore it, even though it's churning my stomach. I begin to shake, not with nerves or fear, but with pure hatred and anger. I'd been listening as Peter had told his story to Alicia. I'm still reeling from the idea that he's been chatting to other psychos and rapists online, bragging about his fucking wall of photographs and God only knows what else.

Plus there's the thing he said about my parents ... was it true? Had they lied about something else? I'll admit that I was curious, but I couldn't let him try and convince me not to kill him. I'd sacrifice not knowing the truth in order kill him. I must keep my focus. I only need to know one thing right now ... and it has nothing to do with my parents.

The knife is still buried deep in his stomach, my fist clenched around the handle, which is slippery because of the amount of blood.

'What's the name of your online group?' I ask calmly.

Without pausing Peter immediately recognises the change in my voice. 'Josslyn, is that you?' he stutters. 'You have to help me. You can't let me die, you hear me. We're meant to be together, you and me forever—'

'The name,' I repeat.

'I can't tell you that.'

I twist the knife and Peter screams, tears leaking from his eyes, mixing with his blood.

'Tell me the truth,' I say as calmly as I can muster.

'The truth?'

'Did you kill Oscar?'

'Of course not, I would never—'

'Tell me the fucking truth. Did you kill him? I want to hear you say it!' I scream at the top of my lungs. My throat burns and my voice breaks.

Peter looks at me solemnly. He begins to cry, proper tears as he stammers his words. 'I did it for us baby. I needed you to come back to me.'

That's all the response I need.

Without a moment's hesitation I grasp the handle of the knife as tight as I can, rip it from his body, causing more blood to spurt out, and then with one quick movement, slice it across his throat. He jerks as blood ejects from the deep cut across his jugular. He's coughing and spluttering, huge jets of warm blood drenching me, but I don't move a muscle. I let it wash over me and watch as Peter slowly slumps down, his head bowing and succumbing to gravity. He gives one last twitch and then he's gone ... he's still ... and very, very ... dead.

I stare at his lifeless body. His eyes are glassy and frozen, his chest perfectly still, his muscular arms bound.

All I can hear is the beating of my own heart. It's deafening in my ears. My brain is fuzzy, as if I'm dreaming and the room is beginning to spin again. I'm violently shaking due to the cold and adrenaline, my teeth chattering.

I don't know how long I stay kneeling beside him, but eventually I attempt to stand up, my legs buckling slightly. The knife is still in my hand. I find I'm unable to let it go.

Alicia is standing beside me as we both look down at our victim.

'Josslyn ...'

'Yes,' I say.

'Are you all right?'

'Yes.'

That's when I hear banging on the door. I'm not sure if it's been happening the whole time, but this is the first time I hear it.

'B-Ben,' I stutter.

My body reacts instinctively and I begin to walk towards the sound of the banging. I unlock and open the door. Ben is standing on the other side. He catches sight of me, covered in blood, holding the knife, and takes a step back.

'Jesus Christ,' he mutters. 'Alicia ... you killed him.'

'No,' I say. 'I did.'

'Josslyn?' He's unable to hide the shock in his voice. 'What did she make you do?'

'Nothing ... she didn't make me do anything. It was all me.'

'I don't know what to do ... tell me what to do,' he begs.

'Help me,' I reply.

Then I collapse to the floor.

My body is still aggressively shaking. I'm in severe shock and I can't control this body any longer. I can hear Ben's sweet, concerned voice echoing all around me, but I can't focus on it. I keep replaying the moment I sliced Peter's throat open over and over like a movie. I've never killed anyone before ... not me, Josslyn. I feel like I've lost a piece of myself, like I've just killed a small part of me along with Peter. Am I a psychopath now? No, I can't be because psychopaths don't feel empathy or guilt ... but yet ... neither do I. I'm relieved and happy that Peter's dead. It's what I've wanted for so long. Then why am I reacting so badly to killing him? I may not be a psychopath, but I'm as sure as hell a murderer.

Ben manages to drag me out of the room, away from the blood, the smell, the pictures and the body, but I can't leave yet, so I fight against him. I want to see her one last time.

I turn and see Alicia standing in the middle of the room. She's covered in blood, the same as me and wearing the torn and stained ball gown. She looks so glamorous even spattered with blood and badly beaten and bruised.

We look into each other's eyes and we know ... things are never going to be the same again. I'm different now. I've taken a life. I am her and she is me, as one forever and always. We share a knowing nod and a faint smile and I close the door on her.

Then I pass out in Ben's arms.

Chapter Thirty-One

Alicia

I open my eyes and find myself staring up at Benjamin. He is cradling me like a child, shaking me to attempt to rouse me. I blink at him, bringing his face in to focus.

'Josslyn,' he says. 'Wake up, wake up. Please wake up.'

'Josslyn is in shock. I suggest we leave her alone to recover.'

Benjamin looks startled for a moment. 'Holy shit ... Alicia ... what happened in there? I was shouting for ages.'

'Soundproofed room,' I reply, by way of an explanation. Even if I had heard him I would not have allowed him entry nor responded to his calls.

I bring myself up into a seated position and Benjamin backs away from me.

'I don't know what to do right now,' he says as he shakes his head slowly.

'I suggest that you do as Josslyn asked and help me.'

'Help you do what? Cover up the fact that you just murdered someone in cold blood?'

'Yes.'

'How can you be so fucking calm right now? Peter was a goddamn human being. He may have been an asshole and a psycho, but he was a living, breathing person and you and Josslyn have just taken all that away ... you're telling me you feel nothing?'

'He deserved it.'

'Look, I know he killed Oscar and he stalked loads of women, but—'

'If you knew the truth about what he has done, then you would be happy he is dead. Trust me.'

'How can I trust you? If what you know is so bad then tell me. I want to understand, I do, but I'm never going to be okay with the fact that you kill people.'

'Then leave.'

'Excuse me?'

'Leave,' I repeat, firmer this time.

'I can't fucking leave, Alicia. I love you. I love Josslyn.' Benjamin screams into his hands and lowers his head between his legs, taking a few deep breaths, ruffling his fingers through his hair as he does so.

I watch him wrestle with his emotions. This is why I am glad that I do not possess them. He appears to be suffering a great deal, clearly torn between doing the morally correct thing and helping someone he says he loves.

'Benjamin, you have two choices. Either you get up right now, walk out of this house and never speak of what happened here and never see me again ... or you can help me dispose of Peter's body, I will tell you the truth and I will be indebted to you forever ... you will have gained my trust, and that is something I have never given freely before. It is your choice. I will not attempt to persuade you either way.'

Benjamin raises his head and looks at me, tears swimming in his eyes. 'What about the choice where I walk out of here and call the police?'

'If you choose that option I will have to kill you. Please do not make me kill you. I will do absolutely anything to protect my sister.'

Benjamin nods. 'I know.'

'Then which option are you going to choose?'

'I choose option number two.'

'Good choice.'

We smile at each other and sit in silence and blood for a few moments. I am exhausted and now that the surge of adrenaline is wearing off the pain is flooding my body at an alarming rate. We are both in a severe state, in need of sustenance and a shower, but there is much work to be done first. That is why we sit and revel in the silence for as long as possible.

Finally, I get to my feet, wincing at the shooting pain in my ribs. Benjamin rushes forwards to assist me, but I shrug him off.

'You don't like it when men help you, do you?'

'I do not like it when *anyone* helps me,' I correct.

'Tell me what to do.'

'Go into the kitchen, find as many cleaning products as possible, put on some rubber gloves if there are any, fill up a bucket with water and find some black bin bags.'

'Then what?'

'You used to be a butcher at university did you not?'

Benjamin tilts his head sideways. 'I don't like the way you just said that.'

'We need to chop up the body.'

'No way. Absolutely not. I'm not chopping up his body. There has to be another way.'

I sigh in annoyance. 'Fine, then we shall burn him in the garden.'

Benjamin gulps, clearly not liking that plan either, but he nods. 'Fine. It's better than chopping him up. What are you going to do while I get the kitchen stuff?'

'I am going to fetch some bed sheets from upstairs to wrap him in for now and then we shall get to work on cleaning the room. We must remove every last piece of evidence, including all the photographs from the walls and ceiling, but we need them, so we cannot destroy them yet.'

Benjamin and I get to work. He gags and shudders when he sees the mutilated body of his former best friend, but does not say anything. He is silent as we work, only stopping to ask for assistance or directions on what to do next.

I wrap the body up in as many bed sheets as I can find while Benjamin begins to take down all the photographs on the walls. There will come a time when these will be shown to the correct authorities, but for now I need the evidence. Benjamin places the items and photographs of each individual woman in separate bags. I intend to search through it later for clues as to who Rebecca is and where Laura is.

Luckily, the guest bedroom that Peter has been using as his shrine does not have carpet covering the floor; it is laminated. Instead of attempting to clean the blood off the laminate Benjamin suggests ripping the whole floor up and burning it. We scrub the walls, ensuring all splashes of blood are removed. The body is wrapped tightly in bed sheets and then covered in black bin bags, bound together with rope. It is laying in the middle of the room, a large inanimate object.

Benjamin finishes cleaning, stops and looks at it.

'So ... you're the expert ... how do we burn a body to ensure he's never discovered?'

'Trust me, I am no expert when it comes to disposing of bodies. Peter disposed of Daniel's body and I buried Alicia under a rotten tree trunk. As for Michael ... I do not know what Peter has done with him, but I assume he will not be a problem now.'

'Who the hell is Michael?'

'I shall reveal all of the details later.'

'Right ...' Benjamin raises one eyebrow at me. 'Let's just get this over with.'

'I suggest we leave him here for the time being. We should get ourselves cleaned up before venturing outside in the garden to burn of him.'

'Good idea. I'll stay here and keep an eye on him while you take a shower.'

'I doubt he will make an attempt to escape.'

Benjamin smiles at my attempt at sarcasm. 'I'd rather not take the chance.'

'As you wish.'

I nod my approval and leave the room. I do feel slightly concerned about leaving Benjamin alone with the body. I do trust him, however I am more concerned for his mental wellbeing and stability. He is not me. He has been through a great deal over the past few days and has lost his best friend, killed by the women he says he loves. Josslyn will recover from the shock eventually, but I am not sure the same can be said for Benjamin. Death changes people in ways that are unexplainable and complicated.

I walk gingerly across the landing towards the bathroom. The pain and exhaustion in my body is overwhelming and I am fighting the urge to find somewhere to lay down and sleep. I immediately remember the layout of Peter's house, having spent several days here with him all that time ago. I reach the door to the bathroom and that is when I hear a scuffling noise behind me and a *meow*.

I turn and see Harrison staring at me. He is sitting in the middle of the hallway, his tail beating angrily from side to side. He is letting out a low hiss and a growl, his fur jet black and shiny, his ears pinned back flat against his head.

'Hello Harrison,' I say slowly. 'Your master is gone. You have one of two choices to make. Either you deal with it and move on ... or I throw you outside to fend for yourself.'

Harrison hisses again, but then appears to think better of his decision, turns and walks away into the main bedroom. He settles onto the bed, but still keeps his dark eyes trained on me. It is clear we have some issues to work through.

Once I have showered I assess the damage to my body in the bathroom mirror. Dark, ugly bruising is beginning to form on either side of my rib cage. There are numerous incisions made by the sharp blade scattered across my arms and legs as well as deep slices from the broken glass on my face. I have a black eye, a badly cut lip and my little finger on my left hand is severely broken, bending at an awkward angle. I prepare myself for the horrendous pain that I am about to inflict on myself as I grasp my finger and snap it back into place. I wince, but only slightly. My body is battered, bruised and weak after days with no food and little water, but my mind is clear: I know what I have to do now. I cannot give up.

Peter is dead, but he has left behind a lasting legacy that I must bury forever. He said he only taught and mentored Michael, but I do not believe him. This online group he told me about contains a plethora of rapists, serial killers and evil human beings that must be eradicated. I feel it is now my job to do this. I must track them down and take them out. If I do not do this then they will come for me. Peter made that exceptionally clear. I am in danger. Josslyn is in danger and so is Benjamin. I must tell Benjamin what I know. For the first time I am trusting another human being to help me. I cannot do this alone.

I find some clothes of Peter's which I put on and hand Benjamin a set also. The t-shirt and tracksuit bottoms are far too big for me, swamping my feminine frame, but I do not care what I look like for the time being. There are much more important things to focus on and worry about at this precise moment. My once beautiful and striking ball gown is beyond repair. It bears the scars and marks from the abuse I have received and will be destroyed, along with Peter's body, in due course.

Harrison follows me down the stairs and into the kitchen, ensuring he keeps his distance from me. I pour myself a glass of water from the tap and drink it straight down, gasping mid-way for a breath. Harrison watches me intently and then circles around his food bowl. I sigh as I place my empty glass on the side.

'I suppose you wish to be fed,' I say, a slight annoyance to my voice. It is typical that I feel obligated to now look after Peter's damn cat, even though the feline despises me greatly.

Harrison hisses at me, but does not stray from his bowl. I search the kitchen cabinets until I locate his cat food. I fill his bowl with kibble and the second bowl with fresh water. The cat stares at me, unwilling to approach his bowl while I am close by, and once I am far enough away for his liking, he begins to eat.

I wait for Benjamin to come down the stairs. I have made us some toast and tea. Harrison has retreated back upstairs after eating his fill.

'Hey,' says Benjamin as he sees me. He takes the plate and mug that I hand to him. 'Thanks. You look ...

better.' He does not mention the overly baggy men's clothes I am wearing or the fact that my face looks like it has been slammed into a door repeatedly.

'How do you feel?' I ask him.

Benjamin appears to be in physically bad condition also. His face is battered and I remember how Peter sliced the skin on his chest with the knife.

'I'll survive. My nose is broken, but otherwise I think it's just superficial wounds.'

I nod, finding that I am relieved.

'Do you need to go to the hospital?' he asks me, as he begins to devour his toast.

'No, however I would appreciate it if you could assist me in setting my finger with some kind of makeshift splint.'

'I'll find something.' He attempts to stand.

'Wait,' I say, stopping him. 'I must tell you what needs to be done now and what Peter revealed to me. It will be difficult to hear, but you must hear it if you are to be of assistance to me.'

'More difficult than hearing that you're actually two people in one body and my best friend is a serial stalker?'

'Yes.'

'It's worse than that?'

'Yes.'

'Fuck.'

Benjamin stands without another word and approaches the alcohol cabinet in the corner of the room.

Peter kept a large selection of alcohol, including whisky, gin and wine. Benjamin pours himself a large whisky and offers me one, but I shake my head no. I wait until he has taken his seat, the large tumbler in his hand.

'Okay ... I'm ready ... I think.'

I begin. I tell him about The Hooded Man, about how he is a serial rapist and how women are slowly coming forwards and revealing their stories. I explain that I have had dreams about him, hallucinated that he has been following me, and about how I was attacked in the dark street the night I was with him and Peter at the bar. I reveal who Michael is and then I tell him about the online group and how The Hooded Man is the leader and that the members show off their conquests and victims for fun and sport. I describe how Peter would not reveal who Rebecca was and, finally, the details regarding Laura. I explain how it is not known if she is alive.

Benjamin listens, sips his drink and listens some more. By the time I finish my speech he has drunk the entire contents of the glass. His eyes are glazing over and his face is as white as a sheet.

'S-so,' he stutters. 'Phil sent some kid to rape you?'

'Yes.'

Benjamin grinds his teeth and the hand that is not holding the glass squeezes the cushion beside him. He is angry. 'If Phil wasn't already dead I'd fucking kill him,' he mutters. 'What happens now? Surely we should call the police, you know, once we get rid of the body ...' He frowns and shakes his head.

'We cannot inform the police yet. Peter told me that these ... people ... will now come after me, and quite possibly, you as well. We must locate Rebecca and Laura. They may also be in danger and they may also know things that may help us. The online group may wish to continue Peter's work or seek revenge on his victims. I cannot be certain. We must find them first, then I will find this group ... and I will take them out.'

'You can't be serious? We're talking about an actual underground secret group full of rapists and murderers ... and you want to hunt them down and kill them?'

'Yes.'

'Do you actually hear yourself right now? Alicia ... you're crazy! It's ridiculous and extremely dangerous. The police are much better equipped to deal with this—'

'No!' I snap. 'I must be the one to do it.'

'Why? Please, explain to me why you're taking on this insane – for want of a better word – death wish?'

I do not respond immediately. I already know the answer to his question. In fact, the answer is extremely simple so I answer as clearly as I can.

'It is my duty.'

'Your duty?'

'Yes.'

Benjamin stares at me for several long seconds. I have never been bothered by awkward silences because I prefer it to conversation, but Benjamin appears to be extremely uncomfortable. He is fidgeting in his seat. He glances into his empty tumbler.

'I think it's time for a top up,' he says as he walks to the alcohol cabinet and refills his glass. He turns back to me. 'I'm never going to fully understand all of this, am I?'

'Quite possibly not, no.'

Benjamin nods. 'I didn't think so ... I mean, I'm already an accessory to murder. I've been tortured by my best friend. The woman I love is actually two completely different people, one of whom is a murderous psychopath hell-bent on hunting down a dangerous group of serial killers.'

'You use that word a lot.'

'What word?'

'Love. Do you even know what it means?'

Benjamin smiles. 'Right, well ... do you ... know what it means?'

'I do not. For all intent and purposes I suppose you could say I love Josslyn, but the emotion is something I am unable to comprehend. Emotion is a chemical reaction in the brain. My brain is wired differently to yours. I am incapable of love.'

Benjamin absorbs my words, but then begins to talk slowly and meticulously. 'Love isn't just a mere chemical reaction. To love someone means that you'll do anything for them, put them first before yourself. It means wanting to be with them all the time and when they aren't there you feel like a piece of you is missing. It means accepting them for who they are, no matter what and to stand by them till the end of time.'

Benjamin's speech echoes quietly around the room. I have never really thought about it before – *love*. It is a word that I always hear thrown around casually, therefore often losing all meaning and respect. Josslyn's parents would say that they loved her and she would respond the same way. Josslyn would tell Oscar that she loved him and he would respond by licking her face (I assume that was the dog equivalent of a response). It is merely a word, but Benjamin has just explained it to me in words I can finally understand and relate to. Recently, a lot of things have happened, things have changed and my world has been turned upside down. The loss of Oscar is something I have never truly thought about until now, nor the loss of Josslyn for that year and a half I spent without her inside my head. I understand now ... I loved Oscar and I love Josslyn and to live without either one of them would be ... and will be ... torture.

I love you too, Alicia.

I stare straight at Benjamin, which quickly makes him uncomfortable.

'What's wrong? Why are you staring at me like that?'

'Thank you,' I say quietly.

'For what?'

'For explaining to me what love really means. I am sorry that I cannot reciprocate your feelings in the way you want me to, but you have truly earned my trust and respect.'

'Wow … t-thank you Alicia, and that's okay about you not loving me back. Maybe one day you will … I mean … not that I expect you to ever love me back, but do you know if Josslyn—'

'I believe that is a conversation you should have with her at a later date.'

'Of course.'

I think I do love him.

It would not surprise me if you did. He is a good man.

Are you giving me your blessing?

Yes.

Chapter Thirty-Two

Alicia

Benjamin and I create a large bonfire in the back garden, douse Peter with petrol and set him alight. It takes several hours for the body to completely disappear, but between us we keep the fire going. Luckily, Peter's back garden is not overlooked by his neighbours so there is very little risk of us being spotted. The fumes from the fire may turn up several noses in the area, but eventually the flames die down and the only evidence that the pile of ash was once a body is a small portion of skull, which I smash into pieces with my foot. We then dig up all the ash, soil and debris and place it in plastic buckets, which we find in a small shed at the bottom of the garden. We intend to take the soil to the nearby rubbish tip tomorrow and dispose of it in the garden waste section.

Once we have finished we place two deck chairs on the patio at the back of the house, pour ourselves a glass of wine each, take a seat and make a toast.

'To ... never being caught,' says Benjamin.

He is smiling, but I know it is a forced one. He is not okay with this and I fear for his sanity when this is all over. We clink glasses and then his phone buzzes in his pocket. He checks it and quickly answers. I watch his face fall as he listens to the person on the other end. It is not good news. He finally finishes his conversation and hangs up.

'My mum ... she's dead.' He slumps in his chair and stares at the setting sun. Something breaks within Benjamin at that moment.

I have never been good at comforting people, so I do not attempt to do so. We just sit in silence and watch the sun set over the horizon, closing a day that we would both much rather forget.

'You should go and deal with your mother's passing,' I finally say.

There is a long silence. I am unable to read Benjamin. He looks as if he wants to cry, but also scream at the top of his lungs.

'No, it's okay,' he eventually says with a gravelly voice. 'I can't leave you to deal with this by yourself.'

'The body is gone. I suggest we both leave this house as soon as possible. I shall go back to yours with the evidence and photographs and wait for you there. We can then discuss our next move.'

'Are you sure?'

'I insist.'

Benjamin nods. 'I ... I need some time.'

'I understand.'

'The hospital wants me to go and fill out some paperwork, but I can do that tomorrow.'

'Go ... now. It is important that you get your affairs in order.'

Benjamin nods again, understanding exactly what I mean. His eyes are empty; hollow. He is broken and it is my fault. His mother is dead and I do not know how to comfort him.

It is not safe to stay at Peter's house any longer. There will come a time, very soon, when he will be reported missing, possibly by his colleagues or parents, and this house will no doubt be searched. We have removed as much evidence as possible. It is not perfect. I expect the police will find traces of blood or foreign DNA one day, but I merely require time.

Harrison is a problem. Josslyn tells me to take him with us to Benjamin's house, but I feel it is too risky. However, if he remains here by himself, he could starve by the time the police arrive and find him. In the end I make the difficult decision to leave him here; however I ensure the cat flap is open so he can come and go from the outside, and I leave plenty of food out for him. Even if I had decided to take him it would be almost impossible to catch him because he still will not allow me anywhere near him. Good luck Harrison.

I return to Benjamin's house. It is late at night, but I know I will not sleep. I am not sure I will ever be able to properly sleep again ... at least not until this is all over. I do not know how long he will be, so I begin to sort through the sordid evidence of Peter's obsession – the photographs, along with other items. I focus on Rebecca and Laura. They are the ones who require my help. I must locate them as soon as possible. I lay out the photographs on the floor of the lounge, surround myself with them, and sit in the middle.

The truth of Peter's obsession is abundantly and horrifyingly clear. These women had no idea that they were being hunted by a mad man, a sick psychopath who enjoyed watching them live their lives. I focus on Laura first – Laura Willis. There are snapshots of her smoking cigarettes, drinking vodka straight from a bottle, dancing provocatively with several different men. It is obvious that what Benjamin told Josslyn about his sister is true – she was/is a wild child. Her life was full of drugs, alcohol and sex. There are also pictures of her naked, proving that at some point, Peter had sexual intercourse with his best friend's sister. There are also naked pictures of Rebecca. He collected us, like trophies, and displayed us on his wall for his own satisfaction.

I read several of Peter's notes:

Laura has disappeared – where? Has she run away from me? Benny tells me she's in India. I shall leave her be ... for now.

I know who Rebecca is now. I am unsure whether to tell The Master. Does he know? Does she know? I must find her mother ...

The Master?

Is that what he called The Hooded Man?

Peter told me that he was the leader of their online group. I must find out what this group is called and where they are based, but there is no mention about it anywhere on his notes. I am not surprised. If it is a secret group then Peter would not be so careless as to leave the name and details displayed on a wall, even if it was in his locked guestroom. He must have the details hidden somewhere. His computer maybe? Earlier, when I had searched his house, I had not seen a computer, nor a laptop. I had found his mobile though.

I reach into one of the black bags and pull it out. It must hold a vital clue of some sort. Everyone's lives are stored on their phones. His password has not changed since the last time: *Josslyn.* Peter should really have paid more attention to his digital security measures ...

I immediately look at the call list, noting that there are calls from Michael up until a few days ago, as well as texts from Benjamin and also someone called Frank Master.

I recognise that name.

You do?

When I first looked through Peter's phone – when I first found out he was my stalker – Frank Master was on his call list and had sent him messages, but I didn't look at them at the time. Oh fuck! I've just remembered ... Rebecca ... she was another one who had sent him texts, but again, I skipped over them because her name didn't mean anything to me at the time. I'd assumed she was a colleague or a girlfriend or something ... shit!

That means that he has been stalking Rebecca for some time.

But who is she?

I believe she may have something to do with The Master, according to Peter's notes. His last few notes on her say he must find Rebecca's mother ...

Why? Who is Rebecca's mum?

I do not know, but I believe she would be a good place to start our investigation. It is possible that she may know who Frank Master is.

Agreed, but how do we find out who this Master guy is ... who The Hooded Man is?

We have his phone number.

Are you saying we should call him?

No. He will call Peter eventually, possibly wondering why he has not contacted him.

And then what?

Then we must be ready.

Benjamin arrives home several hours later. His face is sullen and his eyes are red and puffy from crying. He tells me that his mother suffered a large heart attack out of the blue. She died almost instantly. Apparently she had been asking the staff where her son was before it happened. Benjamin is clearly racked with guilt. While he was being tortured and then disposing of a body his mother was dying. I decline from mentioning that his mother's death appears to be extremely suspicious, especially since she had been recovering well.

Do you think the Hooded Man knows that Peter is dead and is sending us a message?

I cannot say for certain, only that I do not believe in coincidences.

We sit together for a while discussing our options. I fill him in on what I have found regarding Peter's phone and his call log. Benjamin decides to take it upon himself to find his sister, which is even more prevalent now that her mother is dead. I agree to locate Rebecca and her mother.

We have our plan.

However, the next morning the news brings with it a disastrous realisation – I am not safe, not even from the media. Josslyn is being hunted by the police and as soon as I step outside I am vulnerable.

A young broadcaster reads the news headlines:

'A new update has developed in the case of the murder of Daniel Russell. His ex-girlfriend, Josslyn Reynolds, has seemingly disappeared. Her previous residence has been searched and traces of blood have been found belonging to Daniel Russell. She is now wanted for his murder. The latest development being that she could have fled the country before the lockdown started last year. If anyone has seen her or knows of her whereabouts then please call ...'

'Shit,' says Benjamin as we eat cereal together on his sofa. 'You can't be seen outside. You'll have to stay here and lay low for the time being.'

'How am I supposed to track down Rebecca and The Hooded Man if I have to stay inside?'

'Well you can't just go walking about wherever you like! You're a wanted murderer for Christ's sake! Trust me Alicia, you're going to have to think about this seriously.'

'Be quiet!' I snap as the next news headline appears on the television.

'Another rape victim has come forward claiming she was attacked by The Hooded Man, only last week. This is now the seventeenth attack that has been uncovered, all carried out by this mysterious serial rapist. The young girl, who has withheld her identity, has spoken of her ordeal, saying that The Hooded Man was not alone. This is the first instance of the rapist having a possible apprentice. The second attacker also had a hood over his head and did not speak. The victim was raped by The Hooded Man and then the apprentice took over. She was left badly beaten and is now in protective custody and receiving psychiatric treatment. These attacks have spanned the past several decades as more and more reports are being discovered. However, there are still no possible leads as to the identity of The Hooded Man.'

Neither Benjamin nor I speak for several minutes. I continue to eat my cereal, but he appears to have lost his appetite.

'Do you think it could have been Michael or Peter with him?' Benjamin asks me finally.

'I am unsure, however it does not matter now for they are both dead.'

'What if there are more of them? More rapists that he's recruiting I mean.'

'That is why we need to take out the leader. Take him out and the rest will follow.'

'But the Hooded Man and his followers are after you. You're not safe.'

'I am aware. That is why I will find him first. I will be one step ahead of him.'

'How? I mean, how do you contact and find a serial rapist that doesn't want to be found or contacted?'

I dig into the pocket of my jeans and bring out Peter's mobile phone. 'With this. I believe his name is Frank. I am unsure of his last name. It could be Master or that could just be what Peter called him.'

'It sounds like this is some sort of cult following.'

'I believe that is exactly what it is.'

'Even more of a reason to stay the fuck away.'

'As I said before, I cannot allow The Hooded Man to win.'

'What does Josslyn say to all of this?'

'She is in agreement with me.'

'Is she? Really?'

'Ask her yourself.'

I close my eyes and drop my head to my chin.

Chapter Thirty-Three
Josslyn

I slowly open my eyes and look up. Ben is staring at me. It feels good to be me again, to be in this body, even though I still ache all over and my broken ribs are extremely painful. I've finally gotten over the shock ... I think. I mean, can a normal person ever really recover from killing someone in cold blood? I hated Peter with a passion. I wanted to watch him suffer for as long as possible and when I slit his throat and felt his blood spurt all over me I thought I'd feel relief and closure, but I didn't ... and I still don't. I know I won't feel closure until all his sick and perverted *friends* are dead or behind bars. It's my job now to help Alicia find Rebecca and Laura ... and The Hooded Man.

'Josslyn? Are you okay?' Ben asks me.

'Yes, I'm fine.'

'Thank God!'

Ben puts down his bowl of cereal and practically flings himself at me. I'm momentarily stunned as he wraps his arms around me and hugs me. I'm not sure quite how to react at first, but I accept his hug and respond. I breathe in his warm, masculine scent.

I love him. I honestly, truly do, but I just don't know how to love someone. I've never been in love before. Plus – and here's the biggy – I'm not fucking real! And by that I mean this isn't my body and sooner or later I'm going to fade away and become nothing. How can I possibly give myself to this man knowing that I don't have much time left?

Ben pulls away after a few seconds. 'I'm sorry ... I've wanted to hug you ever since I found out about you, but Alicia isn't ... well, she's—'

'She's not exactly a huggable person,' I finish. 'I understand.'

We share a laugh and then sit close to each other, our hands entwined, our legs touching. Ben runs his fingers over the skin on the back of my hand, being careful not to touch my injured finger. His stroke sends tingles up my spine (and I mean *good* tingles). I can feel the sexual electricity pulsing between us. Oh God ... I want him so bad right now! I know that Alicia has given me her blessing, but a part of me is holding myself back and I don't know why.

'So,' says Ben. 'Are you seriously on board with Alicia's plan to track down this group of serial rapists?'

'Of course I am. We're a team. We're in this together. We always have been. Yes, we've had our problems ... like when she lied to me, tricked me and had me cut out of her body ... but she's different now. I know she might seem a bit ... cold ... but I promise you that she does care about you, in her own way.'

'And you? Do you care about me?'

I smile. 'Yes, I do care about you, with all my heart ... whatever that means.' I just can't bring myself to say the L word, but I have a feeling that he knows what I'm trying to say. 'I'm just ...' I continue, 'I'm just not sure we can ever be together Ben. It's too complicated. You love me, but you also love Alicia. I don't know how much time I have left.'

Ben frowns. 'What do you mean?'

Oh shit. How do I explain this?

'Remember when Alicia explained to Peter that I didn't have much time left?'

Ben nods slowly. 'Vaguely, but I didn't really understand what she meant.'

'I mean ... at some point I'll fade away. Alicia said that when the doctors removed me, they didn't remove all of me, but eventually this body will absorb what's left ... like it should have always done. I don't know how long that will take, but one day ... I won't exist.'

Ben stares at me for several moments, clearly attempting to soak up everything I've just said. It sounds crazy to him, it must do.

'Josslyn,' he says slowly. 'Are you absolutely one-hundred percent certain that Alicia isn't just a different personality?'

I stare at him in disbelief. 'I thought you said you believed me.'

'I do ... it's just ... I also believe that there's another, more rational, explanation and I'd like you to see a therapist when this is all over.'

I bite my bottom lip.

Just humour him, Josslyn. He will never understand our situation. No one can. Maybe this is his way of dealing with the fact that you are not really real.

I smile at Ben, but my heart is breaking a little bit. 'Okay, yes ... I'll see a therapist after we finish all this.'

Ben smiles back at me. 'Thank you.'

We sit in silence, the air suddenly fraught with tension. I'm actually completely lost for words right now and to be perfectly honest I feel a horrible sinking feeling in the pit of my stomach. Ben doesn't believe me and he thinks I'm crazy.

'Josslyn ... talk to me,' he says. 'What's going on in there?'

'You wouldn't believe me even if I told you.'

Ouch. I can tell that hit him right where it hurts.

'I'm sorry, I really am. All I know for certain right now is that I love you, no matter what, whether you're crazy, have a split personality, are bipolar or that you're ... not really real. I want us to be together and I know you feel the same way.'

'That's just it Ben ... I'm not sure I can be with you because I don't know how much time we'll have together.'

Silence.

'Let me ask you this ...' he finally says. 'If you knew that you'd have both your legs chopped off tomorrow would you just sit down and do nothing, or would you run and jump and do awesome flying air kicks for as long as possible?'

I can't hold back the laugh that escapes from my mouth. 'Flying air kicks?'

Ben smiles at his own joke. 'You know what I mean.'

'What if I knew my flying air kicks would hurt someone?'

'What if that someone is okay with being hurt by your flying air kicks?'

I glance down at our hands which are still nestled together perfectly. We fit together. I know we do. It shouldn't work ... but it does and right now Ben and I are stuck together in this terrible mess. No matter what he may or may not believe ... maybe I should give us a chance.

'Okay,' I say at last. 'Let's do some awesome flying air kicks ... for as long as we can.'

Ben smiles as he brushes a stray piece of hair behind my ear. We lean in and as our lips touch I feel an excited jolt of *something* flow through my body.

We leave our cereal to get soggy and spend the morning exploring each other's bodies, temporarily forgetting that we are injured, both physically and mentally. It doesn't matter. Nothing matters right now except the way his skin feels against mine, how his lips taste and how ... complete he makes me feel.

Later that morning Ben and I are in his shower, soaping each other up. I can't stop touching him (not there! Well yes there, but ...) I just mean that I love the way he feels and how warm his body is. I've always enjoyed having sex, but I've never connected with a man the way I've connected with Ben, not just sexually and physically, but emotionally too. I'm pretty sure that Alicia is mentally rolling her eyes at me, but ... Ben and I just ... work. I can't explain it. I know it's weird and quite possibly you may think I'm a freak (or that he's a freak), but whatever this is ... it works and I never want to let him go.

Ben kisses me, hot and heavy. We've just spent the best part of three hours having sex, but he still can't get enough of me, nor I of him. I know that sooner or later we'll have to return to the real world and deal with all the ugly truths and the disastrous consequences, but right now we're revelling in each other's company, trying to forget the hell we've both been through over the past few days. We need each other.

I finally pull away from his lips, needing to breathe as the water from the shower has been cascading down from above. I laugh and throw my head back as the water streams down my chest. He kisses my chest and then moves down to my nipples.

Oh boy.

Okay, so after another hour we finally emerge from the shower, thoroughly spent and clean (well, physically clean yes, but we did do some very dirty things). Ben heads downstairs to make us a cup of tea while I get dressed.

Are you finally finished?

Holy fuck! You scared me. Please tell me you weren't aware of all of that? Oh God, I feel dirty again ... this is wrong. Oh fuck! Did you enjoy it? Did you like it when he used his tongue and ...

Stop! Calm the fuck down. I retreated into the depths of our mind for a while to allow you your privacy.

Okay, I'm sorry ... it's just ... are you sure you're okay with this? I mean, you've slept with him too.

Let us not get hung up on semantics.

But—

Trust me, Josslyn. I am okay with it. I am unable to give him what he wants. What we had was just about sex. You can give him more than that.

Okay ... thank you.

Now ... if you can keep it in your pants for two seconds ... we have work to do.

Right ... of course.

Alicia tells me the next phase of her plan and then I go downstairs to see Ben in the kitchen. He's only wearing a pair of boxers and it's all I can do to not rip them off him again.

No, stop it Josslyn ... focus.

'Hey you,' says Ben.

'Hey ... um, so I need to talk about some serious stuff for a moment.'

Ben puts down the coffee cup he was about to drink from and turns his full attention to me. 'Should I be worried?'

'Well that depends.'

'On what?'

'On whether or not you'll agree to breaking into my old house where my parents used to live and looking through their attic.'

Ben blinks several times. 'Well, I'm already an accessory to murder so breaking and entering should be no big deal ... but why exactly do you want to look through their attic?'

For some reason I thought he'd take more convincing.

'Before Peter died he said something ... something about my parents. He told me that they lied to me about more than just my adoption and I need to know whether it's true or not.'

'I still don't understand what—'

'I found out that I had a twin sister when I looked through a box of my old baby things in the attic. I found an ultrasound photo and a teddy bear, but there was other stuff in there too ... stuff I didn't even look at. I think the answer may be in that box. When Alicia sold the house she said she didn't have it emptied and the new owners just moved straight in. There's a chance that the box could still be in the attic, but I can't just walk up to the new owners and tell them I used to live there as they may put two and two together, so we have to break in.'

Ben nods slowly, but doesn't say anything.

'If you want to walk away right now I'll understand. I know it's a lot to take in and I know I'm asking a lot from you.'

'No, I'm with you ... I was just thinking that we'll have to watch the place first and make sure they're out of the house. Then maybe break a window or something to get in—'

'Or I could use my old key. I always kept one hidden in the back garden. We just have to hope that they haven't had the locks changed.'

Ben smiles. 'Of course you did. When do you want to leave?'

'Today.'

'Right ... I'll go pack some things.'

'There's one more thing ... once we've got the box and come back here then I need you to go and get Oscar. I can't travel abroad, it's too risky. I need you to get him cremated over there and bring his ashes back.'

Ben walks towards me and kisses me on my forehead. 'Of course I will.'

I look up at him and smile. 'Thank you. I don't know what I'd do without you.'

Ben hugs me tight, but doesn't say a word. I sink into his chest and listen to his heartbeat. I'm putting this man through absolute hell and I feel so guilty. I wish he'd never gotten himself involved. The last thing I ever wanted to do was drag him down with me. I don't know how this is all going to end, but a part of me knows it won't be a happy ending all neatly wrapped up in a bow.

'I'm sorry you're stuck with a psychotic killer,' I say at last.

I feel Ben inhale sharply. 'You're not a psychotic ... well, I mean, you are ... but ...'

I laugh softly. 'It's okay. I know how crazy this all is.'

'Yeah, it's a little crazy.'

We stand and hug in silence for a few moments.

'Ben?' I ask.

'Yes, Josslyn.'

'I can feel myself slipping away. I think Alicia's going to have to take over for a while. She'll be better at breaking into my house anyway.'

We look at each other and smile.

'How long will you be gone this time?'

'I don't know.'

'Just make sure you come back to me, okay?'

'I will ... and I'll always be here ... for as long as I can.'

We kiss and then I'm gone. I'm going to miss him.

Chapter Thirty-Four

Alicia

Benjamin still has his arms wrapped around me. I immediately back away from him and he allows me my space.

'Alicia,' he says slowly.

'Benjamin.'

Silence. I turn to leave the room to go and pack some things for our trip.

'Alicia, listen ... I know we ... the other night ... I know it was you who came into my room. At the time I didn't know about you and Josslyn, but I know it was you. Is me being with Josslyn ... is it okay?'

I turn and look at him for several seconds with my evil stare. I can see that I am causing him to feel uncomfortable. I will not lie ... I do care for Benjamin, but it is impossible for me to love him the way he wants me to love him. I care about him too much to cause him any suffering. He appears happy with Josslyn. They need each other. I have never needed anyone.

'I gave Josslyn my blessing and so I will give you my blessing also. I am not always present when you are together. I can adjust. In fact, we will all need to adjust, but yes, I am fine with it.'

Benjamin smiles slightly at my use of the word *fine*. 'I do still love you Alicia, but Josslyn ...'

'I know.'

'We just ...'

'I know. You do not have to say it.'

Benjamin and I nod at each other; a mutual understanding.

'Do you know when she'll be back?'

I sigh. 'Josslyn is weak. I do not know the answer to that question. We have been trying to build up her strength and tolerance, but I am not convinced it is working. If anything, it appears to be making her weaker.'

'How long has she got left until she ... until she ... not that I think it'll happen, but if what you say is true then—'

'I do not know. I am sorry.'

'So one day it could just be you and me.'

'Yes and when that day comes I shall leave you.'

'What! You can't!'

I hold up my hand to stop him from talking any further. The phone in my pocket has begun to vibrate – Peter's phone. I can tell that Benjamin wishes to continue our conversation; however I ignore him and glance at the screen.

It is him.

The Hooded Man.

Frank Master.

My breathing is steady. I am surprised at how calm I feel as I press the answer button. I am not afraid of him. I do not answer with a greeting, as is the usual custom. I merely hold the phone to my ear and wait ... I can hear breathing, slow and steady, and then ...

'Hello, Alicia.'

'Hello, Frank,' I reply bluntly.

'I have been looking forward to speaking with you. I have heard a great many things about you.' His voice is deep, rough and mature. He speaks formally, something I can relate to. 'You may have a lot of questions for me.'

'I only have one ... who are you? Your real name.' I can hear shuffling and movement on the end of the phone. There is possibly someone there with him, but I cannot be certain.

'My name is not important.'

'I believe it is.'

'My name is Frank Blake, but you can call me ... *Father.*'

The word echoes around my head. Josslyn hears it too. I am momentarily stunned and the shock must be abundant on my face because Benjamin has stepped towards me, a look of concern on his face. I hold up my hand again, a warning to not take another step closer.

Father.

Frank Blake – The Hooded Man – the serial rapist ... is our father.

'Now that I have your attention, Alicia ... listen closely.'

Read the final book in the

"My ... Self Series"

My Real Self

Available from Amazon

eBook / Paperback / Kindle Unlimited

Did you like this book?

I really hope you enjoyed reading My True Self, the second novel in the "My ... Self" series.

If you have, please consider leaving me a review on Amazon and Goodreads, share a review on your social media pages and tag me, share my book to any book clubs you may be a part of or recommend my book to friends and family.

Reviews are massively important, especially to self-published authors. They help find other readers who may enjoy the book and spread the word to a wider audience.

For a FREE Novella – My Bad Self, set four years before the first book, sign up for my monthly newsletter at:

www.jessicahuntleyauthor.com

Connect with Jessica

Find and connect with Jessica online via the following platforms.

Sign up to her email list via her website to be notified of future books and her monthly author newsletter:

www.jessicahuntleyauthor.com

Follow her page on Facebook: Jessica Huntley - Author - @jessica.reading.writing

Follow her on Instagram: @jessica_reading_writing

Follow her on Twitter: @jess_read_write

Follow her on TikTok: @jessica_reading_writing

Follow her on Goodreads: jessica_reading_writing

Follow her on her Amazon Author Page - Jessica Huntley